LOVE ON
LAVENDER LANE

What Reviewers Say About Karis Walsh's Work

Set the Stage

"Settings are an artwork for [Karis Walsh] as she creates these places that feel so real and vivid you wish you could hop in a car or plane to go walk where her characters are to experience what they get to on the pages of her book. …Her character work is as good as the places she's created so they feel like realistic people making the whole picture enjoyable."—*Artistic Bent*

"…a fun romance. It made me want to go this festival, which I'd never had any interest in before. *Set the Stage* is worth a read for fans of romance or theater."—*The Lesbrary*

"I really adored this book. From the characters to the setting and the slow burn romance, I was in it for the long haul with this one. Karis Walsh to me is an expert in creating interesting characters that often have to face some type of adversity. While this book was no different, it felt like the author changed up her game a bit. There was something new, something fresh about this book from Walsh."
—*The Romantic Reader Blog*

You Make Me Tremble

"Another quality read from Karis Walsh. She is definitely a go-to for a heartwarming read."—*The Romantic Reader Blog*

Amounting to Nothing

"Karis Walsh is known for quality books. Her characters are likable and well developed, her stories have interesting/realistic dialogue. She is one of my go-to authors for an easy, enjoyable read."—*The Romantic Reader Blog*

"Great characters, excellent narration, solid pacing, interesting mystery, lovely romance. Everything worked for me!"—*The Lesbian Review*

"As always with Karis Walsh's books the characters are well drawn and the inter-relationships well developed."—*Lesbian Reading Room*

Tales From the Sea Glass Inn

"Karis Walsh has an appealing and easy writing style that always makes her stories a pleasant read and a keen eye for human frailties that captures the interest. Here she pulls out the quirks of each woman and shows us who they are and what they struggle with in swift brush strokes."—*Lesbian Reading Room*

"*Tales from Sea Glass Inn* is a lovely collection of stories about the women who visit the Inn and the relationships that they form with each other."—*Inked Rainbow Reads*

Love on Tap

"*Love on Tap* by Karis Walsh is a contemporary romance between an archaeologist and an artisanal brewer. That might sound like an odd match, but thanks to the author's deft hand, it works very well and makes for a satisfying read."—*The Lesbian Review*

"Karis Walsh writes excellent romances. They draw you in, engage your mind and capture your heart. …What really good romance writers do is make you dream of being that loved, that chosen. Love on Tap is exactly that novel—interesting characters, slightly different circumstances to anything you have read before, slightly different challenges. And although you KNOW the happy ending is coming, you still have that little bit of 'oooh—make it happen.' Loved it. Wish it was me. What more is there to say?"—*The Lesbian Reading Room*

"This is the second book I have read by this author and it certainly won't be my last. Ms. Walsh is one of the few authors who can write a truly great and interesting love story without the need of a secondary story line or plot."—*Inked Rainbow Reads*

"I liked this book, I really did. There was something about it that pulled me in and held my attention. Karis Walsh is an expert in creating interesting characters that often have to face some type of adversity. I love that she gives them strength to persevere in spite of this."—*The Romantic Reader Blog*

Mounting Evidence

"[A]nother awesome Karis Walsh novel, and I have eternal hope that at some point there will be another book in this series. I liked the characters, the plot, the mystery and the romance so much. Danielle Kimerer, Librarian, Reading Public Library (MA)"—*Library Thing*

"[A] well paced and thrilling mystery revolving around two enigmatic women."—*Rainbow Book Reviews*

"…great characters and development, a wonderful story line, lots of suspense and mystery and a truly sweet romance."—*Prism Book Alliance*

Mounting Danger

"A mystery, a woman in a uniform and horses…YES!!!!… This book is brilliant in my opinion. Very well written with great flow and a fantastic plot. I enjoyed the horses in this dramatic saga. There is so much information on training and riding, and polo. Very interesting things to know."—*Prism Book Alliance*

"Karis Walsh easily masters the most difficult pitfall of a traditional romance. Karis' love for horses and for the Pacific Northwest is palpable throughout and adds a wonderful flavor to the story: The beauty of the oceanside at Tacoma, the smell of horses, the dogs, the excitement of Polo, the horses themselves (I am secretly in love with Bandit), the sounds of the forest. A most enjoyable read for cold winter days and nights."—*Curve*

Blindsided

"Their slow-burn romance is a nuanced exploration of trust, desire, and negotiating boundaries, without a hint of schmaltz or pity. The sex scenes are sizzling hot, but it's the slow burn that really allows Walsh to shine. ...The deft dialogue and well-written characters make this a winner."—*Publishers Weekly*

"This is definitely a good read, and it's a good introduction to Karis Walsh and her books. The romance is good, the sex is hot, the dogs are endearing, and you finish the book feeling good. Why wouldn't you want all that?"—*The Lesbian Review*

"Karis Walsh always comes up with charming Traditional Romances with interesting characters who have slightly unusual quirks."—*Curve*

Wingspan

"As with all Karis Walsh's wonderful books the characters are the story. Multifaceted, layered and beautifully drawn, Ken and Bailey hold our attention from the start. Their clashes, their attraction and the personal and shared development are what draw us in and hold us. The surrounding scenery, the wild rugged landscape and the birds at the center of the story are exquisitely drawn."—*Lesbian Reading Room*

"I really enjoy Karis Walsh's work. She writes wonderful novels that have interesting characters who aren't perfect, but they are likable. This book pulls you into the story right from the beginning. The setting is the beautiful Olympic Peninsula and you can't help but want to go there as you read *Wingspan*."—*The Romantic Reader Blog*

The Sea Glass Inn

"Karis Walsh's third book, excellently written and paced as always, takes us on a gentle but determined journey through two womens' awakening. ...Loved it, another great read that will stay on my re-visit shelf."—*Lesbian Reading Room*

Worth the Risk

"The setting of this novel is exquisite, based on Karis Walsh's own background in horsemanship and knowledge of showjumping. It provides a wonderful plot to the story, a great backdrop to the characters and an interesting insight for those of us who don't know that world. ...Another great book by Karis Walsh. Well written, well paced, amusing and warming. Definitely a hit for me."—*Lesbian Reading Room*

Improvisation

"Walsh tells this story in achingly beautiful words, phrases and paragraphs, building a tension that is bittersweet. As the two main characters sway through life to the music of their souls, the reader may think she hears the strains of Tina's violin. As the two women interact, there is always an undercurrent of sensuality buzzing around the edges of the pages, even while they exchange sometimes snappy, sometimes comic dialogue. *Improvisation* is a true romantic tale, Walsh's fourth book, and she's evolving into a master romantic storyteller."—*Lambda Literary*

Harmony

"This was Karis Walsh's first novel and what a great addition to the LesFic fold. It is very well written and flows effortlessly as it weaves together the story of Brooke and Andi's worlds and their intriguing journey together. Ms Walsh has given space to more than just the heroines and we come to know the quartet and their partners, all of whom are likeable and interesting."—*Lesbian Reading Room*

Risk Factor—Novella in Sweet Hearts

"Karis Walsh sensitively portrays the frustration of learning to live with a new disability through Ainslee, and the pain of living as a survivor of suicide loss through Myra."—*The Lesbian Review*

"Another satisfying and exciting short novel. This one was set in an unusual setting, and covered an emotive and at times emotional subject. The characters although strong were very different woman, and both had individual weaknesses. The author used these differences to create an interesting and touching story line."
—*Inked Rainbow Reads*

Visit us at www.boldstrokesbooks.com

By the Author

LOVE ON LAVENDER LANE

by
Karis Walsh

2019

LOVE ON LAVENDER LANE
© 2019 By Karis Walsh. All Rights Reserved.

ISBN 13: 978-1-63555-286-7

This Trade Paperback Original Is Published By
Bold Strokes Books, Inc.
P.O. Box 249
Valley Falls, NY 12185

First Edition: March 2019

CREDITS
Editor: Ruth Sternglantz
Production Design: Susan Ramundo
Cover Design By Jeanine Henning

CHAPTER ONE

Paige Leighton turned to the next page in her neatly printed business plan and continued to review her assessment of Kenneth Drake's commercial real estate firm. With no small effort, she ignored the thin wisp of hair that had escaped from her antique silver clip and was tickling the side of her cheek. Irritating. She kept her hair at just the right length to be smoothed back and held in place at the nape of her neck. Not long enough to be considered a ponytail, and not so short she felt the need to fuss with it during meetings. Like today.

Every aspect of her appearance was intentionally designed to give clients the impression that she was strong and in control, as well as to minimize the amount of time she needed to fuss over herself. When she had first started as a business consultant's assistant, she had experimented with different styles and colors of suits. Now, as an independent contractor and sole employee of Leighton Consulting, she had settled on a wardrobe full of expensive but basic black pants and jackets, collared white shirts, and a few metallic clips for her hair. Nothing beat black-and-white and a sleek hairstyle for a display of power and simplicity.

Kenneth excused himself to answer his cell phone, and Paige took the opportunity to tuck the misbehaving lock of dark brown hair back into place. Her stylist had been unusually chatty last week—relating something about her baby learning to walk, or was it her dog learning to sit?—and she had seemed intent on continuing to cut Paige's hair until she finished telling her story. Paige had been mentally wandering along a beach dotted with palm trees and had returned her attention to the mirror just in time to stop the rest of her hair from following the strands from the left side of her face to the floor.

She pushed the hair off her face again just as Kenneth turned toward her and came back to the table. Great, she was going to have to resort to using a handful of bobby pins until her hair grew out again. She'd look like a twelve-year-old getting ready for a ballet recital. She injected a more forceful, confident tone into her words as she continued her presentation, even though she realized it wasn't really necessary. Her client was obviously impressed by her work and didn't seem to care that her hair wasn't perfectly in place.

He leaned back in the black leather chair when she finished and tapped the edge of the folder on the glass conference table. "How long will it take to make all the changes?"

He spoke in what Paige thought of as *boss voice*. Most of her clients had the same mannerisms, those of people who were accustomed to giving orders and having subordinates fall silent and listen whenever they spoke, then laugh at the appropriate time or rush off to do whatever task they had just been given. Her proposal was aggressive and would cause significant upheaval in the company, but Kenneth should be able to sell it to his board and employees just through force of voice alone.

"The initial personnel shifts can be completed within two weeks, but you should give the second phase of restructuring job descriptions and responsibilities at least six months, to minimize confusion. Otherwise tasks might be duplicated or slip through the cracks entirely." Paige tried to ignore the tinge of guilt she felt, as annoying and unproductive as the hair curling over her cheekbone. No matter how cutthroat she and her clients were, she always tried to minimize the number of staff who would lose their jobs under her new regimes. The problems her clients' businesses were facing, however, were usually connected to overstaffing and underutilization of a few key players. And that meant pink slips and severance packages. "My contract covers the extended period of readjustment, so feel free to call me in if you have any questions or want to make any changes to the plan."

"Perfect. We'll get started right away. More coffee?"

Paige struggled to keep her face neutral. "Sure. Thank you," she said, silently apologizing to her stomach lining. Kenneth's coffee was undoubtedly expensive but bitter as hell. She got a sense that he wanted to chat, though, so she accepted the drink and promised her esophagus a bottle of antacids when she got home.

Usually at this point in her consultation, business owners and managers were ready to shoo her out, either to get started immediately on her suggestions or to get away from the discomfort they felt in the face of her evaluation of their companies. Those latter clients probably fed her proposals to an industrial-strength shredder as soon as she was out the door. Of course, they always had cause to regret that decision a few months later when they were filing for bankruptcy, but by then she had been paid and was moving on.

Thriving, streamlined businesses never hired her, but ones close to the brink did. If they didn't choose to follow her drastic plans, they often went under within a year—a fact that made her feel proud and sad at the same time. Kenneth's company had seemed successful on paper—in terms of number of sales and clients—but it hadn't been showing the expected results in profits. Paige was confident she had found the worst of the leaks and plugged them securely.

He handed her a full mug without much room for adding the copious amounts of cream and sugar that would make the brew palatable. She stirred in as much as she dared, not wanting to add a coffee-stained shirt to her hair fiasco. Kenneth took a seat across from her and rested one ankle over the opposite knee, leaning back in the casual but posed position of *boss at ease.*

"My daughter's birthday is coming up soon. This spring, sometime," he said with a wave of his hand.

Paige took a careful sip from her too-full mug. His phrasing was odd. Who referred to a daughter's birthday by a vague season and not a specific date? She joked to herself that maybe he was worried Paige would steal the daughter's identity if she had too much detailed information. He surely couldn't have forgotten the actual day of her birth.

"I'd like to hire you as her gift. Your services as a business consultant, of course."

Paige set her mug on the table, focusing on watching the movement of her own hands as she struggled to contain a completely unprofessional burst of laughter that wanted to escape. His first sentence had implied that this polished businessman intended to purchase *her* as the present, which was ludicrous. The second cleared up the misinterpretation but still seemed equally funny to her. The gift of her professional services didn't strike her as a heartfelt present from a loving dad.

Maybe it was a practical one from a father who didn't remember his daughter's birthdate?

"What type of company does she own?"

Kenneth waved his hand vaguely through the air again. "She has a little farm in the Willamette Valley, near McMinnville. She grows...herbs or something New Agey. Certainly nothing that would cover the property taxes and high cost of living in those fancy small towns that are within commuting distance of Portland. The last time I talked to her, she tried to sound confident and not at risk of losing the place, but I think she might be fooling herself. I tried to talk her into selling before she gets too deep in debt and finding a job with a regular salary, but she's too stubborn."

Paige's mind seesawed between Kenneth's appallingly dismissive attitude toward his daughter's business and a sudden vision of leaving the city behind and driving to McMinnville for a paid vacation. The daydream won for the moment, and Paige pictured herself behind the wheel of a convertible, her hair loose and blowing in the wind, and her dog Dante grinning in the passenger seat. Somehow, the weather was sunny, warm, and springlike in her mind, even though she had only mentally traveled a few miles from Portland's overcast skies. The air in her mind was fresh and filled with the green scents of growing things and fertile soil. She could walk Dante through vineyards and stop for samples of wine. Visit her old college roommate Sarai.

Of course, Paige didn't own a convertible. She might be able to convince herself of the practicality of renting a car instead of racking up miles on her own if the trip from Portland would take more than two hours. She sighed and brought herself back to the conference room, where the heat was turned to a dehydrating level to counter the cold, rainy Pacific Northwest spring weather. Which was barely discernible from the cold, rainy Northwest winter. She shook her head. If she wanted a sunnier destination, she'd need to travel a lot farther than McMinnville.

"I really don't know anything about the agricultural industry," she said, but the argument sounded weak to her. She could study. Research. The same thing she did every time she took a new job and made her client's business concerns and passions her own, at least during the term of her employment. She hadn't been familiar with Kenneth's industry when she was first hired, and now she would feel comfortable teaching a class on commercial real estate at the local college. Did she *want* to learn everything there was to know about New Age farming, though? Not particularly. "And how can I save her money if she doesn't have much staff to fire?"

Kenneth laughed at her joke even as she cringed internally at her flippant reference to the people who would soon lose their jobs here because of her recommendations. "I know this isn't your usual type of client," he said, gesturing broadly with his hands. "I was hoping you would take the job as a favor to me."

Paige took another sip of her coffee, giving herself time to think. She would surely get more clients because of her work at Kenneth's company, but not because he liked her and recommended her to others. Other managers and owners would be watching the firm over the next few months, studying its bottom line and determining whether her advice translated to more financial success. Then they would see that her input had added value to the company. A lot of value, in the form of dollar signs. And they would hire her.

Eventually.

Paige rubbed at a drop of coffee that had spilled on the table, but she ended up smudging the glass more than cleaning it. While she had been building her reputation as a consultant with her own firm, she experienced the expected highs and lows in terms of workload. She'd get a new client and work tirelessly to create a prospective plan for them. Then she—and the people who were considering hiring her—would wait to see how well her ideas worked. Those downtimes always came to an end, but she hated being in the middle of them. Idle, with an emptiness that she longed to fill with research on her next venture. She never quite knew what to do with herself in those middle places.

Working for Kenneth's daughter was an answer, but not a great one. Paige had no idea what to expect. Would she be as cutthroat as her father, or a flake, as he seemed to imply? Or maybe a witch who used her herbs to make love potions and spells to make ex-lovers go bald? Paige could only hope—that would at least make for some interesting research.

"It's an intriguing proposition," she said. "I'm sure I can find ways for her to cut costs by either diversifying or specializing, although I can't make a business concept that doesn't have intrinsic potential work, no matter what I suggest. Usually, I only take clients that have the elements for success buried somewhere in their companies." Then she knew they would thrive, as long as they followed her proposals. If Kenneth's daughter was facing a weak market with an undesirable product, Paige would never be able to fix the broken parts short of telling her to start from scratch and try something else.

Kenneth propped his elbows on the table and leaned toward her. "Truthfully, that's the reason I want to hire you. If you tell her the farm idea's a bust, then she might be more inclined to take your advice than mine and get out of it while she still can."

Paige frowned. "So you *want* me to fail."

"Of course not," he said, but it was accompanied by a smile and a nod of his head, as if he was relieved she understood. "I want you to succeed in helping her move toward a more financially responsible future."

Her initial irritation with his dismissive attitude had taken a back seat to the convertible-fresh-air-spring working-vacation daydream, but now annoyance moved to the forefront of her mind again.

"I'll do it," she said. It wasn't the type of work she wanted, and it definitely wouldn't lead to useful contacts for future jobs. She'd help Kenneth's daughter, though, but not in the way he wanted. She'd do her best to make the farm as profitable as it could be, and only as a last resort would she try to convince this woman to give up her dream and sell her farm, if it proved to be something she really cared about. Paige's aggressive tactics might be more suitable for the boardroom than a garden patch, but how different could it really be? Business sense was business sense, no matter the location.

❖

"So I'll be spending a few weekends in McMinnville helping someone named Kassidy and staying in Portland during the week, in case Kenneth needs me to help during his transition period." Paige toyed with the fragile stem of her wineglass and watched Evie to see how she would react. Paige wasn't sure if she should ask Evie to go with her or not. She was planning to make this a vacation as well, after all, since she rarely left town and figured her work on the farm could be handled quickly and efficiently, leaving plenty of time to taste wine and sightsee. At least, to do whatever passed for sightseeing in the country. Looking at trees? Taking walks through nature? Dante would love those, but Paige was decidedly ambivalent about them. She usually preferred her nature to come in the form of paved walking paths that wended through city parks.

"Are those bobby pins in your hair? I hope you didn't pay your stylist since she cut you too short," Evie said, taking a small bite of her grilled salmon. "Anyway, I get that you want to keep your client happy by taking on this job with his daughter, but it's a dead end. Unless you're planning to hand out business cards to every hobby farmer hovering on the outskirts of Portland, of course."

Evie laughed at this comment, and Paige covered up her lack of response by taking a sip of her merlot. Why did everyone want to belittle Kassidy's profession? Even though Paige had no interest in cultivating either plants or plant-growing clients, she didn't feel a need to put down the farming community in general.

"I thought it would be nice to get out of the city for a bit. Plus, I don't have any other jobs lined up right now, and I hate to sit around and do nothing."

"I've been thinking of getting away, too," Evie said, fiddling with her asparagus and not looking at Paige. "I thought I'd drive up to Seattle and visit some friends. Do some shopping and see what's new in the art galleries. I've been meaning to redecorate my bedroom, so I want to find a new painting to hang in there. Or maybe a collage."

Just like that...Paige realized she wouldn't be asking Evie to go to McMinnville with her—and Evie wouldn't say yes even if she did. Paige didn't need to hear the precise words to recognize that she was one of the things Evie would be removing from her bedroom when she redecorated. No eye contact. Decisions that sounded as if they'd been made for a while now, but this was the first Paige was hearing about them.

She couldn't complain or act too affronted, though, since most of her own sentences—like Evie's—had started with the word *I*. It was all very civilized and drama-free, like the rest of their relationship had been. They had spent a pleasant six months together, and now it was time to move on. Paige exhaled in a long sigh, which she tried to cover with a small cough because too much of her sense of relief was evident in it.

"I think some time in Seattle sounds great. For you," she added quickly, in case Evie thought she was trying to include herself in the trip.

Evie met her gaze again and gave her a smile that had as much relief etched in it as Paige's sigh. "And I'm sure McMinnville would be great for some people. I'll bet you die of boredom there, though."

Paige shrugged. "That's why I'm coming back to the city during the week. Short doses of country life shouldn't prove fatal."

Evie made a skeptical-sounding noise. Paige watched her as she attacked her meal with gusto now, apparently relieved that their breakup had been simple and nonconfrontational, and no longer too nervous to do more than pick at her food.

Evie was everything Paige should want in a woman. She was smart and a successful interior designer—*her* business never had any need for Paige's professional assistance. She was gorgeous. Well-read. Informed on current events.

Not the most romantic list of attributes, but then again, Paige wasn't looking for flowers, pink hearts, and love notes left on bathroom mirrors. She and Evie had never defined their relationship, and Paige preferred it that way. She wanted nothing more than heated, explosive beginnings, ambiguous but pleasant middles, and vague, unemotional endings. Exactly what she had gotten with Evie.

She felt sort of hollow, but she couldn't tell if it was because she and Evie were through or because it was simply the way she always felt when she finished a consulting job and faced the stretch of empty days before she got to work again.

"Are you going to start your farming research soon?" Evie asked.

"Not yet. I don't even know what she grows there, so I'll wait until I see the place before I start formulating any sort of plan." Paige always preferred to begin a new job without any preconceived ideas about how she wanted to fix a business. If she didn't go in with a blank slate, then she might overlook key issues that were unique to the individual firm. In the case of Kassidy's farm, Paige didn't have any biases in place because she didn't know what she'd find in McMinnville. Kenneth might have been correct about the herbs, but given his indifferent attitude, Paige thought it was just as likely that Kassidy was a chicken farmer or even something else entirely.

Paige would find out soon. She'd observe the farm, locate the areas of mismanagement, and formulate a proposal just like she always did. She might not have a job with a high-end corporate client right now, but she at least had a temporary place where she could channel her energy and attention. She suddenly realized how hungry she really was and, like Evie, turned to her dinner with renewed enthusiasm.

Chapter Two

A burst of steamy fragrance filled the kitchen when the chopped garlic hit sizzling oil in the heavy enamel pan. Kassidy Drake stirred the mixture, careful not to burn the garlic, and then added a large plateful of diced chicken. While the meat browned, she returned her attention to wiping the last few morels with a damp tea towel and slicing them into thin half rounds. She added the mushrooms and a few leaves of sage from her garden to the pan and breathed in the earthy blend of aromas as the ingredients finished cooking.

Kassidy didn't have an abundance of fresh vegetables available to her this early in the growing season, but the ones she had been able to scrounge from her yard and some nearby woods made up for the lack of variety with a depth of flavor. She took the Dutch oven off the heat and set it on a trivet on the counter, somehow managing to fight the temptation to stand by the kitchen island with a fork and eat everything right now, all by herself. Then she wouldn't have anything to bring to tonight's potluck, but she could always stop by the grocery store and pick up a premade veggie tray. She smiled at the thought. Her friends from the neighborhood farming community wouldn't recognize her if she wasn't carrying a dish of something homemade.

She scraped the chicken mixture out of the pan and returned it to the heat, moving through the process of creating a meal with the comfortable ease of long familiarity. She had been cooking since she was six, and she somehow continued to enjoy it as a hobby even though it had been an overwhelming responsibility when she was a child. She had started with burnt grilled cheeses and undercooked scrambled eggs, gradually teaching herself what she needed to know in order to feed her siblings and her mother—as well as not burning down the house. Cooking equaled love to her. And she hadn't done more than microwave a frozen dinner since Audrey left.

Of course, she hadn't done much of anything since Audrey left. Kassidy slid a large hunk of butter into the still-hot pan and let it sizzle and sputter until it started to look a little foamy. Tonight's get together was good for her beyond just getting her into the kitchen again, she decided, as she beat a blend of all-purpose and hazelnut flours into the butter. She had spent more time talking to the grafted plants in her greenhouse than her friends for the past couple of months, and her hermit-like behavior had gone on long enough. Sure, she had needed time and space to heal, but now she was scared of how much distance she had put between herself and other people.

The toxicity of her relationship with Audrey had snuck up on her, but the moment she realized how dysfunctional things had become, she severed the relationship without a backward glance. Audrey had seemed honestly perplexed by the breakup, and maybe she hadn't been consciously aware of what she was doing to Kassidy. That didn't make it better, though. Kassidy had opened up to Audrey and shared parts of her childhood that made her vulnerable. Audrey had used that information to punish Kassidy every time she got angry, withdrawing from Kassidy and distancing herself with a cold, emotionless expression.

Kassidy added milk to the pan and whisked with more vigor than was necessary, splashing herself with a few drops of hot liquid. She took a deep breath and calmed her movements. She had reacted to Audrey's silences in ways that were deeply ingrained in her. She had apologized, cooked Audrey's favorite foods, left her small gifts. Eventually, Audrey would turn to her with that dazzling smile again, and all would be forgiven. At least Kassidy hadn't taken very long to recognize the old patterns, and she had pulled herself out of the messed-up game the moment she clearly saw what was happening.

Old habits died hard. The proverb had stuck around for ages because it was true. Kassidy uncorked a bulbous glass jar and sprinkled a palmful of dried purple buds into her hand. She scattered the Sharon Roberts lavender over the surface of the steaming milk and was rewarded with the sudden release of a calming floral scent. A few sprinkles of freshly grated nutmeg, some twists of black pepper, and the béchamel was done.

She strained the liquid to remove the lavender pieces before mixing the chicken with the sauce, then covered the pan and set it aside to cool. She had already packed a small army of tiny puff pastry cups, and she'd assemble the hors d'oeuvres at the party. She had to be more vigilant with her romantic relationships and not let them lead her down the path she had taken with Audrey—and one or two past girlfriends—but she didn't need to maintain the same distrust and carefulness around her friends. She knew she could rely on them for anything, just like they could turn to her without hesitation. And given the challenges they all were facing with increasing taxes and fickle markets, they needed to band together as much as possible if they wanted their artisan community to survive. And it *had* to survive. The world would be a much grayer place without it.

Kassidy shook her head, trying to ignore—just for tonight—the near constant worry she felt when she thought about the future of her farm. She felt a little better when she focused on the fate of the community as a whole, because then she didn't feel so overwhelmingly alone when she contemplated her financial situation. She went into her bedroom and pulled off the sauce-splattered shirt and soft flannel pants she had been wearing while she cooked. She tossed them into the clothes hamper and put on a pair of faded jeans and a gray T-shirt that showed a frowning cartoon grape holding an empty wine bottle upside down with the words *I'm crushed* underneath the image. She wouldn't have to worry about empty wine bottles tonight, though. Over half of the members of their local business community were connected to the wine trade in some way, and all of them would be sure to bring plenty of bottles for everyone to sample. She added a thin sweater because the early spring evening promised to be a cool one and hurried out to the car with her heavy containers of food.

The drive from her rural farm to Drew and Jessica's tasting room in downtown McMinnville was a quick one. Most of the businesses except for a few pubs and restaurants along the small main street were closed for the evening, and the strings of colorful lights around the Bête Noir's large paned windows provided a splash of brightness in the deepening dusk. The party was meant to give the local farmers and artists a chance to gather together after the quiet isolation of the winter season and before the bustle of spring and summer arrived, but no tourists or other passersby would be turned away from the welcoming room, the plentiful glasses of Oregon's pinot noir, and the lavish food.

Kassidy's stomach growled at the thought of food. She had spent hours fussing over her chicken dish but hadn't had anything to eat since her breakfast of fruit and a cinnamon roll. She gathered her bowl of sauce and boxes of pastry off the back seat and crossed the street. Once inside the store, she hesitated in the doorway for a moment, blinking as her eyes adjusted to the light and as her mind adjusted to the presence of the crowd that filled the room. The winter had been a lonely, dreary one, and she felt overwhelmed by wall-to-wall people.

Not for long, though. Drew was at her side before she had a chance to give in to her initial reaction and escape back into the anonymously dark evening.

"Ah, our lavender keeper has finally arrived," he said, bending down to kiss her cheek and take the containers out of her hands in one smooth movement. "This smells heavenly. Does anything need to be reheated or prepped?"

Kassidy felt the knots that had been forming inside her loosen. She had needed privacy while she healed and shored up her personal defenses again, and now she was ready to be back in the world. Among friends who cared about the same things she did and who cared about her, but who never intruded on her privacy as a person.

"Thank you, Drew," she said, giving his arm a squeeze, grateful for more than his offer to help with the food. "They don't need reheating. Just put a scoop of chicken in each of the pastry cups, and that'll be perfect."

"Will do. Now, go find Jessica and make sure you try a glass of the reserve. She's been moping because she hasn't seen you for ages." He held her food with one hand and used the other to turn her toward the corner of the room and give her a gentle push toward the bar.

Jessica was waving at her, so Kassidy bypassed the loaded food table with a longing look and headed toward her friend. Jessica was an ex-model who had come to the Willamette Valley to do a photo shoot, met Drew when she stopped to taste some wine, and never left. She still had the ultrathin physique and angular cheekbones of a high-fashion model, but a ruffled peasant blouse and genuine smile softened her look. She came around the bar and gave Kassidy a tight hug.

"Don't even," she said, slapping Kassidy's hand away when she reached for one of the prefilled wineglasses. She took her place behind the counter again and surreptitiously poured some wine out of a bottle hidden under the lip of the bar. "We've already sold out of most of this year's Best Bête, even though Drew just announced it a few weeks ago, but we put a couple bottles aside to share with special friends."

"Thank you," Kassidy said, touched by the gesture. Drew and Jessica were giving her more than a glass of fancy wine. This gift encompassed all the time and effort and passion they put into their winery, and Kassidy took the time to fully appreciate it. The color of the wine was deeper than the less mature ones in the glasses on the bar, but it was still the clear burgundy of Oregon's ubiquitous pinot noir. She had been surprised by the flavor of these wines when she first came to the Willamette Valley because she had expected the lighter-colored wines to lack dimension and flavor. If she hadn't recognized how wrong she was before, then tonight's wine would have clearly shown her the error in her thinking. She sipped it slowly, savoring the strong taste of cherry and the underlying hint of earthiness. She had been transplanting some new varietals this week and had marveled at the rich, healthy smell of the soil and how substantial and nourishing it felt in her hands. Drew and Jessica had captured that in a glass.

"I taste Oregon," she said, and Jessica grinned at her.

"Exactly," she said. "Every year the wine gets better and tastes more like a place instead of just a handful of anonymous grapes."

Jessica turned away for a moment to hand glasses to a couple Kassidy didn't recognize. She noticed more drop-in traffic than she had seen last year. Word must be spreading about the so-called private party. When Jessica looked back at her, Kassidy saw an expression of concern on her face. Here it came…

"How are you doing? We haven't seen much of you this winter, and I've been worried. I was going to come by, but I didn't know if you needed some time alone after…"

Her words trailed off, but Kassidy knew exactly what she meant. The community was too small for it to have gone unnoticed when Audrey had moved in with her, and then moved out again not long after.

"I'm fine," Kassidy said, forcing a smile. It didn't feel convincing, so she covered it by taking another drink of her wine. She nudged the conversation out of the personal sphere. "I've been keeping busy, expanding the number of plants I have in the north field and experimenting with some new varietals."

"I think it's a good idea for you to experiment with someone… oops, I meant *something* new," Jessica said, apparently not fooled by Kassidy's deflection of the conversation from personal to business related subjects. "If you ever need a friend to talk to about these varietals, or anything else, I'm here for you."

Kassidy smiled and thanked her, but she knew she wouldn't accept the offer, even though she was grateful to receive it.

"Ugh, here comes Alexandra," Jessica said, looking over Kassidy's shoulder. "She always compliments our wines while managing to let me know how much worse they are than her own."

Kassidy laughed and held up her glass. "You should give her some of this. That'll shut her up."

"No way. She doesn't deserve its deliciousness." Jessica topped off Kassidy's glass with more of the reserve and nodded toward the food. "You should get something to eat before everything is gone. Plus, you might want to be out of the line of fire in case I dump a glass of wine on her head."

"Your wines are too good to be wasted like that," Kassidy said.

She slipped away as Alexandra approached the bar, and turned her attention to the food. Finally. Jessica's dire prediction about everything being gone wasn't holding true, and the table was overflowing with offerings from all the local farms and restaurants, showcasing the best products they had. The invitations sent by Drew and Jessica had included a small decorative card used to identify the dish, and Kassidy had written *Lavender Chicken Cups* on hers and put it in the box with the pastries. She found it on the table where Drew had placed it next to an artfully arranged plate of her hors d'oeuvres.

In the center of the table, looking sadly out of place among the gourmet dishes, was a large bag of tortilla chips and a jar of salsa. There wasn't a handwritten card next to this selection, since all one had to do was read the bag to know what it was. Kassidy moved around the table, putting a small taste of everything around the edge of her plate. Spicy onion pakoras from Sarai's Pakistani restaurant. Panzanella with bright red tomatoes, vibrant green strips of basil, and chunks of what was surely homemade bread, glistening with a hefty drizzle of Everett and Brian's olive oil. Tiny rhubarb and pear tarts from the Moorhouses' orchard. When she finished the circuit of the table, she added a huge pile of chips in the middle, topped with a generous dollop of salsa.

She happily crammed a loaded tortilla chip into her mouth and looked up just in time to see a woman watching her from the far corner of the room. Kassidy swallowed the chip and looked away quickly, but she could still picture the woman in her mind with a disturbing clarity of detail. She was standing next to Sarai and some other local restaurant owners, seeming to be part of their conversation but still looking like an outsider. She held her wineglass like someone unfamiliar with the tenets of wine tasting, cradling the bowl so her hand would warm the liquid instead of holding the stem. Kassidy tried to fixate on that fact instead of letting her mind wander to the stranger's shiny brown hair and the way it curled across her jawline and barely brushed her shoulders. Her hazel eyes that had held a look of amusement, as if she was carrying on a private and funny conversation with herself while she observed the world around her. Kassidy was struck by how much she wanted to know what thoughts were taking place inside her mind.

Experiment with someone new. Jessica's advice leaped unbidden into her mind. No way. Kassidy wanted to focus on what was old and comfortable. Her farm, her solitude, her privacy. Salty chips and earthy wine. The smell of lavender. She put all her attention on the plate of food she was holding, resolutely banishing the image of a beautiful stranger from her thoughts.

Paige was feeling out of place. Oddly disjointed, as if she had entered another dimension instead of merely driven to a town that was a couple hundred miles from her own. Not because she had been shunned for being an outsider, but because she had been welcomed in with open arms. She had been to parties before, of course, but never ones that were as equally welcoming to people wandering in off the streets as they were to invited guests. She had come with her friend Sarai, but she saw random people stumbling through the door as if inexplicably drawn to the lights and crowds, and they were gathered into the fold by their hosts as if they were long-lost family members.

Sarai had said it was a potluck but insisted Paige didn't need to bring anything. Paige had, of course, ignored her advice and brought what would be a nondescript and acceptable appetizer at any other party. Chips and dip. How could she go wrong? Ha. At least she hadn't opted for the bottle of Italian wine that had been her second choice. Paige thought she should probably feel embarrassed, but instead she had an irresistible urge to laugh every time she looked at the table with its ring of elegant hors d'oeuvres surrounding her plastic bag of chips.

And then a goddess had descended from the heavens and accepted her offering. Well, not a goddess. A beautiful mortal woman wearing a cute T-shirt and incredibly well-fitting jeans. With asymmetrical hair that walked a fine line between being light brown and honey blond, tucked neatly behind one ear and softly curling a little longer over her other cheek. Eating chips and salsa as if it was as perfect an example of epicurean delight as anything else on the table.

Paige couldn't stop herself from walking over to the table, even though she tried. She had just broken up with Evie—or what constituted a breakup in their overly subtle relationship. She was in town to work, not to engage in some sort of ill-conceived fling. She had no idea what to say to someone who would be at this kind of party.

All too soon, she was standing right behind her chip-munching goddess with no idea how to initiate a conversation. The woman smelled intoxicatingly wonderful, with an aura of something floral and delicate surrounding her, and the scent obviously had the ability to make Paige completely lose the ability to form words. *Talk about the food. Make a joke.* The woman was obviously not a food snob, so she'd surely appreciate a little self-deprecating gourmet humor from the outsider who had brought store-bought chips.

"Hi," she said, rolling her eyes internally at her awkwardness.

The woman turned around quickly, as if surprised to have someone approach and talk to her. At a party filled with a crowd of people. Paige wasn't sure why she should be startled, since she must be accustomed to having random women fling themselves at her all the time.

"Hi."

Paige gestured at her plate. "Do you like those chips? I picked them myself just this morning."

The woman looked toward the door, then back at Paige, seemingly trying to decide between the two options she faced. Luckily, she chose Paige and gave her a small but pulse-affecting smile. "I'm surprised to see them this time of year because I thought they were only harvested during football season. You must use a lot of fertilizer to keep them crisp after February."

"Yeah, I really pile it on," Paige said. She was rewarded for her small joke when the woman's shy-looking smile turned into a real grin, making her nearly drop her wineglass. She had been beautiful when she had been eating chips with a slightly rapturous expression, but once her nose scrunched with laughter, Paige was lost. She needed to keep this conversation going and find more ways to make her laugh. If they joked around long enough, Paige might dredge up enough courage to ask her out, even though she was feeling decidedly out of her element in this community.

Paige turned to the table for inspiration and luckily found it right in front of her. She gestured toward a plate of creamy discs labeled as Herb and Garlic Chevre. "I'm guessing this town has outlawed microwaves, but if we can find a wood-fired oven in the back we can make some nachos."

The woman shook her head with an exaggerated sigh. "And here I thought I was talking to a real gourmet. Nachos need to be made with shredded orange cheese from a plastic pouch. You didn't happen to harvest any of that, did you?"

Paige mimicked the deep sigh. "Sorry. I picked my orange cheese vines clean a couple months ago. Blame it on the Seahawks for making it to postseason."

They shared another smile, and Paige moved on to the next platter of hors d'oeuvres as a source for her jokes. If she worked her way around the table and kept talking about food, an invitation to dinner would seem like a natural segue from their banter. Halfway around, ask for her name. After the circuit had been completed, ask for her phone number. Paige loved an organized plan, and she struggled for something comical to say about the dainty pastries on the next tray. "Look at this one. Lavender chicken. Who puts perfume in food, right?"

She picked up one of the little puff pastry cups and crammed it in her mouth, more to stop herself from saying something stupid than because she wanted it, but once she started to chew she was hooked. The flavors exploded in her mouth, filling her with earthy and floral notes as if she had taken a very deep, delicious breath while standing in the middle of a forest. "Oh my God, this is amazing. Is it really lavender? I expected it to be nasty and perfume-y, but it isn't."

She paused, giving the other woman a chance to add to the conversation while Paige swallowed the tasty morsel and snagged another pastry cup. She was met with only silence, and when she looked around, she was standing all alone.

"Huh," she said. Hadn't their conversation been going well? Paige had thought the woman's laughter seemed genuine, but maybe she had been merely humoring her and waiting for a chance to escape. Paige ate the second hors d'oeuvre as a consolation prize and picked up a third as Sarai walked over to her.

"Oh, good. You got a chance to meet Kassidy."

Paige choked on her third appetizer. "What? When?"

"The woman you were just talking to," Sarai said, with a confused-looking frown. "Didn't you say you were here to work with Kassidy Drake? Something to do with her lavender farm?"

Shit. Had she really just insulted her new client's product directly to her face? And in a completely unwarranted way, since it was wonderful?

Paige sighed. This was why she always met with clients in their boardrooms and offices, where they usually had a placard announcing their names and titles. That way she could pick them out of a crowd and be sure not to inadvertently cram her foot into her mouth. She supposed she should count herself as fortunate because Kassidy's hors d'oeuvres had been at the beginning of Paige's attempt to joke her way around the table and not at the end, when her comments might have been paired with a request for a date. If that had been the case, Kassidy might have dumped the jar of salsa over Paige's head instead of simply walking away from her. Paige ate another lavender chicken cup, just to ease the feeling of anxiety creeping over her. She had some serious groveling to do tomorrow when she went to visit Kassidy's farm.

Chapter Three

Paige pulled to the side of the road and parked next to the Lavender Lane Farm sign. She wasn't quite ready to face Kassidy in person yet, so she decided to get a tourist-eye view of the farm first.

A thick hedge of large domed shrubs lined the street, with spiky green stems and small dots of deep purple. The plants were almost a yard high and would likely be stunning when in full bloom. Paige got a glimpse of the neat rows of shorter plants beyond the border and a small cottage in the distance. The place was beautiful—like its owner—and Paige wished yet again that she could go back in time and not say anything derogatory about lavender. She had replayed the evening over and over in her head, always imagining a different scenario than the one that actually took place. She had called Sarai from the road yesterday, and when she was invited along to the party, she had been more concerned about getting some food to bring than with finding out about Kassidy Drake. She had mentioned Kassidy's name but must have given Sarai the impression that she knew all about her new client. Unfortunately, she had been missing the key parts of the equation, including Kassidy's occupation and what she looked like. Of course, knowing that she was entering a realm dedicated to the Slow Food movement would have been helpful, too.

Oh, well. She couldn't change what had already happened, but she could move forward and make the best of the situation. While completely ignoring the fact that she had been awkwardly angling toward Kassidy as a potential date last night, against her better judgment. She was here to work and she had just broken up with Evie, she reminded herself yet again. Even though the dissolution of their relationship hadn't induced any trauma in either of them, she still wasn't ready to jump into another cycle of meeting someone, getting bored, and moving on. Luckily, the only woman who had managed to make her rethink her decision was her new client.

She needed to focus on the business aspect of Kassidy's life, not on her sexy blue eyes or the way she had eaten Paige's chips and salsa as enthusiastically as if they had been rare truffles or some other exotic treat. Paige brought her full attention to the farm and her first impressions of it as she stood facing the road with her hands on her hips. She hadn't seen many cars since leaving McMinnville and following the rural streets to Kassidy's farm, and she hoped this would change in tourist season. For now, though, she enjoyed the peace and quiet, and she let Dante out of the ancient Tercel so he could explore with her. He smiled exuberantly, tongue lolling out to one side, as she unbuckled his safety harness and set him free.

The young dog gamboled around her legs for an exhausting few minutes, nearly tripping her up. He was a rescue dog, of uncertain origins, and the love of her life. He seemed to be partly black Lab, but his ears were huge enough—and his energy level frantic enough—to make Paige suspect a crazy Chihuahua or two in his convoluted gene pool. Paige watched him run in circles for a few minutes and wondered if part of Evie's decision to move on was connected to the realization that if Paige became a fixture in her life, Dante was part of the package. The two of them had never gotten along.

In a heartbeat, Paige went from feeling parentally indulgent of Dante's show of energy to panicked when he took off toward the rows of lavender near the entrance to the farm and started digging with abandon. He flung an uprooted plant to the side and moved on to the next as she ran after him, conflicted between getting him to stop and returning the discarded plants to their now-empty holes.

After destroying a dozen or more plants, he stopped suddenly and stared toward the farmhouse. Paige breathed a sigh of gratitude and hastily shoved the bushes into the ground, doing her best to cover the roots, but her relief was short-lived because Dante took off, running away from her and down the lane toward the cottage.

Paige stood for a moment, staring after her dog with dirt clumping off her fingernails. She was tempted to cut her losses and go back to Portland right now. She already needed to apologize for insulting Kassidy's food, and now she had to add Dante's indiscretions to the list. She climbed in the car with weary resignation, wiping her muddy hands on some fast food napkins she had stashed in her glove compartment. The compartment door refused to shut completely when she was finished, and she drove slowly up Lavender Lane with it bumping noisily at every rut in the road.

Paige parked near the cottage and got out of her car again. She slowly turned in a circle and stared at the farm. There was no sign of Dante, but she saw seemingly endless rows of mounded lavender bushes, stretching out and away from her in tidy lines. Some were bright green and others had a silvery tinge to them. Most of the early buds on them were a deep purple, but some were pink or lighter shades of lavender. She hadn't expected such a variety of colors. A smaller cottage—trimmed and painted to be a tiny replica of the main house—sat on the edge of the main farmhouse's garden, which was as different from the exact rows of the fields as it could be. It was already a riot of color, even early in the spring, and it had the wild, crowded look of an English garden. All sorts of lavender shades were there, as she expected, but there were also splashes of red poppies and yellow daisies, and numerous other plants she couldn't identify, massed together in one glorious tangle.

She completed a 360-degree view of the farm and arrived back at the farmhouse, where she saw Kassidy standing near the open front door watching her with crossed arms and a wary expression. The lower half of the door was streaked with mud, and given the way her day was going, Paige figured Dante was the cause of the mess. *Please don't let it be any worse than a muddy door.*

"I don't suppose you've seen a dog running around," she said, trying to slip back into her usual professional demeanor and tone of voice, as if most of her business meetings took place on farms and involved disobedient pets. "I seem to have misplaced mine."

Kassidy gestured over her shoulder, and Paige stifled a groan as she walked up the steps and joined her in the doorway.

The farmhouse's living room was gorgeous, with a plush cream-colored couch and two elegant bergère chairs upholstered in stripes of deep rose and cream. The wooden frames of the chairs were stained in a deep cherry tone to match the hardwood floors, and a thick beige and pale rose rug neatly framed the sitting area. A few colorful and interesting touches kept the room from looking overly matchy-matchy. Throw pillows in lilac and light blue, some framed photographs of the farm, and what seemed to be an enormous dark wicker picnic basket sitting next to one of the chairs, covered with magazines and bits of mail.

Paige was silent as she admired the room. It was beautiful and transported her mentally to the South of France as long as she didn't dwell too much on the muddy paw prints leading across the lovely rug, directly to where Dante was sprawled on the couch. He seemed enormously pleased with himself, as if he appreciated the aesthetics of the room and was happy to improve upon it with his presence.

Paige covered her mouth as her urge to laugh at the scene overrode her dismay. "You probably shouldn't have let him inside," she managed to choke out.

"Gee, you think? I heard a noise at the door and when I opened it, he ran past me. I didn't exactly invite him in."

Paige cleared her throat. "I am really sorry. I'll pay to get the couch and rug cleaned. And the chair."

"Don't worry about it. Once the dirt dries, it'll be easy to vacuum. I live on a farm in a state where it's usually raining, so it's certainly not the first time I've had mud tracked into the house. He scared my cat, though." She pushed Paige's shoulder, playfully knocking her over the threshold and into the room. "Go ahead and laugh. I can tell you're trying to hold it in."

Paige wasn't sure if it was the physical jarring or Kassidy's words that made her release control of her composure, but she bent over and put her hands on her knees, laughing until she had to wipe a few stray tears from the corner of her eye. Kassidy didn't seem as amused as she was, but she chuckled softly. At least she wasn't calling the police to report a pair of dirty trespassers.

"Sorry," Paige said again, gasping for breath. She was proud of her ability to see humor in most situations, but more often than she liked, the tendency to collapse in inappropriate laughter was awkward when it happened in front of clients or girlfriends. Hopefully, Kassidy wouldn't hold it against her since she wasn't the one paying the bill for Paige's services. "It's just so awful that it's funny. I was coming here to apologize for last night, and now this..." She waved her hand weakly toward the mess.

"Are you going to tell me what field he destroyed, or shall I be surprised when I discover it on my own?"

Paige straightened up. She felt calmer since she didn't have to fight her laughter anymore, and only an occasional giggle seeped out. "He dug up one or two...or maybe twelve plants at the end of the driveway, near the Lavender Lane sign. I put them back, though, so they should be fine."

"Mm-hmm." Without saying any actual words, Kassidy managed to convey her doubts about Paige's ability to save her mangled lavender bushes. She pointed at Paige's arms. "I can see you tried, at least."

"Oh. Ugh." Paige looked at the stained sleeves of her blouse. It had been bright white when she left the bed-and-breakfast this morning, and probably never would be again. She had removed most of the loose dirt from her hands, but they were still gray and her short fingernails were a mess. She unbuttoned her cuffs and rolled the sleeves to her elbows to hide most of the mud.

Kassidy walked down a hall and returned with a fluffy blue towel. "There's a hose by the garden gate. Why don't you rinse him off while I try to get my poor cat to come out from under the bed."

Paige walked across the room and caught Dante's collar, belatedly realizing she had left her own muddy set of prints next to his. She took him outside to the hose and rinsed the mud off his paws and her black flats before drying them both with the towel. The process took some careful maneuvering since she didn't dare let her dog loose in the garden. She spent her few minutes of alone time reminding herself that she was here to do Kassidy a favor. The benefits she could provide by refiguring the running of the farm would far outweigh the trouble of cleaning a sofa and a carpet. And a chair, and possibly a scratched door.

She got back to the farmhouse and kicked off her shoes on the porch. Kassidy was standing in the middle of the living room holding a cat, and Dante strained against Paige's hold, trying to reach them. She shut the door behind her and gripped his collar with both hands. When Kassidy had mentioned a cat, she had immediately pictured a Persian or something equally fancy and pedigreed. Something suited to the décor of the house, and possibly purchased because it blended well with the color palette.

Kassidy knelt on the floor and nodded for Paige and Dante to come closer. She set the cat down and the two animals briefly touched noses before the cat jumped onto the back of a chair and started cleaning his patchy tiger-striped coat. He was missing part of an ear and he had the face of a boxer who had gone one too many rounds. Dante pulled himself free and jumped onto the seat of the cat's chair, curling into a ball with his chin on his paws.

"What happened to him?" Paige asked. She had been trying to come up with a politer way to ask the question, but she decided she'd missed the chance for tact and decorum. Might as well go the direct route.

"Don't make fun of him." Kassidy frowned at her and went over to stand by the cat, scratching his chin and petting Dante with her other hand. "He had a tough life out there, before I got him."

"I've heard McMinnville has a lot of trouble with cat gangs."

Kassidy kept her head turned, looking at the animals, but Paige saw the hint of a smile she was apparently trying to hide. "It's pretty bad. The dropout rate at obedience schools is astronomical. You'd be wise to avoid dark alleys and fish markets while you're in town. Anyway, I heard this horrible yowling one night, and when I went out to see what was going on, he streaked into the house. He hasn't expressed the slightest interest in going back out since."

Of course not. Why would he want to leave you? Paige was surprised by the sudden thought. It was reasonable to believe the cat would prefer living in a nice, safe house rather than outside, but Paige's consideration had been more to do with being around

Kassidy than being in this house in particular. She kept her tone light and ignored the entirely too personal way she was thinking about Kassidy. "You really need to be more careful about opening your door every time you hear a noise. You never know what will come inside."

Kassidy looked her up and down. "I'm beginning to realize..."

"Very funny. So, what's his name? Bruiser? Bugsy? Prince Fuzzyboots?"

"Kipper," Kassidy said. "We have a lot of *K* names in my family, and it was the first one to come to mind."

"Best he stays inside. He won't get a lot of street cred with a name like Kipper." Paige paused, distracted by Kassidy's obvious affection for the animals. Of course Kassidy liked her own cat, but she paid just as much warm attention to Dante, regardless of his disastrous entrance into her life.

"His name is Dante," she said, before realizing she hadn't introduced herself yet. She'd started in on the lavender joke last night before she had a chance to exchange names, and her arrival today hadn't gone any more smoothly. "And I'm—"

"Paige Leighton. I know."

She frowned. Had Kassidy's father called her about Paige's impending visit? She had been under the impression that his involvement ended when he deposited the money in her account. He didn't know his daughter's birthday or what type of farm she had, and Paige was frankly a little surprised that he even had Kassidy's phone number.

"Sarai called," Kassidy said, as if she could see Paige trying to figure out who had given her name. "She asked me to forgive you for last night because you didn't know who I was and because you ended up eating the entire tray of chicken cups."

"They were really good," Paige said with a shrug. "And I only ate ten or so. I expected them to taste like—"

"Perfume. Yes, you mentioned that."

"Well, at least you left before I was able to ask you out. That would have made today really awkward," Paige said. She had probably made Kassidy feel vulnerable and hurt with her comments, so she decided to share her own embarrassing ulterior motive from their interaction to even the playing field.

Kassidy turned a deep shade of pink and avoided meeting Paige's gaze, but the smile still hovered around the corners of her mouth. "You're right. That would have been awkward. Thank goodness I am completely unaware that that was your intention." She gestured toward a door leading out of the living room. "I was just making some lunch for us. Do you want to come with me and make fun of the ingredients I'm using, or would you rather wait here with the animals?"

"I'll wait here." Paige sat on the clean side of the couch and Kipper immediately hopped off the chair and onto her lap. Dante followed and jumped onto the cushion next to hers. She called to Kassidy's retreating back, "Remember, I like extra cologne in mine."

Kassidy shook her head as she pushed through the swinging door and into her kitchen. Once she was alone, she leaned against the counter and took a deep breath. She had spent her entire life seeking calm. Even her relationship with Audrey, with all its dysfunctionality, had been a fairly steady and predictable affair, with no extremes of passion or any other emotion. That was part of what had drawn her to Audrey in the first place.

Paige was something different altogether. She had already messed with Kassidy's ordered life, and they hadn't even been formally introduced until moments ago. When other people had expressed surprise about lavender's culinary uses, she had always taken the opportunity to explain about the different cultivars and their characteristics. But Paige made one snarky comment last night, and Kassidy had rushed out the door as soon as her back was turned. Once she was outside in the cold night, she had realized how easy it would have been to laugh at Paige's comment, introduce herself, and talk about her beloved lavender plants. By the time she had come to her senses, though, she felt too silly to go back inside. She had been on her own too long before the party, and maybe she had been looking for a chance to escape.

She wasn't about to admit it to Paige, but the idea of a date had been on her mind, as well, during their conversation at the party.

Paige had been funny and sexy and easy to talk to. Despite her initial desire to flee when Paige approached her, Kassidy had been attracted to her and relaxed in her presence. Combine those reactions, and they were enough to scare Kassidy right out of the party.

But Paige had followed her home. Kassidy walked over to the ingredients she had been assembling when she'd heard Dante's frantic scratching at the front door. She had hopefully sounded relaxed and unfazed when she spoke with Sarai about Paige, but she had felt turmoil inside. She wasn't ready to date, especially not someone who made her feel too many emotions at once, but she had ignored her internal warnings and had prepared a nicer meal than the frozen pizza she had been planning to microwave for herself, just because she heard that a stranger was coming over to her house.

Kassidy rolled some fresh dough into two rough ovals and topped them with a garlicky kale pesto before putting them into the preheated oven. This really wasn't much more effort than using a microwave, she decided, as she put some greens in a bowl and topped them with candied hazelnuts, chunks of strawberries, and a little crumbled feta. She certainly wasn't putting out more effort than she would for any other guest in her home. The meal had nothing to do with the way Paige's eyes crinkled with laughter at the slightest provocation, or the pleased expression she had worn when Kipper jumped on her lap. Kassidy was merely being a good host.

She poured extra virgin olive oil, red wine vinegar, and a little sugar in a cruet and shook it harder than was really necessary, pausing to wipe some splatters off her counter before adding dried mustard and poppy seeds. She shook it more carefully this time and poured the dressing over the spring greens.

The scent of fresh bread and herbs greeted her when she opened the oven door and removed the flatbreads. She drizzled them with some more of the olive oil, then arranged everything on two plates. She would have to spend a long time restoring her living room to a state of cleanliness and her emotions to a state of peace once Paige and Dante left. She might as well fortify herself with some good food and wine before she got to work.

Chapter Four

Kassidy put the plates of food on a small table in the alcove off the living room. It was too chilly to eat in the garden, and she wanted to keep an eye on the animals in case they started to brawl. Although, after getting his fur ruffled at Dante's abrupt entrance earlier, Kipper seemed to have accepted the dog's presence with the confidence of a cat that knew he could win a battle if necessary.

Paige scooted the cat off her lap and got up, hurrying over to help. Kassidy opened a bottle of wine and poured two glasses while she watched Paige arrange plates and napkins on the table. If Sarai hadn't called to let her know Paige was coming, Kassidy probably wouldn't have recognized her right away since she looked so different than she had last night. Instead of casual jeans and a long-sleeved T-shirt, she was wearing expensive-looking black dress slacks and a neatly pressed white shirt—patchily white now, after her adventures in Kassidy's lavender fields. The soft curls Kassidy had briefly let herself imagine touching last night were slicked back and held hostage by a metallic clip. She looked dressed for a boardroom meeting rather than a trip to a country farm.

"This looks delicious," Paige said. "I hope you didn't go to any trouble."

"Not at all," Kassidy said with a dismissive gesture. "I was making food for myself anyway." She neglected to mention exactly what kind of food she had planned to make. She had just bumped her dinner meal to lunch instead. The microwave pizza would be waiting for her tonight.

Paige took a bite of the flatbread. "Mm. I can barely taste the lavender in this. It blends in with the other flavors very well."

Kassidy somehow managed to swallow her wine before laughing. "There isn't any lavender in it. I don't put it in everything I cook, just because I grow it here."

Paige laughed, too. "You shouldn't have told me. You had me believing you were the master of subtlety."

Kassidy chewed a forkful of salad. "So are you going to tell me why you're really here? It seems excessive for a simple apology, and Sarai was sort of vague about it on the phone. She seemed to think we knew each other."

Paige watched her intently, as if trying to gauge her reaction. "I know your father. I did some consulting work for his firm, and he hired me to do the same for your farm. It's a birthday present. Surprise!"

The last word was spoken with an injection of enthusiasm, complete with an awkward flourish of jazz hands. Kassidy could see something underlying Paige's cheerful smile, though, as if she was aware of tension between Kassidy and her dad. How much did she know about Kassidy's personal business? She ate some more bites of salad, not really tasting anything but trying to get her equilibrium back.

"My birthday is in June," she said.

Paige shrugged. "Well, I'm between clients right now, so it's an early present."

Kassidy gave up the pretense of enjoying her meal and sat back in her chair, her arms crossed over her chest. The more believable explanation was that her dad had forgotten when her birthday was. Since Paige was carefully avoiding eye contact, she probably realized it, as well. Kassidy didn't care for her own sake, since she had grown up with her dad's absentminded approach to fatherhood, but she hated having anyone else witness his lack of concern for her.

"What kind of consultant are you?"

She knew her tone sounded snippy, but Paige didn't seem deterred.

"General business," she said. Her tone of voice and facial expressions changed as she switched to a discussion of her profession. She suddenly seemed as detached and unadorned as the clothes she was wearing, and Kassidy found herself missing Paige's sharp gaze and ready laugh. "I observe companies and suggest ways they can improve in efficiency, structure, production...whatever is appropriate for the industry they're in."

"So you tell companies which employees they should fire?"

Kassidy saw a brief flash of something unreadable flit across the professional mask Paige was now wearing, but it disappeared with a shrug.

"Sometimes, yes. But I also advise in other ways. Some clients need to restructure certain aspects of their companies. Combine some job requirements or divide others among more employees. Maybe invest in specialized training. Also, successful businesses don't always take advantage of expanding markets and changing industry climates because they get complacent. They might function well for another five or ten years after missing significant opportunities, but they eventually fall behind their competitors."

Kassidy nodded. Her dad had always been successful, with flashy apartments and cars and an extravagant lifestyle. She was surprised to hear he needed a consultant, but Paige's last example made sense to her. "That's what you did for my dad, isn't it?"

"My final proposals are often multifaceted," Paige said ambiguously, still managing to sound like an impersonal brochure come to life. "I never share the results of my consultations with anyone but my client."

Kassidy gritted her teeth. The thought of her dad intruding on her business, implying she was failing somehow, was bad enough. But for Paige to give him access to all her private information, all the things Paige decided she was doing wrong? No way.

Paige reached forward and rapped her knuckles on the table, pulling Kassidy's attention back to her. "You would be my client, Kassidy. Your dad paid for this as a gift, but the contract is in your name, and all privileges of confidentiality belong to you."

"That's good to hear," Kassidy said in a determinedly casual tone, trying not to let her face show how much Paige's assurances meant to her. The very fact that Paige had felt the need to tell her this indicated that she knew Kassidy's relationship with her father wasn't a typical loving one. If Kassidy admitted how much she wanted to keep her affairs private, she would be revealing too much of herself to a relative stranger.

She paused and collected herself. Paige wasn't Audrey. She might sense that Kassidy and her dad were distant, at best, from each other, but she had just promised she wouldn't use the information she got from Kassidy to expose the details of her business to her dad. If Kassidy could trust what Paige was saying, of course. She felt she could based on her instincts, but her gut had been wrong before.

She stared out the window at the rolling field of lavender behind the house. Her dad had gone away soon after the twins had been born, leaving Kassidy to take care of them and her mother, who barely managed to get out of bed most days. The first few times she and the twins had gone to his new Portland apartment for visitation weekends, she had hoped for at least a few hours with a responsible, present parent. She had soon learned to give up those expectations. Now, his intrusions into her life always caused her to feel stress and anxiety rather than the joy she would have experienced as a child.

She toyed with the delicate, wilting greens with her fork. She had to deflect the attention away from her childhood and family life, and Paige offered the perfect opportunity. She might be able to manage high-end corporate clients, but she was out of her element on the farm. She'd have nothing of use to contribute here besides humorous commentary about cooking with lavender.

"These skills you have, do you really believe they're transferable from a massive commercial real estate firm to a boutique farm? To be honest, you don't seem to know the first thing about lavender. I wouldn't be surprised if I found the ones you replanted upside down, with their roots waving in the air."

"Hey, give me a little credit for having common sense." Paige dropped her businesslike persona for a moment and laughed, with a slight blush reddening her cheeks. "Well, I'm pretty sure I put them back the right way. Purple dots in the ground, sticklike parts in the air. Right?"

Kassidy couldn't stop her answering smile. "Brilliant. Now I have no hesitation handing over all my business decisions to you."

Paige grinned. "Actually, you're right. I don't know anything about growing lavender or selling it, or even why people want to buy it. But that's what makes me so good at what I do. I observe without bias, learn like a beginner, and always see answers and options that people with entrenched ideas and beliefs seem to miss."

Kassidy shook her head. Paige sounded more real now, and less like a publicity video, but she still didn't seem to understand Kassidy's situation. "I don't have a bunch of employees to fire. I hire a few people to help me during harvesting, but I do most of the work here on my own. You can't magically lower my property taxes or turn my product into a money-earner like real estate or the newest technology. It's lavender. It's wonderful, but the potential is limited."

Paige clapped her hands together. "Exactly. You see limits. I come in with fresh eyes and see possibilities. That's what I *do*. It doesn't matter if you're making hundreds of dollars a month or millions. The process is the same."

Kassidy managed to stop thinking about her own issues—her farm, her meddling father, her determination to keep her private affairs *private*—and noticed the almost passionate way Paige talked about her consulting business.

"If you're this good at figuring out how to run a corporation, why don't you have one of your own? Why spend your life helping other people make money when you could, according to your own humble assessment, take any type of business and make it a success?"

Paige was silent for a moment. She kept her smile in place while she scrambled for a way to answer Kassidy's question. She had been an economics major at Reed and had gone on to get her MBA, but she had never found a niche for herself. She was good at injecting herself into other people's lives for a short time, subsuming their interests and learning what she needed to know before making her recommendations and moving on. She just didn't have anything she cared about on her own, which was part of the reason why she hated being between jobs. This one certainly wasn't ideal, and Kassidy wasn't a willing client, but Paige needed to be absorbed in learning. Lavender seemed to be an interesting enough topic, and Kassidy's farm could obviously use her help—after all, what business couldn't?

"My skills seem better suited to consulting," she answered vaguely. "Most of my clients are too personally involved in their businesses to adequately evaluate them. I can come in as an outsider, with a certain detachment, and see possibilities others might never consider."

She sighed and took a bite of salad, relieved that she had turned an uncomfortable personal question into a plug for her business. She needed to remember the wording she had used and put it on her website. She gave herself a mental high five. Way to turn a personal defect into a slogan.

Kassidy shook her head and finished off a triangle of flatbread. "The things you say make sense, but I still don't see how they'd apply to my farm. There's only so much you can do with lavender, unless you're an alchemist and can turn it into gold."

Paige spread her hands in a frustrated gesture. "You're providing proof for what I'm saying every time you open your mouth. You keep talking about what can't be done, while I'm here to show you new markets you've never even considered."

Kassidy rolled her eyes. "You're persistent. I'll give you that."

"And you're stubborn. Determined to follow your own path even if it leads you to bankruptcy. Losing your farm. Are you really willing to give up a chance to improve your financial situation just to make a point to your dad?"

"So my choices are either accept your help or declare bankruptcy?" Kassidy pushed back from the table and stood up. "I'll take the third option and keep the farm going on my own. I've done a damned good job so far, and I have a community of people around me who are supportive and who understand what it's like to run a business like mine. If I need help—which I don't—I'll turn to one of them."

Kassidy went into the kitchen, leaving the door swinging wildly behind her. Dante and Kipper followed her, dodging through the door on one of its swings. Paige gently set her fork down on her plate, not trusting herself to keep hold of it because she felt tempted to throw it at the wall in frustration. Why was she fighting so hard? Kassidy obviously didn't want her help, and Paige—despite her arguments to the contrary—wasn't fully convinced she would be able to offer any useful assistance. The entire place was covered with lavender plants. Either they sold for enough money to make a profit or they didn't. There didn't seem to be enough variables to offer a chance for drastic improvement.

Paige rubbed her temple, hoping the headache she felt wasn't the onset of a migraine. She undid her barrette and ran her fingers through her hair, releasing the tension caused by the tight hairstyle and letting her curls brush against her neck. Maybe Kassidy didn't need a drastic improvement in her farm's situation. Maybe a few cut corners or an as-yet unexplored source of revenue would be enough to help her cope more comfortably with her taxes and other expenses. Paige loved learning new things, and her interest was piqued by Kassidy's farm and by the local community. And she never turned down a challenge. Besides, she had only finished Kenneth Drake's proposal a week ago, and she was already frustrated by the lack of direction and substance she noticed in her life when she wasn't working. She needed something to do.

She got up and stacked her plate with Kassidy's. Her reasons were valid, but they weren't the full truth. She had felt a desire to support Kassidy during her meeting with Kenneth, even before she met her. The feeling had intensified today when she saw hurt flash across Kassidy's face before it was hastily hidden behind a scowl. Paige's attraction to Kassidy belonged on the list of reasons why she should run away from this job, but at the same time, it made her want to stay. She could be professional and ignore her feelings, especially since they were clearly not reciprocated.

Paige was about to go into the kitchen and request a truce when Kassidy came through the door, holding it open as the animals followed her through. She handed Paige a Fudgsicle.

"Peace offering," she said, sitting down again and unwrapping her own bar. "There isn't any lavender in it, in case you're wondering, although it might be a tasty combination."

Paige smiled, feeling the sharp edges of her headache soften with Kassidy's words. She sat in her chair, and Dante came over and rested his chin on her knee. Kassidy looked like she wanted to say more, so Paige remained silent and rubbed Dante's ears.

"It's just…well, the only time he expresses any interest in my business, it's to tell me to sell the farm and do something more worthwhile. Something *he* considers to be more worthwhile. And now his birthday present—sent months early and by proxy, for God's sake—is just another way for him to express his belief that I'm incapable of managing my own farm."

"He hired me first, to help *him*," Paige reminded Kassidy. She didn't fully understand the family dynamics in play here, and she wouldn't insult Kassidy by telling her that her instincts were wrong, and her father really did believe in her. He didn't, and he expected Paige to nudge Kassidy toward giving up her farm. She planned to do the exact opposite if Kassidy gave her a chance. "He wanted to improve his company and he believed I was the right person to help him do it. He's not offering you help that he wasn't willing to take on his own."

Kassidy frowned. "I hadn't thought of it that way." She took a bite of her dessert and drummed her fingers on the table. "So if I decided to let you work your consultant magic here, what would happen, exactly?"

Paige smiled. Now they were getting somewhere. "Well, I'd like to observe you for a few days." She cleared her throat, distracted by the thought of an all-too-personal type of observation. She started talking faster to keep her brain occupied with work and not the image of Kassidy traipsing through lavender-scented fields. "Watch you work on the farm, I mean. So I get an idea of the routines and processes you have in place. I try to keep my research to a minimum until I see how my clients' individual businesses are run because each one is unique, even if it's based on a similar industry or model. If I do too much research before I have a chance to observe, I'll only be learning what worked for someone else and might be tempted to push an agenda without understanding how it will fit your situation."

"That makes sense," Kassidy said, nibbling on her empty stick and sounding slightly annoyed because she had to agree with what Paige was saying.

Paige stared at Kassidy's lips for a long moment before she managed to look away. She focused her attention on the cabinet against the wall to her right, trying to concentrate on the way the green paint had been distressed until the knotty wood showed through beneath the wash of color. It was a pretty piece, and somewhat interesting, but it required a determined effort to keep her attention on it and not on Kassidy's mouth.

"So, um, yeah. I'd need to see your books, of course. And I'll want to visit other—"

"My what?"

"Your books. You do keep track of spending, profits, deductions, and all that, don't you?"

"Of course. But that seems very intimate."

Paige sighed. Her headache was coming back. "I promise I'll be fully clothed while I look at them."

"Not that kind of intimate." Kassidy hesitated, carefully centering the stick on the discarded wrapper and folding it up with a series of pleats. "How about this. You come here early tomorrow morning, and I'll show you around and explain how the farm functions. Then you can give me a suggestion about how I can improve what I do. If it seems reasonable, we'll talk about revealing my finances."

Paige stared at her in disbelief. "So you want me to audition for a job I already have?"

Kassidy spread her hands. "Think of it as a trial period to see if we work well together."

Paige might be attracted to Kassidy, and she might admire the beautiful place she had created, but she had a suspicion that working together wouldn't be easy for either one of them. Mostly for her. Still, she had invested too much time to back down now. Hadn't she just been thinking about how much she enjoyed challenges? That had been a stupid thought.

"You don't sound positive about my chances. Maybe I should go back to my initial plan, before I knew who you were, and ask you out instead."

"I'd say the odds are pretty even for both options," Kassidy said, keeping her eyes lowered and biting her lip as if to hide a smile. "Neither one seems like a good bet at the moment."

Paige grinned, not fooled by Kassidy's assessment of her chances. She smiled at the suggestion of a date but had looked ready to flip the dining room table on its side when Paige mentioned looking at the farm's accounts. Paige knew which choice she wanted to make. Asking Kassidy out, though, would be selfish and short-term, given Paige's usual relationship style. Helping her with her business would benefit Kassidy in the future. Really, no matter how tempted she was, Paige had only one option.

"Fine," she said. "I'll be here bright and early, ready to wow you with my advice."

"Good. I'll prepare to be dazzled."

Chapter Five

Paige drove the ten-mile circuitous route that bypassed the town of McMinnville and brought her to a valley south of Kassidy's farm, where the winery and bed-and-breakfast where she was staying was located. She was tempted to download every book she could find about lavender growing and use the downtime between now and tonight's dinner with Sarai to come up with some ideas to toss at Kassidy tomorrow. She'd resist, though, and not just because it felt like cheating. She would surely find some useful advice in a book, but she'd be throwing off her usual rhythm when faced with an unknown client and industry. She had to keep her long-term goal in sight—to help Kassidy's farm realize its unique potential—and ignore the desire to show off by sounding like an expert after one day of study. She wouldn't fool Kassidy with hastily acquired knowledge. Instead, she would impress her the way she always did during a consultation. She would let her own instincts guide her advice, not another farmer's suggestions.

She would, however, check out some local businesses. She was desperately lacking the community perspective she had after years of working in Portland. She understood corporate trends and conventions in the city even if the particular businesses she worked for were unfamiliar at first. She was out of her depth in this farming and non-chain-business culture.

Besides, she needed something to do besides sit in her room or wander through the vineyard. She appreciated how beautiful it was, with rolling hills and arcing rows of leafy vines, but she could only take so much quiet time. She'd taken Dante for a long walk this morning and would get him out again before dinner, but she had to find something to occupy her mind before she went crazy.

Once they got to her room, Dante got a drink from his water bowl and curled up in the dog bed that had been provided by the inn. Paige immediately started to take off her stained clothes. She had hoped her usual work uniform would help her remain distanced from her attraction to Kassidy and her all-too-personal embarrassment over messing up their meeting last night. The effect had been somewhat spoiled by the impromptu lavender replanting session and subsequent chase after Dante.

She carefully folded the dirty outfit and opened the closet to find something more casual. She chose a pair of khakis and a thin navy sweater and dressed quickly before sitting on the bed where she had tossed a stack of brochures from the lobby. Luckily, there were plenty of options to keep her occupied when she was in town and not directly working with Kassidy. Being in Kassidy's presence was far too distracting, and Paige decided she'd minimize their time together as much as she could. Once she had an idea of the systems in place at the farm—and once Kassidy allowed her access to the holy account books—Paige would be able to do most of her work on her own, either here or back in Portland.

Paige leaned back against the pillows and gazed out the window. She could see the entire eastern slope of the vineyard and its thick border of fir trees through the massive panes. Even though the trees were tall, the house was set high enough for her to have a great view of the sunrise. She had expected the place to have a shabby, country feel to it, but it was surprisingly elegant and modern. Her room was filled with gray. Gray comforter over ivory sheets. Gray and tan travertine tile fireplace and floating shelf. Sitting area chairs upholstered in gray and white geometric patterns. Gray dog bed. The place reminded her of her own apartment, with its neutral color palette and clean lines.

An image of Kassidy's living room, with its bright colors and more eclectic style, superimposed itself over the scene in front of her, complete with streaks of mud on the rug, and Kassidy smiling as if she didn't care what kind of mess Paige's dog made of her beautiful home. Paige stood up abruptly. She had to get out of this room, with its lack of television and abundance of quiet. She had to get her mind off Kassidy, unless it was to focus on her in an impersonal, business-related way. She might try to find an apology gift for her while she was out, though, but that didn't really count as thinking about her. Maybe a state-of-the-art carpet cleaner. She grabbed a few brochures at random, picked up her pile of muddy clothes, and called Dante to come with her.

She came down to the lobby and was greeted by the cheerful man at the reservation desk.

"Nice to see you, Ms. Leighton. I hope you slept well last night. Can I interest you in a wine sample? I don't believe you've tried our Syrah yet."

"Not right now, but thank you," Paige said. She was plied with wine samples every time she passed by the front desk, no matter who was on duty. It was an effective marketing tool. She hadn't really enjoyed the taste of their wine, especially when compared to Drew's selection last night, but she had already bought two bottles seemingly against her will, driven by the friendly force of the employees' enthusiasm. They'd make nice gifts for clients, at least.

"Shall I pack a picnic lunch for you? We have some tables set up along the path through the vineyard."

"No, but thank you," Paige said again. She bit back a laugh, wondering how many snacks and libations he would offer if she just stood here and let him run through every amenity the winery and inn had in its arsenal. She hurried on to make her own requests, so he didn't have to keep guessing what would make her happy.

"Can you recommend a dry cleaner? And I was hoping I could use the dog yard for an hour or so while I do some sightseeing. I have brochures," she hastened to add, before he started listing recommendations.

He pulled a map across the counter and circled a spot in downtown McMinnville. "This dry cleaner will be open all weekend.

And you're the only guest with a dog right now, so feel free to use the yard anytime you want. Does your dog want a bone?"

"I'm sure he would," Paige said. If she gave the same *no, but thank you* answer to that offering, Dante would probably bite her in the leg.

She took the map and bone and put Dante in the small fenced yard with a promise to take him on a long walk before she went out to dinner later. She left him crunching happily on his treat, sitting half in and half out of the doghouse. When she had read about the inn being pet-friendly, she hadn't realized how seriously they took the statement. Dante had received a complimentary basket of goodies that rivaled the one she had gotten. He had his fancy bed, water and food bowls, and access to this nice yard with a shelter in case it rained. The staff even provided dog walking and exercise services, although Paige didn't think she would need them. Dante could go with her to Kassidy's, providing a much-needed way to get Paige's mind off Kassidy's gorgeous hair and curves since she would need all her faculties about her to keep him from destroying entire rows of lavender.

After Paige dropped off her dry cleaning, she wandered through the small old-fashioned downtown area. Historic buildings were given new purpose, and their street-level windows revealed upscale boutiques that were an interesting contrast to the stoic brick facades. Artisanal crafts and edibles filled the majority of the shops, from soaps to baked goods and art galleries to microbreweries.

Paige couldn't tell for certain whether the abundance of products worked together to provide an environment in which they all did well, or if the competition would make it difficult for most of the individual suppliers to thrive long-term. She jotted down her question in the notebook she had bought for this job. She used a new one for each client, keeping track of her impressions in the beginning, the topics she needed to master during the middle, and her conclusions once the consultation period was nearing its close.

The Lavender Lane Farm notebook was mostly empty so far, with only Paige's initial impressions after talking to Kenneth and a page of notes about Kassidy she had written last night. The part about Kassidy was a bit too flowery to be included in a business notebook, and admittedly written after Paige had had a few glasses of wine. She needed to tear out the page and eat the evidence.

Now, though, she was fully in command of her emotional response to Kassidy. Or, at least, she was determined to ignore it until the job was done and she was out of Kassidy's life. She wrote a reminder to investigate the longevity of the more successful businesses in town before putting the notebook in her back pocket and entering a shop dedicated to olive oil called OreOil. She wasn't convinced this detour would help her with the Kassidy project, but she was intrigued by the single-minded focus of the store and curious about what could possibly be on the shelves besides bottles of olive oil.

A bell jangled when she walked through the door, which featured the business's name on it alongside a picture of an oriole, and a man came out of the back room. He was wearing dark-rimmed glasses and three layers of shirts, all apparently chosen to be intentionally mismatched. Paige would never put together a yellow sweater, blue plaid button-down shirt, and white T-shirt, but the look somehow worked, and the guy looked like he should be standing in line at some hot new hipster club in the city rather than behind a counter in a small-town olive oil store.

"Welcome to OreOil," he said, giving her the same hearty type of greeting she had gotten at every establishment in McMinnville, from the clerk at her bed-and-breakfast to the teen working at the dry cleaners. "I'm Everett. Are you browsing, or would you like to taste some olive oil?"

Paige bit back the urge to honestly voice the question in her mind about who could possibly want to taste plain olive oil. She had learned her lesson about that last night when faced with perfumed chicken. Her initial reaction had been wrong then, so she might as well go against her better judgment and at least try his product.

"I'll give it a try," she said, curious about how it would be served. On bread? Drizzled over a slice of ripe heirloom tomato?

Or in a cup. She took the tiny paper container he handed her and looked suspiciously at the shimmering green liquid inside. This couldn't be good for the digestion.

"This is one of our more delicate oils. Cold pressed, of course, like all our oils. You'll notice it has a light texture and a bright, grassy flavor."

Paige scrunched up her nose and took a sip, expecting to merely notice that it was oil, and therefore not a typical beverage option. Everett walked her through the process with several samples, though, mentioning bitterness and spiciness and even different vegetables at just the right time to help her identify what she was tasting. He also explained the process of harvesting and milling the oils in between handing her more samples, and she found the experience much more educational than she had expected. Still, her mouth felt greasy, and she wouldn't need lip balm for the rest of the month.

Once she had finished drinking her oils, she wandered through the little shop, amazed by the number of items made with olives. There were bottles of oil for sale, packaged in fancy wooden crates with the name of the store stamped on them and also sold individually for a lower price. Colorful jars of olives packed in flavored brines were stacked alongside some other pickled vegetables. An entire wall was devoted to skin- and hair-care products. Paige picked up a bar of olive oil soap flecked with deep blue lavender buds and sniffed it. The scent was strong, and definitely in the perfume-y category. Very different from the flavor in Kassidy's chicken.

"Ah, that's one of our most popular fragrances," Everett said when he noticed her holding the soap. "The lavender is grown locally, of course, by our resident lavender keeper."

"Lavender keeper," Paige repeated with a smile. "Do you mean Kassidy Drake?"

"Yes. Do you know her? She's as lovely a person as the plants she grows."

"She is," Paige agreed. "I mean, I assume she is. I just met her once."

Well, twice, but Paige decided not to include the party incident. They hadn't exactly exchanged names, so it didn't count as a real introduction.

"What do you recommend as a gift for someone who loves cooking?" she asked, determined to change the subject at least as far as Everett knew. She decided not to say the gift was for Kassidy.

He came over to the display of oils and took three small crates off the shelf. "You really can't go wrong with any of these. The Select oils are well suited to cooking because they're heartier and they won't be overpowered even with meats and spices. This second package has oils that are sweeter and more delicate in flavor. They're good for baking or for drizzling on food after it's cooked. But these unfiltered oils are my personal favorite. The last sample you had was one of them. They aren't for everyone since they are less refined, but someone who loves fresh produce and a real local flavor would probably appreciate them."

"This one will be perfect," she said, pointing to the crate of unfiltered, cloudy oils. She had liked the rawness of the sample she'd tasted, and she had a feeling the strong flavors would blend well with lavender.

She added a jar of citrus-flavored olives packed with Cipolline onions and hunks of preserved lemons, as well as the bar of soap, and paid for her purchases, thanking Everett for the time he had spent with her. She went to a few more shops in the downtown area, including a bakery where she bought a loaf of Italian bread to complement her olive and onion midnight snack and realized she needed to hurry back to the inn if she wanted to walk Dante before she went to dinner.

She thought about her shopping trip as she wandered through the vineyard with Dante, making occasional notes in her book while never taking her attention completely off her dog in case he decided to excavate again. She had been in stores like the ones she had visited today before this, but she had never paid much attention to them beyond the products they sold. If they had something she wanted, good. If a chain store had it for a better price or had something mass-produced she wanted, also good. Today's experience, though, had been as much about the people as what they were selling. Everett, the staff at this winery, and the other shopkeepers were passionate about their products, and this passion coupled with their expertise made the urge to buy their products nearly irresistible. Paige had brought packages of food and other items back to the room with her, but the memories of being in the stores and the information that was shared with her were what she had been willing to pay for.

Dante pulled free, dodging under a vine and into the next row over from hers, and she dropped her notebook and hurried after him, catching sight of the bright yellow breast of the meadowlark he had flushed. She caught hold of him again and led him back to the path where she retrieved her now-dusty notebook. She put it in her back pocket and finally let her thoughts turn to the more discomfiting feelings she had experienced today. She wanted to push them aside, but she had to face them and then let them go because it didn't do her any good to live with regrets or might-have-beens.

She had originally decided to pursue economics in college and an MBA because she wanted to be exactly the type of business owner she had met today. Maybe not on this small a scale or in this tiny a town, but with the same grand passion she had seen in every business in McMinnville this afternoon. She had struggled when she was a recent graduate, though, to find a concept or interest or angle unique to herself, some way she could make her own mark in the world, but she hadn't been able to come up with anything. Nothing.

She was good at quite a few things. She was reasonably good at most sports, able to master the work in any academic class she took, confident and approachable enough to be elected to any school office she had pursued. But none of it was personal. Each endeavor was just a series of skills to learn, and she never cared about any of it beyond a superficial level. Superficial. She hated how much the word defined who she was in a very uncomfortable way, even though most people only saw the successes she had on the surface of her life.

Paige checked the time on her phone and turned Dante back toward the inn since she only had half an hour before she was supposed to be at Sarai's. Kassidy had asked her why she didn't have her own business, and Paige wouldn't admit the real reason. The peripheral ones were enough, and they told a small portion of the truth. She had taken a job at a consulting firm because she had wanted to get exposure to a variety of businesses, hoping to find the one that resonated with her. She hadn't, but at least she had been good enough at observing companies and fixing what was wrong with them to make a living at it.

Hopefully, she could do the same thing here. Help Kassidy mobilize her passion and get the farm performing to its highest potential. Learn a little about lavender along the way. And then move on to the next business that needed her help.

CHAPTER SIX

Kassidy answered the call on Skype and smiled at the image filling her screen. She felt as if she was looking in a mirror at herself. If she was six years younger and cut her own hair with the dullest gardening shears in her shed.

"Hey, K," her sister Kayla said, rubbing her eye with a knuckle and yawning.

"Hey, K. Late night?"

"And early morning. The Pearsons' mare colicked again, and then I had to go to Jane's to check her gelding because you know how paranoid she gets when show season is almost here. I just got back here to the office and heard Kyle's message."

Kassidy smiled and didn't bother to remind Kayla that she didn't know either the Pearsons or Jane. Her sister had a habit of talking about her clients as if everyone knew who they were. Kayla cared so much about them and their animals, they seemed like family to her.

"So, who's this spy Dad sent to your farm? Should I come up there, or did you get rid of her?"

Kassidy sighed. She shouldn't have mentioned Paige's visit when Kyle called last night. She had spent her early years taking care of her twin siblings, and somewhere during their time in college they had turned the tables and appointed themselves as her protectors. Apparently using the mafia model as their inspiration.

"She's not a spy," Kassidy said. A good spy would have researched Kassidy and known what she grew, thereby missing the opportunity to call her chicken perfume-y. Or maybe that was all part of Paige's evil plan to throw Kassidy off the scent. Dante was probably in on it, too. Kassidy pressed her lips together, trying not to laugh at her thoughts when her sister was looking so worried and exhausted. "I checked her out online, and she's a legitimate consultant. A very expensive one. Besides, if Dad wanted to know about the farm, he'd just ask something straight out, like how much money did I lose last month, or do I really think people can make a living selling weeds."

Kassidy had spent more time than she wanted to admit on Paige's website, reading her bio, which was sparse and impersonal, and the rave reviews from satisfied clients. And, possibly, staring at the photo of her. She was dressed similarly to the way she had looked when she came to the farm yesterday, minus the mud splatters. Kassidy thought she looked much better a little messy and not as put together as she did on the website.

"Are you listening to me?"

"What? No. I mean yes. What did you say?"

"I asked if you told her to get the hell off your property and go back to Portland."

Kassidy laughed at her sister's imperious tone. She was soft-spoken and gentle with animals, but when it came to defending Kassidy, she could get carried away.

"I'm going to hear her out, and if I think she can help my business, I'll let her." Until she said it out loud, Kassidy hadn't realized that she was leaning toward working with Paige. Not because she was beautiful and seemed ready to fill a room with laughter, but because her portfolio was impeccable.

Kassidy nodded at herself. Right. Just go on believing *that*.

Kayla visibly took a deep breath, apparently gearing up for a lecture, but Kassidy didn't have time to hear it.

"Look, K, our past is not her fault. I'm not going to give up on a chance to improve my business just because I'm mad at Dad for not being a better father. Now, you go and get some sleep. I'll call you and Kyle tonight. If you don't hear from me, then she probably bludgeoned me with a shovel and buried me in the north field. The ground is softer there. Bye."

She ended the call before her sister could say anything else, and then she shut off her computer and phone. When one twin called, the other was sure to follow, and Kassidy didn't feel like being tag-teamed by them. Paige would be here soon, and she wanted to have everything ready for her visit.

She picked up a sheaf of papers and a black marker and went to sit at the kitchen table. Kipper wound around her legs several times before settling on the chair opposite her, where Paige had sat yesterday. Kassidy tried to focus on the paperwork in front of her, but she had too many memories pressing on her, triggered by her conversation with Kayla.

The twins saw their dad in a much different light than she did, without all the complexity and mixed emotions. To them, he had always been distant and uninvolved, even when they had visitation days at his house. He had left when they were babies, but Kassidy had been six. It wasn't as if she had a plethora of happy memories of the three of them as a family before the twins came, but at least her dad had shouldered some of the responsibilities that her mother was usually unable to undertake. They had eaten mostly takeout and had a housekeeper do most of the regular chores, and Kassidy had been free to be an unencumbered—albeit lonely—child. And the months before her mother gave birth to the twins, she had been nearly depression-free, in what Kassidy now recognized as a false euphoria brought on by hormones. But at the time, Kassidy had only known it as the brightest time of family togetherness she had ever experienced.

Which made her mother's relapse after the twins were born even more difficult to bear. Kassidy had adored them and couldn't understand why they had been the catalyst that tore her family apart when they should have banded even closer together for the new babies. Her father hadn't been able to handle the depression, not able to comprehend the depth of the illness Kassidy's mom was experiencing, and he had responded by leaving. Sure, they had the money he sent, but Kassidy was promoted to household manager and surrogate mother before age seven.

She'd never regret the relationship she had with Kayla and Kyle, and she refused to let her life be ruled by bitterness toward her parents, although some days it was easier than others to rise above it all. Paige's abrupt arrival in her life, with her connections to Kassidy's father, made for one of those less bearable times, when too many memories clambered to the surface even though they were better off left on the sludgy bottom of her mind.

Kassidy managed to focus enough to finish marking up the papers right before she heard Paige's car pull up in front of her house. Really, given the fees she charged her clients, she should have been able to purchase a new car after every job instead of driving the Tercel that looked about to shudder to its death. Kassidy couldn't remember the last year they had even been manufactured. Maybe the irrepressible Dante made buying a fancier car seem like a foolish idea.

Kassidy tucked the papers into a cabinet drawer and went out to meet Paige, ignoring the lighthearted jump in her heartbeat at the sight of her. She was here for business purposes only, and if she didn't impress Kassidy with her suggestions, she would be sent back to Portland. Pushed along by the twins and their cattle prods if she wouldn't go willingly. Paige was laughing when she got out of the car, and for all Kassidy's determination to be unaffected by her, she responded to Paige's happiness in a completely unprofessional and trembling kind of way.

"I know I put those back right-side up yesterday," Paige said, shaking her head and grinning at Kassidy. "You went out and changed them, didn't you?"

Kassidy returned her smile and shut the front door behind her. She had gone down to the road yesterday afternoon and replanted the bushes Dante had mangled so their roots were waving in the air. The prank was uncharacteristic of her, and she had surprised herself when she actually followed through after coming up with the idea. She had known Paige would be amused by the joke, and that had been enough to convince her to do it. She'd bring the bushes in tonight and take cuttings from them since Dante's exploits—or perhaps Paige's attempts to fix them—had resulted in too much root damage for the plants to survive.

"The first thing I'll teach you today is what parts of the plant go below ground. We farmers call them *roots*."

"Very funny. We need to make sure your lavender business does well because you wouldn't make a living as a stand-up comic." Paige went around to the passenger side of the car and got Dante out, complete with collar and retractable leash. He promptly dragged Paige onto the porch so he could greet Kassidy.

"He must have twenty feet of leash to play with. Will you be able to reel him in fast enough if he starts digging?"

"Let's hope so, but if not, I'll buy you another present. Here's one for yesterday." Paige handed her a bag from Everett and Brian's store. "I hope it's the right kind for you. Everett described them, and I thought this sounded most like something you'd use."

Kassidy opened it and saw the cloudy gray-green of her favorite olive oil. "This is perfect, thank you. The bottle I used to finish the flatbread we had for lunch yesterday is almost empty."

They were quiet for a moment, and Kassidy desperately searched for a way to get past the warm feeling she had because of the gift and get back to seeing Paige as a business partner, or coworker, or consultant. Whatever reminded Kassidy that Paige was only here temporarily—possibly only for the day, but at most for a few weeks. Fortunately, Dante spotted a wren flitting through the garden hedge, and Paige's attention was fully turned toward controlling him. Kassidy put the bag on the patio table and followed Paige.

"If you can manage to wrangle him in this direction, we can start with the drying shed," Kassidy said, gesturing down the gravel path toward a large yellow barn. Once they were walking, Dante settled down and stayed between the rows. The lavender plants came up to the very edge of the trails, filling most of the available acreage on this part of the farm.

"Do you need to have this much space between rows?" Paige asked, stopping to look at the field to her left, spreading behind the house and up the gentle hill.

"Yes. The plants need room between them for drainage and room to grow. If they're overcrowded, they might be stunted or develop a fungus." She crossed her arms over her chest. "Was your amazing piece of advice going to be to move all the plants closer together? Because it wouldn't be good for the plants and certainly wouldn't be time or cost effective for me."

"Yeesh. Do you really think I'm going to suggest you uproot your entire crop and move it a few inches to the right? I have to ask a lot of questions, and some of them might seem basic or intuitive to you, but just answer and let me do my job."

Kassidy looked at Paige, who had her hands on her hips. If she was trying to look stern, however, the effect was ruined by the way she was swaying back and forth as Dante tugged on his leash. Kassidy uncrossed her arms.

"We look like we're about to brawl in the lavender fields."

Paige grinned and relaxed her stance, as well. "I had my share of mucking about in your fields yesterday. Once we're done with the initial observations, I'm hoping to do the rest of my consulting from a distance, as far away from the dirt as I can get."

"Not too far away, I hope," Kassidy said before she could stop the words. She cleared her throat and searched for a way to change the tone of what she had just said. "I mean, this isn't some big, impersonal corporation that you can study online."

Paige's grin widened. "So you're saying you want me to take a more personal, hands-on approach to this job?"

"No hands required," Kassidy said, holding up her own as if to ward off Paige's advances, even though she hadn't moved. "And no flirting."

"Oh, I thought you were the one flirting with me when you begged me not to leave."

"That's not what I…" Kassidy stopped. She seemed to have lost this round and she decided to give up and change the subject. The thought of consulting with Paige via email—or not at all—should have been a welcome one, but she had a feeling Paige's humor would be stripped away if she had a chance to censor herself in professional emails.

Kassidy gestured for them to move forward again, even as her mind moved backward to recapture the thread of their conversation before her uncomfortable comment about Paige going away. What had Paige been saying? Something about asking stupid questions? "I'll try to answer your questions without sarcasm, no matter how inane they sound. I wouldn't want to impede the *artiste*'s process."

Paige bumped Kassidy with her shoulder as they walked. "I'm certainly not an artist, nor am I the prima donna in this relationship." She waggled her finger between herself and Kassidy. "Now what's the black stuff between the rows? Do you keep the baby plants under it?"

Kassidy glanced at Paige but couldn't tell if she was joking or not. She decided to assume Paige had never stepped foot off the city pavement before and truly had no idea what happened on a farm.

"It's landscape fabric. A weed barrier, so I don't have to mow or pull weeds between rows."

"Is it expensive?"

Kassidy hesitated, ready to flail her arms in the air and tell Paige she would be crazy to suggest Kassidy cut corners by not using the fabric. With no small effort, she kept her voice and her hands calm. "Yes, especially for the good stuff. The cheaper barriers are thin and let quite a few weeds grow through. But I save significant time by not having to do much upkeep to those areas. Plus, it's easier to harvest and care for the plants when the rows are clean and accessible."

Paige nodded. "See? That wasn't so hard, was it?"

"It was torture," Kassidy said, opening the door to the drying shed. Her first instinct was to shut Paige down at every hint of advice, before she could intrude on Kassidy's territory and try to change her methods, and Paige must have seen the struggle she had gone through before answering the question civilly. At least the antagonism she felt when defending her farm's practices made the thought of a long-distance consulting arrangement seem more palatable. "I'm going to have an ulcer by the time we're through with this tour."

She walked through the nearly empty room, letting the lingering scent of lavender—intensified in the enclosed space—soothe her.

Most of the shed was crossed by low beams where she hung bundles of lavender and let them dry. She had sold most of the stock the year before but still had quite a few bundles left on the wooden tables. She had been experimenting with crafts, and she watched Paige wander around the room, poking at lavender wreaths and wall hangings.

Paige held up a cylindrical collection of lavender stems, interspersed with only an occasional brilliant blue flower and tied with a raffia bow.

"This is pretty," Paige said, rolling her eyes as if Kassidy needed help interpreting her sarcastic tone. "Did the rest of it die?"

Kassidy laughed. It did resemble a pile of leftover sticks. "You use it as kindling. The smell is lovely, especially when exposed to the heat of a fire."

Paige sniffed at it and nodded, silently agreeing with Kassidy. Most of the other craft projects were self-explanatory, and Paige looked through them without comment. Kassidy was torn between interrupting her perusal to ask her what opinions she was forming about Kassidy and her business, and remaining silent while she took pleasure in watching Paige explore. Kassidy chose silence, even though she was supposed to be picking Paige's brain professionally today, not standing there feeling squirmy inside at the sight of Paige's graceful fingers as they brushed over a frond of lavender or her intense hazel eyes that seemed to notice everything.

Like now, when Paige looked at her and noticed her staring. She felt her cheeks flush and hastily turned back to the lavender.

"I don't sell these finished products, but I was experimenting with different drying techniques and cultivars. I started out with only a quarter acre of the varieties I used for these crafts last year and doubled it this year. I sell the dried bundles to florists and a local hobby shop."

"Did the sales go well?"

Kassidy nodded. "The market is limited around here, but I sold what I had. The crafts are labor-intensive, but the drying process is simple."

Paige came over and handed Dante's leash to Kassidy. "I need to write," she said, with a distracted inflection in her voice. As soon as Kassidy had control of Dante, Paige produced a small notebook from her pocket and began writing furiously, stopping now and again to stare into space before starting again. Kassidy didn't think she had given Paige enough information to produce such copious notes. Maybe they weren't all about the farm, and Paige was writing a shopping list or short story.

Or a novel. Eventually, though, Paige waved in her direction. "You said something about cultivars. Different kinds of lavender? Explain it to me."

"Oh, um, okay." Kassidy took a moment to collect her thoughts because she had been transfixed watching Paige work. Kassidy had expected her to be detached and cool, looking at the farm and then barking out some glaringly obvious suggestions. Paige seemed to be absorbing the passion of the place, somehow, until she seemed to be the one who was obsessed with lavender, and Kassidy was a bystander.

"I grow about fifty varieties of lavender on the farm. Most of them are *Lavandula angustifolia* varieties because they grow well in the microclimate of this farm and they have a nice sweetness to them. They're good for perfumes, cooking, fresh arrangements, and crafts. I sell most of the harvest to perfume manufacturers, and they distill the oil. I also have some varieties that have a stronger scent, with hints of camphor. Those are good for hair-care products, soaps, that sort of thing. I distill them on my own, but only on a small scale, and I sell the oils to locals who make those types of products."

Kassidy's lecture came to a halt. She was mesmerized by the transformation in Paige as she absorbed the information and it flowed onto the notepaper. Kassidy edged closer and tried to look at the notes, but the writing was too sloppy for her to decipher.

Paige circled her hand in the air, gesturing for Kassidy to continue. "What's different about these new crafty plants?"

"Some types of lavender are great for drying because they hold their color well and have interesting shapes. The new ones I added aren't great producers of essential oils, but they're beautiful in fresh and dried arrangements."

Paige stopped writing abruptly and looked at Kassidy with a sheepish smile that couldn't quite hide the thrill of learning something new she had talked about during their lunch the day before. "If I'd thought about it at all before I came here, which I never did, I would have thought there was only one kind of lavender. I can see the hints of different colors in your fields, but I didn't realize the varieties had different qualities."

"There are almost five hundred varieties," Kassidy said, wrestling Dante toward the back door of the shed and away from the half-empty bag of potting soil he had discovered in the corner. "Angustifolias, lavandins, stoechas. Some are generalists, and some are specialists, just like people."

"And it's up to the lavender keeper to find the perfect use for each one."

Kassidy grinned. She wasn't sure how Paige had discovered her nickname, but she liked hearing it from Paige's mouth. She made a determined effort to get her attention off whatever else Paige's mouth might be able to do to her and opened the door, getting back to her tour.

CHAPTER SEVEN

Paige trailed after Kassidy as they covered the eight acres of Lavender Lane Farm. Dante trotted obediently at Kassidy's heels—the traitor—while Paige filled the pages of her notebook with ideas for the farm, topics she wanted to research later, and phonetically transcribed names of the many cultivars. Kassidy knew each one, of course, pointing at barely flowering bushes and rattling off Latin names, countries of origin, and uses for the plant without hesitating or needing to consult some sort of farm schematic.

The day had started as a series of general impressions for Paige. The spring morning was reasonably warm, but the clouds had been slowly drifting in from the north and looked as if they might bring rain later on. Paige had worn regular weekend clothes instead of her typical business outfit, since she didn't need to spend her entire consulting fee on dry cleaning when most of what she was doing here consisted of mucking around the farm. After the first hour, she was glad to have on the thick Reed College hoodie and sturdy hiking boots. The paths were exposed to the wind on the slopes of the farm, and even though they were well-maintained and reasonably flat, Paige noticed the effects of the steady inclines and declines in her thighs as they moved from field to field.

The plants had looked uniform to her at first glance, aside from some color variations, especially since many of them hadn't started flowering yet and the earlier bloomers still showed only the merest hints of color. From a distance, the plants appeared dusted with purple, but a closer view showed individual, tightly closed buds. After Kassidy's explanation of the different varieties, however, Paige had begun to notice the unique characteristics of the cultivars. She might not know their names yet, but she could tell when they moved from a row of one type to a different one. She took notes about things like bracts and peduncles, trying not to laugh at the words because she wasn't sure how Kassidy would react. She was funny and lighthearted in a lot of respects, but every once in a while she reverted to her prickly, defensive mode.

It wasn't just the lavender. Kassidy changed in Paige's view, too, as the tour progressed. At first, Paige was focused only on her sensory perceptions of Kassidy. The distinctive scent of lavender blended with some unknown aromas that Paige had already come to associate with her. The faded green sweatshirt with its stretched-out collar that revealed Kassidy's smooth skin and sharp collarbones. The jeans with permanent mud and grass stains on the knees, slouching low and sultry on her hips. She fit on her farm like the focal piece of a puzzle, matching the beauty and elegance of the herb she grew. The farm, Kassidy herself. They were an experience and not merely a place and a person, like an Impressionist painting come to life.

As Paige took notes and listened to Kassidy talk, she started sorting her impressions under several specific headings. She was accustomed to the experience of seeing themes emerge from the tangle of new information, and she let the process happen without trying to force it. Kassidy had called her an *artiste* in a joking way, but Paige knew her consulting abilities had nothing to do with art. It was just common sense combined with a desire to organize information. There was nothing romantic or creative about it.

Not like Kassidy's vocation. Before today, Paige would have lumped farming into the general category of physical labor, but after hearing Kassidy talk about her plants and how she chose, grew, and used them, Paige saw the farm as more like a clay pot waiting to be molded than a field to be ploughed. Kassidy used as much intuition and experimentation as research and knowledge in her choices.

Paige shook the cramps out of her writing hand as they finished the wide arc around the house—the center of the farm—and went inside a huge greenhouse. She had pages of notes and normally would have taken a break for a couple days to review and think about them before returning to finish her observation at a company. Sometimes she spent weeks during this phase, but she didn't want to stop. She tried to convince herself it was because she only had weekends in McMinnville and needed to condense her work into a shorter period of time, but she wasn't fooled by that reasoning at all. She could easily spend hours, no matter how much it hurt the tendons in her note taking hand, standing close enough to Kassidy to drink in the scent of her and listen to her talk.

Kassidy might not be as forthcoming as Everett and some of the other business owners had been about their products, but she shared the same type of passion. Paige had originally thought Kassidy was only reticent with her because she was connected to her dad and here on a mission to make changes where none were wanted, but she started to change her mind as she learned more about the business. Kassidy held herself apart from more people than just Paige. Her community, her customers...she seemed to appreciate and like them, but she maintained a distance from them all.

Paige looked around the cavernous greenhouse, noticing that only about a fifth of the tall workbenches running the length of the room showed any sign of use.

"So this is where you plant the seeds?" she asked. She noticed the expression she had seen on Kassidy's face after just about every question Paige asked, as if she was fighting the urge to roll her eyes dramatically and sigh, *You don't have a clue, do you?*

"It's a reasonable question," she said with a laugh. "Don't look so pained by it. What do you do if you don't plant seeds, then, clone them?"

Kassidy smiled, turning a becoming shade of pink. "Sorry, it seems to be a reflex whenever you say something." She paused, and then frowned. "I guess I'm still feeling defensive, like my dad sent you here to criticize the farm. It makes me want to contradict you, no matter what you say."

Paige was stunned into silence. Not because Kassidy was so quickly able to figure out the underlying reasons behind her determination to argue every point with Paige, but because she was willing to truthfully admit it. Honesty deserved honesty in return.

"Your dad hired me to act as your consultant, but I think his real agenda was for me to fail and advise you to sell." Paige held up a hand to stop Kassidy before she could interrupt her. "You have every right to be angry and indignant, and I can only guess what kind of a father he's been for you, but I really believe he has your best interests at heart."

"*That's* your great advice? To quit?" Kassidy's expression clearly showed her disbelief and hurt feelings, and Paige stepped closer and took Kassidy's free hand in hers.

"God, no. I was just letting you know the subtext we've got going on here, because if we keep ignoring it and being defensive, it'll only get in our way." Paige took a deep breath, lacing her fingers through Kassidy's in a very unprofessional way. She needed to keep them connected, stop Kassidy from running out of the greenhouse and shutting her out. She had been forming the intention to help Kassidy bridge the distance between herself and her customers and community, and instead Paige was closing the gap between the two of them. The move wasn't professional, but like Kassidy had pointed out, this farm had little in common with an impersonal corporation. Maybe Paige could allow herself a little leeway.

"Your dad wants you to be secure and safe. To a man like him, that means having a conventional job and a reliable paycheck. Those things symbolize happiness for him, and he doesn't understand that you see the world differently. You can be angry about that if you want, but you shouldn't turn down what I can offer because of hurt feelings."

Kassidy inched away but didn't let go of Paige's hand. "Tell me right now. After all this time showing you around the farm, are you just going to tell me to sell it and give up?"

Paige started in surprise. She had been so focused on taking notes about ways to help Kassidy develop her business, and she had thought her enthusiasm was obvious. "No. I'm already coming up with ideas that will help you maximize the potential you have here. I don't know if it will be enough to make you as profitable as you need to be, or if you'll be willing to follow my advice. I'll need to see some numbers to get a better feel for your profit margin and how we can improve it."

Kassidy scoffed. "Yeah, right. I'm supposed to trust you with my financial information. I really should make you go through my books while you're naked, because then we'd be even in terms of exposure."

"More of your flirting." Paige shook her head with a dramatic sigh. "First you act devastated about me leaving the farm, and now you expect me to be naked while I'm here. Very unprofessional, Ms. Drake."

Kassidy raised their linked hands and looked at them pointedly.

"Message received." Paige laughed. She gave Kassidy's hand a slight squeeze and dropped their contact. It was a tough choice between letting go of her and pulling her closer, and Paige didn't have the willpower to keep touching Kassidy and not wanting more. Especially if she was going to toss around words like *naked*. At least Kassidy looked embarrassed by what she had said, or maybe just surprised that she had said the words out loud.

"So why don't we keep to our original deal and finish the tour, and I'll give you a sample of what a consulting guru can offer. If you like it, we go forward, clothing optional. If not, I go home."

Kassidy hesitated, and then nodded. "All right. But our clothes stay on."

"We can debate that point later," Paige said with a smile before switching back to the business at hand. She enjoyed teasing Kassidy but didn't want to overwhelm the conversation with innuendo. "So, this is where you clone your little lavender babies?"

Kassidy laughed. She started talking again, seeming to regain control over her emotions as she discussed her beloved plants. "I propagate plants by taking cuttings from ones in the field. It only takes a few weeks for them to root, which is much faster than starting from seeds. Plus, I can rely on getting consistent qualities, like color or oil production, in the new plants. It takes about three years before the newly propagated plants are producing at full capacity."

Paige nodded, filling another page in her book and relieved to have something to do with her hands, keeping herself from thinking of excuses to touch Kassidy again. She shouldn't have reached out to her, but she had needed to make Kassidy listen to what she was saying.

Why? Paige wasn't sure. She had been back and forth about this job from the start. She maybe should have let Kassidy storm out of the greenhouse, like she had obviously been ready to do. Let her deal with whatever childhood pain she carried inside on her own, without Paige butting in. Paige flipped to a fresh sheet of paper while Kassidy described how to take cuttings from plants. Paige really *should* walk away from this, but she already had so many notes it would be a shame to let them go to waste. And she couldn't leave before she managed to sniff out the magical combination of scents in Kassidy's perfume.

Paige paused, her attention finally back on her job and off Kassidy. Or, at least sixty-forty in favor of the job.

"If you're using cuttings to save time over seeds, why not go one step further and buy plants from a nursery? I know I've seen lavender plants for sale, and I'm guessing there are wholesale markets for business owners."

Kassidy didn't go through her eye-rolling, sighing display this time, and Paige counted it as a win. Either her question was reasonable, or Kassidy was slowly beginning to trust her. Paige assumed it was the latter.

"A lot of the varieties I grow aren't available in local markets, especially the more specialized and unique ones. I try new ones all the time, which I couldn't do if I relied on what a nursery supplier has to offer. Performance isn't always predictable since some types do well in the microclimate and soil here on the farm, while others don't seem to take to it. If you went five miles down the road and planted the same varieties, the results might be quite different. So sometimes I just need to experiment and see what happens. Besides, you can't always trust that the plant you get in a nursery is really what it's supposed to be. Growers who don't know what they're doing might be careless with cuttings, or not recognize the differences among cultivars. If they're propagating from seeds, there's always the chance the new plant won't match the parent one because bees or hummingbirds might have transferred pollen to them from a completely different type of lavender. It's more reliable when I do it myself."

Paige wrote *bees* in her book and circled it before adding the other information. "Why are there so few plants in here? You have room for a lot more." Paige gestured toward the far tables. Only the ones closest to them had neat rows of pots on them.

Kassidy shrugged. "I've already planted at least half of the cuttings. I only make enough of them to fill the rows I have in mind for the new plants, or to replace old and unproductive ones."

Kassidy and Dante led the way back to the house while Paige trailed behind, finishing her scrawl of notes.

"Why don't we sit out here?" she asked when they got back to the patio. The clouds were thicker, but the day was still dry. "Dante's still got some of that potting soil on his head, and I'd rather he didn't bring it in your house."

Kassidy perched on the chair next to her, warily looking at the notebook. Paige laughed at her expression.

"I promise I didn't write *Kassidy is a bad lavender farmer* over and over in it," she said, coaxing a grin out of Kassidy and a slight release in her tense posture. "I have lots of notes, but they're still raw. I need to do more research and ask more dumb questions before I really have a sense of the direction I'd suggest for the farm. But I do have my audition piece ready, if you still want to hear it."

"Go ahead," Kassidy said with an exaggerated tone of indifference.

Paige took the lavender soap she had bought from Everett's store and set it on the table in front of them.

"This is your lavender, isn't it?"

Kassidy picked up the bar and looked at it before nodding, as if Paige might be asking a trick question. "Yes. I told you I sell lavender to local producers of soaps, hair products, that sort of thing."

"Can you tell me what's wrong with this?" Paige tapped the bar with her finger. She was teasing in a way, happy to have the tables turned for a brief moment and to be the expert instead of the student.

"Well, it smells good and makes your skin feel soft. I'm guessing those aren't your main criticisms?"

"Kassidy, where is your name on this? It should be on here at least two times." She pointed at the name on the bar. "This should say Lavender Lane Farm Olive Oil Soap, not just generic lavender soap, and the farm's website should be on the back."

"But Everett and Brian make the soap, and they paid for the lavender."

Paige shrugged. "Your name should be on every product made with your lavender. Charge a little less for the oils and ask for a cut of the profits, if you'd prefer. But don't sell the right to future marketing or any future sales. You made a set amount for the lavender, but it ended there. If people use this product and like it, they'll never be led back to the farm to try something else."

Kassidy frowned. "They're my friends. I couldn't ask them to…"

"Right," Paige said, figuring Kassidy had stopped midsentence because she didn't know how to finish it. "You wouldn't be hurting them at all, would you? You'd be working together to promote both businesses, because you can sell the soap from your website or at the farm, too. Being friends with them doesn't mean you can't show yourself and your product the respect you deserve."

Paige watched Kassidy as she seemed to internally struggle with Paige's advice. She probably wanted to be able to dismiss it with a derisive laugh and tell Paige to go away, but she couldn't help but see the logic in the advice. Paige had surprised herself with the concept last night, when she had been staring at the bar of soap and wondering why she felt compelled to do something about it. She knew her hesitation arose because she was accustomed to teaching businesses how to outsmart, outsell, and outperform their competitors. That would never work with Kassidy because of who she was and because of the collaborative nature of the local community. Paige had been right to look into the context of

Kassidy's business yesterday, even if she still was fairly ignorant about the specific product she contributed to it.

Kassidy mumbled something under her breath.

"What did you say?" Paige asked.

"I said it makes sense," Kassidy said, enunciating each word. "There. Are you happy?"

Paige laughed and pressed a hand to her heart. "Ecstatic. I feel as if my life's work is now justified."

Kassidy smacked her in the arm. "Now what? Do you have more brilliant ideas to share?"

Paige shook her head. "If we're going to work together, I need to get back to my regular process. I have to go back to Portland tomorrow, and while I'm there I'll start organizing the notes I have and do some research. We can connect on the weekends when I'm here, and then I'll make adjustments to my direction as necessary during the week. A few sessions of this, and I'll have a proposal for you. Do you promise to follow the advice I give you, without question?"

"No."

"Fair enough. I shouldn't have bothered to ask." Paige grinned. She felt the usual excitement about the upcoming period of exploring a new subject, but it was tempered by the strange and sudden thought that she'd rather not go home to the city. On her drive here, she had been anxiously counting the hours before she could return to civilization. Kassidy seemed to have an amplifying effect on her, intensifying whatever emotions Paige was feeling at the time. She'd be better off getting away from McMinnville and restoring her equilibrium before they tackled the rest of this project. Even though she had playfully joked about putting distance between them, Paige decided it was exactly what she needed.

"I want you to make a list of every product made with your lavender and send it to me." Paige readied herself for the next battle. "And I really will need to see some numbers."

"Okay." Kassidy got up and went into the house, and Paige nearly fell off her chair in shock.

Kassidy shut the door behind her to keep Dante from following her into the house and leaned back against it. She felt exhausted from the day. Talking about her dad with Paige had made her weary because Paige forced her to see his side of this whole mess. It was much easier to just feel angry about his lack of parental skills than to look at things from his perspective and feel compelled to forgive him a teeny bit for wanting her to sell the farm because he cared about her in his warped, distant way.

And Paige wore her out because she was so damned friendly and understanding. Even her flirting seemed to be timed so it put Kassidy at ease when she was getting wound too tight. She wasn't sure if Paige meant the sexy things she implied, or if it was only a tactic to break the tension, but Kassidy sure as hell couldn't imagine Paige acting this playful with Kenneth Drake or any other high-powered executive. Maybe it was meant for Kassidy alone...

Still, she wanted to hate Paige and everything the situation involved, wanted to toss her off the farm and go back to the way she was accustomed to managing her life. She didn't want to change anything, so why did Paige have to come up with such a smart idea? Kassidy had desperately tried to come up with an argument against Paige's soap-based logic and hadn't been able to think of a single one.

And now she had to hand over her accounts, as promised. She went over to the drawer and got out the paperwork she had been working on when Paige arrived. She had printed everything out instead of taking the easier route and emailing Paige the files because she had wanted to redact her more personal expenses. A large part of the salary she gave herself went to providing support for her mom, and she didn't want Paige to see it. She would probably argue that Kassidy should ask her dad for help, even though, based on their divorce decree, his legal obligation had ended with child support. Her mom had some government assistance, but she needed the help Kassidy could provide.

Kassidy took a deep breath, prepared to fight Paige over this, and stepped outside again. Paige was lounging back in her chair, soaking up the stray glimmers of sunlight, and Kassidy paused a moment to watch her. She had seemed like she hadn't belonged yesterday, even though she had been wearing some of the farm's mud on her tailored business clothes, but now she looked at home here. She had one arm draped over the chair and she was gently rubbing Dante's ears. They looked as if they had stopped for a break after doing some farm chores.

Kassidy shook her head. It was an illusion. Paige might fit in as a temporary guest, but never as a permanent resident. Kassidy tossed the stack of paper on the table with enough of a smack to startle Paige into an upright position.

"Here you go," she said.

Paige picked up the stack and started shuffling through the pages with an unreadable expression on her face. Kassidy launched into her explanation.

"I have some expenses that are private. I need to have them itemized because I get tax breaks, but they're non-negotiable, and frankly, none of your business. I would have deleted them altogether, but then the totals wouldn't have made sense. If you refuse to work with me over this, then…"

Kassidy stopped talking when she realized Paige was laughing.

"There are redactions. This is awesome." Paige held up a sheet of paper with thick black lines streaked across it, as if Kassidy didn't know what she was talking about.

"You're not angry?"

Paige wiped her eyes, still chuckling. "I love it. The top-secret dossier of the lavender farm. Trust me, I don't want to know what's really written here. I'm sure the reality will never be as funny as the expenses I'm going to imagine."

Kassidy tried to stop herself, but she had to join in Paige's laughter. "I didn't want you to find out about the lavender smuggling operation I have going."

"I suppose you've genetically modified the plant clones to bloom with tiny spy cameras, and you're using them to infiltrate foreign governments?"

"I plan to put a lavender plant on the desk of every top official by the end of the year." Kassidy grinned in relief, happy to avoid the confrontation she had been expecting.

Paige shuffled the papers together and tapped the side of her nose. "Your secret's safe with me. Just watch out for double agents."

"Where do you think I got the plants hanging in my drying shed?"

"This made my day," Paige said. She got up and bopped Kassidy gently on the head with the papers. She was still laughing when she got in her car and drove away. Kassidy sat at the table for quite some time, worrying about how much Paige's visit had brightened her day, too.

CHAPTER EIGHT

K assidy sat at her rolltop desk, with Kipper sprawled across her lap, and clicked through a selection of fonts before choosing one with just the right amount of flourish and elegance. She was fully embracing Paige's advice and designing mock-ups of labels for every product she could find with her lavender in it. Each one prominently displayed the name of the farm or company that had produced it, of course, but now the plain *lavender* was replaced with the full name of her own farm. She would leave the final design options to her clients, but at least she now had some samples to bring when she talked to them about the new marketing scheme.

She felt a sense of pride as she scanned through the images she had created. Mainly because everyone would now associate these products with her farm, and she was very proud of the quality of herb she grew here. Whoever rubbed lavender goat's milk lotion on their dry hands or lit a lavender beeswax candle would now know who was responsible for the calming, beautiful scent they were experiencing.

She was also a little bit proud of herself for embracing this change to her business model without too much of an effort. She liked her life to be steady and predictable because she had never known that type of comfort as a child. Now, her world was…pleasant. Tidy and even-keeled, barring the occasional lapse of judgment when she introduced new variables, like Audrey, into her life. Paige's arrival had threatened even more upheaval, but Kassidy's worries had been unfounded. Paige's suggestion had turned out to be an easy one to follow, and Kassidy was wholeheartedly following through with it.

Kassidy added her farm's website address to the sample labels. She had been meaning to update the site for some time now. Had it been weeks or months since she had added new content? She couldn't remember. She was tempted to work on it now because she had a feeling it would be Paige's next suggestion. Kassidy stopped herself before she logged on as administrator. If she made it more current and appealing now, then Paige might be tempted to look further for changes Kassidy should make. Might as was well leave her a nice, meaty, out-of-date bone to chew on. She would demand that Kassidy fix it, and—since she had been planning to anyway—Kassidy could smugly give in and follow Paige's instructions. Everyone was a winner. Paige wouldn't feel as if her time and expertise had been wasted when Kassidy listened to her advice. And Kassidy would escape from the experience with a new marketing tool and a website on which to market. Since none of the changes had anything to do with the actual running of the farm and lavender growing, Kassidy was a double winner.

Kassidy leaned back in her chair and scratched Kipper's chin until his whole body was vibrating with his raspy purr. Now that she had the Business Consultant Paige situation under control, she could allow herself to sort of miss Paige the person. She had spent the days since Paige went back to the city noticing things that would have made Paige laugh. It had become almost a habit for her to spot an amusing situation or hear a funny story and file it away mentally for the next weekend. She probably would never relate all of them to Paige, and they weren't as humorous when she revisited them later and out of context, but the game was fun for her. She was smiling more than usual, and some of her friends had even commented on her changed outlook. Each time, Kassidy just said something vague about it being spring, but she knew the real reason for her smiles. She would be relieved when Paige was finished in McMinnville and went home, since some of those smiles were the secretive, lost in a fantasy about Paige naked types, but she hoped she would never lose the more innocent ones that came from finding pleasure in the world around her.

Managing to turn her thoughts back to her business, Kassidy finished the labels and printed them out. She had filled each of the rolltop's cubbies with a small wooden tray decoupaged with floral-patterned wallpaper samples, and she pulled one out of its slot and neatly stacked the labels inside. She closed her laptop and rolled the top of the desk down, separating the station where she did her paperwork from the rest of the room. Finally satisfied that everything was back in its place, Kassidy scooted Kipper off her lap and went into the kitchen to make lunch.

She mentally reviewed her day while she gathered ingredients for a sandwich. Plant cuttings in the east field. Check. Fix the clogged drip line near the drying shed. Check. Make labels. Check.

She laid thick slices of gouda and roasted turkey on a ciabatta roll and slathered it with too much mayonnaise. She made up for the bad calories by adding a couple extra tomato slices and some crispy lettuce leaves. After lunch, she needed to clean and stack the pots from the cuttings and play around with a new idea she'd found online for a dried flower craft.

She was just about to sit at the kitchen table when she spotted a minivan coming up the drive. *Ugh. People.* During the tourist season, she usually kept a barrier across the entrance to her farm with a sign stating she was not open to the public. Her customers and friends knew enough to move the cones and come up to the house, and some intrusive tourists did the same thing. This early in the spring, though, she had thought she was safe from drop-in visitors and her driveway was unguarded.

She plopped into her chair and sat perfectly still, hoping the people would turn around and leave since there was no indication that the farm was prepared for anyone to stop by. There were no signs about parking or pricing, no farm host to greet them. Undeterred by the lack of welcome, the family started climbing out of the van. Kassidy groaned as she watched two adults and three children get out. And now they were hauling a grandmotherly type out of the back seat. What was it, a clown car?

Resigned, Kassidy got up and put her sandwich in the fridge with a sigh. She had been up since dawn and she was really hungry. She forced a smile onto her face and went outside to shoo the people away.

"What a beautiful farm." The woman came over to greet her as soon as she came out the door. "We're the Wilsons."

Kassidy noticed with dismay that the three kids had dispersed like dandelion fluff and were now running through the rows of lavender. She realized too late that the woman had given all their first names, as if Kassidy would possibly need to know them.

"I'm Kassidy," she said, filling the void when the woman stopped talking and looked at her expectantly.

"Are you the owner? What a wonderful place to live. It's so peaceful."

Mrs. Wilson didn't seem concerned about the way the little Wilsons' shouts were destroying that peace.

Kassidy kept smiling even though the expression felt more forced by the second. "Yes, it's usually very quiet," she said. Mrs. Wilson smiled and nodded.

"I'm more of a wholesaler and not really set up as a tourist stop," Kassidy said. She made a waving gesture toward the car, as if conducting a marching band, but the Wilsons apparently were unable to recognize hints.

"Oh, we don't mind. We just came down for the day from Vancouver. Do we just pick our own, then?"

Kassidy's smile vanished at the thought of them tearing up her plants. Funny how cute it had seemed when Dante had done it, yet how terrifying it was to think of this family running rampant among her babies. "God, no. I mean, no." She frantically tried to come up with an alternative. She could give them the address of a nearby nursery, but she had a feeling they wouldn't leave willingly. She needed to give them something, make them happy somehow, and then get them to leave.

Mr. Wilson came up with Boy Wilson in tow. "Do you have a bathroom?"

Jesus. Kassidy opened and closed her mouth a few times in panic, gulping for air while she tried to come up with a way to keep them out of *her* house and *her* bathroom. Her mind was almost spinning too frantically to remember the small restroom in the shed, and she clutched her chest with her hand in relief when she thought about it.

"Yes. In here." She walked over to the small shed next to the driveway. She had meant to clean it out and turn it into a garden retreat, or possibly a guest cottage for a visiting twin, but she hadn't done anything with the interior yet. The outside had been painted in yellow with cream trim to match the exterior of her house and the drying shed, but the inside space was filled with farm clutter. She stepped around some large enameled containers and a broken birdbath, picking up a stray hoe and propping it against the wall. She opened the small door in the back, hoping there weren't too many spiders inside. Unless, of course, the presence of spiders would encourage a hastier departure.

Once the child was shut inside, she turned her attention back to the rest of the family. She was thinking more clearly now. She was ready to tackle the Wilsons Have Invaded My Home Catastrophe.

She started by softening her abrupt dismissal of the question about picking lavender. "The plants aren't blooming yet, so there isn't anything to pick, but I have some dried lavender you can use for crafts or for decorations. They're really pretty. I'll get some for you."

She jogged to the drying shed and gathered an armload of lavender sheaves. She spun around and nearly dropped them when she realized the family had followed her.

"What nice benches," Mrs. Wilson said. "Here, Mother, come sit over here. Girls, which of these crafts do you want to make?"

Okay, this was happening. Kassidy latched onto the only positive she could find in the situation—Paige. She would tell her this story, embellishing in places, even though it was horrible enough not to need much exaggeration. She could picture Paige laughing hysterically, commiserating with Kassidy's dismay at the antics of the invading family of Wilsons. The anticipation of sharing this with her almost made it bearable.

Boy Wilson and his father joined them, and the two older kids started play fighting, pretending some lavender wands Kassidy had made were spears. She stepped in between them and dropped the lavender bundles back on the table, passing them out to the family.

"What would you like to make?" she asked the older girl, who was still holding the wand as a weapon. "Those are nice to hang in your closet or put in a drawer with clothes. They'll make everything smell like lavender. Or you could make a wreath or a swag like this one to hang on your wall."

She went to another table and returned with a box full of ribbons, twine, and lacy bags for sachets, doling out the items until she had everyone working on a project. Surprisingly, the kids settled in without a fuss and listened to her instructions as she moved around the table, helping them tie knots and weave ribbons. The scent of lavender filled the barn, released as fingers crushed the flowers and broke the stems.

Once the Wilsons had their creations in hand, they seemed willing to let her herd them back to their vehicle. At first, she refused to take any money since this wasn't really part of her business, but Mr. Wilson seemed prepared to argue with her indefinitely. She finally agreed on twenty dollars for the lot, mostly to get them to leave. It was well below market price, but it seemed to satisfy the family. Besides, she had a feeling Paige wouldn't be happy about her giving away lavender. She didn't have to tell Paige how much she was paid—it would probably be enough that she at least took a little money for her time.

The family piled back into the van, calling out thank-yous and threats to tell all their friends about Kassidy's farm. She smiled and waved, determined to have a metal gate installed before any of those friends could find her place. She closed her garden shed and returned to the house to hurry through her lunch before getting back to her routine chores. She'd had enough crafting for the day, though, and spent some time instead weeding between plants, where the landscape fabric didn't reach.

❖

Kassidy put her makeshift barrier of cones in front of the entrance to her farm later in the evening when she went out. She wanted to pick up something to bring home for dinner from one of the downtown pubs, and she decided to stop at Bête Noir on the way. The tasting room was closed for the night, but she could see Jessica wiping down the bar in the back, and she tapped gently on the glass.

Jessica smiled and waved when she saw Kassidy and hurried over to let her in. She kissed her on the cheek and closed the door behind them.

"You're right on time," she said. "Drew and I were just about to sit down and have a glass of wine."

"I don't want to intrude," Kassidy said, especially sensitive to the thought of barging in on her friends' private time after having the Wilsons interrupt her lunch today. She handed Jessica a pastry box and put her hand on the doorknob. "I just wanted to bring this for you and thank you for the party last week. I'm sorry I left without saying good-bye."

"We were worried about you. I didn't know what had happened to make you rush out." Jessica opened the box, releasing a sweet scent of honey and lavender. "Is this baklava? It smells divine. Sorry, I'm still worried and want to know you're okay, but I desperately need to eat this right now."

She grabbed Kassidy's arm and pulled her back to a small seating area behind a display of wine bottles. Drew came out of the back room with a broom and dustpan, but he set them down and came over to greet her.

"Drew, we need a wine that goes with baklava," Jessica said. "Work your magic."

"Let me taste it first." He snagged a piece and chewed slowly before snapping his fingers. "Mm. Delicious. I know just the bottle."

Jessica shook her head. "He would have known without tasting it. He just wanted to get an extra piece." She offered the box to Kassidy, and she took a small piece because she wanted to try it with whatever Drew selected. She had already eaten more than enough today when she had made the dessert, trimming the ends to make them even and conveniently getting to eat all the discarded parts. The combination of walnuts, pistachios, local honey, and her own lavender water was decadent and irresistible. She only made this confection when she needed to give someone a gift, because if left on her own in the house with it, she'd have eaten much more than the edges.

"Now, tell me why you left in such a hurry the other night. I saw you talking to that gorgeous friend of Sarai's. Did she say something to make you go away?"

Kassidy made a noncommittal noise. "I guess I was overwhelmed by the crowds," she said, sharing at least a partial truth without needing to go into detail about her sensitivity to Paige's innocent comment. "I spent too much time in hibernation this winter and felt like I needed some air."

Jessica ate another triangle of baklava. "I knew I should have come over to see you after Audrey left. I didn't want to bother you if you wanted your privacy, but I should have listened to my instincts and visited anyway."

Drew came back with a dark bottle and three small wineglasses on a tray. "But now you're back among us," he added to the conversation, "and we're not letting you go again. I don't think you've tried this yet. It's our port, made from our cabernet sauvignon grapes. Lightly sweet, with hints of chocolate and fig that should go beautifully with the baklava."

Jessica laughed and patted his knee. "He's been describing wine to tourists all day, and he can't turn off the commentary."

Kassidy grinned. She took a bite of her pastry and followed it with a sip of the port. It wasn't as heavy as she had expected, and the depth of flavor stood up well to the dessert. "Yum. You always get it right, don't you?"

Before Jessica could return to the subject of Kassidy's lonely winter, she jumped in and told them the story of the Wilsons and their unexpected visit. The subject change was successful, and soon Drew and Jessica were sharing some of their more humorous moments with customers in the shop.

"What did that woman want today, Drew? Oh, that's right. She wanted to know if we had a wine that didn't taste so winey. Drew gave her a glass of water and said it was made from a new, clear grape we were experimenting with."

Drew laughed. "I usually try to be more tactful than that, but she had been annoying from the start. I think Alexandra paid her to come here and criticize everything."

Kassidy shook her head. "At least I only have to deal with it when they break past my barrier. I can't imagine dealing with the public every day like this."

"It can be a real pleasure to talk about wine all day, but you always need to be *on*. Even if our closed sign is out and the door is locked, they expect you to open up and serve them if they spot you through the window." Drew waved at their seating area. "That's why we have to sit out of sight if we want to relax at the end of the day."

Kassidy sank into the conversation, laughing along with their stories and sipping the excellent port. She might have hidden away all winter, isolated with a broken heart, but at least she was learning from her mistakes. She wasn't heartbroken because Paige had gone back to Portland, but if she was being honest with herself, she had to admit she missed her. It was only residual loneliness after sharing a weekend with someone, anyone. Nothing to do with Paige herself, of course.

At least tonight Kassidy had recognized her need for companionship and, instead of hiding at home, had sought out the company of her friends whose conversation kept her from thinking about Paige at all. Or at least a little less than she had when she was alone.

Chapter Nine

Paige spent the first two days of her time back in Portland calming employees at Kenneth Drake's firm. She had suggested he take six months to implement every facet of her proposal, and of course he had interpreted her words as a command to completely overhaul his company in one week. Apparently, everyone had left on Friday in a daze after receiving a stack of memos with terse explanations of altered job descriptions and amended corporate policies. Naturally, then, they had entered the building in an uproar on Monday morning.

Paige had hoped for a slow transition back to city life, especially since she and Dante had been delayed by a list of short hikes she had found in a guidebook and hadn't gotten back to her apartment until well after dark. She had taken the long way back to Portland, heading south to Salem, and then east to Silver Falls State Park. She and Dante had hiked until dusk through dense, mossy woods. They had finally gotten back to the car, damp from brushing through bracken ferns and thick grass, exhausted but happy.

She had planned on a day of recovery before stopping by Kenneth's to check on his progress, but her morning of sleeping in wasn't to be. By late afternoon on Monday, she even welcomed Kenneth's nasty coffee because it helped her get through an endless stream of meetings without yawning too often. By Tuesday, she was immune to its effects and desperate for something even stronger.

Along with the large group meetings with vice presidents and other executives, Paige worked her way through a list of every person on staff and made sure she spoke with each one individually. After two days of reassurances and detailed explanations, she felt drained but was confident that the employees' concerns were addressed. She wasn't sure they would all stay through the transition, but they were at least aware of the new direction the company was taking and would hopefully give Paige's plan a chance. She could only do so much with her advice, no matter how accurate and effective it was. Once she had presented a proposal, she also needed the entire company to be on board to make it work in real life. And she needed a boss who carefully helped his employees through the process.

At least she had two of the pieces in place—her solid proposal and now the acceptance of the company's people. The boss was still the wild card, and she hoped he would take advantage of his second chance and be more sensitive with his staff.

She spent most of Monday and Tuesday nights, when she wasn't at the office, drawing up a fresh timeline for Kenneth, this time with precisely detailed dates for each step in the process of restructuring the company. She had apparently been too vague for him before, and now she specified exact days and times for each move he had to make. Changes of this magnitude required finesse, and Kenneth had about as much of it as a shovel to the side of the head.

She brought him the revised proposal on Wednesday and was shown directly into his conference room. She hadn't dealt with him much during the week since her top priority had been the shaken employees. She expected him to look as haggard as she felt, but he bounded into the room with a big smile. It had to be prolonged exposure to the coffee.

"Morning, Paige. Nothing like shaking up the status quo to revitalize a company, is there? It's invigorating."

Paige couldn't come up with a polite way to answer him, so she stayed silent and concentrated her effort on not gaping at him in disbelief. If she hadn't delved into the financial statements for the full history of the company, she would never have believed he could have run a successful business for as long as he had. Fortunately for him, he had somehow surrounded himself with an amazing team, and they were the reason he still had a business to salvage when Paige had come on the scene and identified the trends he had missed in the past few years, the lack of company support for training, and the key duties that had slipped through the cracks and weren't being fulfilled by qualified people.

"Here's the new proposal," she said when she felt able to speak without telling him he was crazy. She slid the folder over to him when he sat down on the opposite side of the table. "I have copies for every department head and I'll go over the details with each of them today."

She wasn't making the mistake of giving him sole ownership of the project again, even though it was his company. It was *her* proposal and her reputation on the line if the company self-destructed during the transition phase. She had recognized how valuable his management team was, and she should have shared the proposal with all of them from the start instead of trusting Kenneth to take care of the transition on his own. She had misread his confidence as competence. She had, at least, learned a valuable lesson from this.

"Good, good," he said, putting the folder aside and leaning his forearms on the table. "Bit of a rough start, but we'll get everyone on the same page. So, did you meet Kassidy this weekend? I was thinking you could find a place for her in the new structure. Manager of something or other."

Paige closed her eyes and tried counting to ten. Then backward. She sighed. Nothing less than counting to one hundred would do the trick, and she didn't have enough time for that when he was waiting for her to speak.

"Yes, I met her. She's a lovely woman and she manages a beautiful farm where she grows lavender. You should visit her sometime. I think you'll be impressed."

"Lavender? She can't possibly make a living selling flowers."

Where was that shovel? Paige wanted to do some head bashing of her own.

Thanks to Kenneth's heavy-handed business tactics, Paige hadn't done nearly as much research into the Kassidy project as she had anticipated doing this week, but as soon as she was finished handling the crisis here, she would make up for it. She had seen enough of Kassidy's accounts—once she had stopped laughing at those cute redacted lines—to realize this farm had the potential to make Kassidy reasonably wealthy. Paige hadn't realized how much money there was in the lavender business, but she was developing more respect for the artisan enterprises that some corporate people like Kenneth dismissed so condescendingly.

"I've been doing some research, and it's a viable enterprise. She's already doing quite well, and I believe I can help her make it even more successful."

"I'll consider *you* successful if you get her to cut her losses and come work for me. She's smart enough to go far, and she shouldn't throw away her potential on some country farm."

Paige told herself to ignore his comments, but her tired mind and body shifted into autopilot and took control of the situation. She stood up abruptly. "And you shouldn't throw away your chance to really know your daughter. She's wonderful and bright and hard-working. You're right that she's smart. Smart enough to follow her dream and sensible enough to make it a reality. Maybe someday you'll take the time to get to know her for who she is, instead of trying to make her into someone she isn't."

She picked up the pile of folders and shoved them in her briefcase. "Instead of worrying about *her* business, you should concentrate on your own," she added, backing toward the door. "Fourteen of your employees sent out applications over the weekend because you rushed these changes, and most if not all of them are likely to get serious offers from other companies. You have the potential to lose some really good people if you don't convince them to stay and give the restructuring a chance. Now, if you'll excuse me, I have a meeting with your CFO."

Paige left the room and managed to make it down the hall and into the bathroom before her briefcase dropped out of her shaking hand. Where had *that* come from? She had always been able to count on herself to behave as predictably and neutrally as her black-and-white outfits when she was on a job. Even in her personal life, she never reacted like this even when she had the right to.

She leaned her hands on a sink and stared at her reflection in the mirror. Her cheeks had a little more color than usual, but otherwise she looked like her familiar, composed self. Her hair was tidy, her shirt was snowy white, her hazel eyes returned her glare with a measured, steady gaze. There was turmoil inside, but no one would ever have known if she hadn't given it a voice. Why hadn't she been able to control her words as easily as she usually did?

She turned away from the mirror and crossed her arms protectively over her chest. Yes, Kenneth was an ass about his daughter's business, but it wasn't any of Paige's concern. And although she'd only known Kassidy for a short time, she was damned sure Kassidy wouldn't want Paige fighting any battles for her with her dad. The outburst had been purely selfish, because she felt she had to get the words out before they clawed their way through her chest. The words wouldn't change who Kenneth was or how he had raised Kassidy. They were useless, empty.

But, damn, had they felt good to say.

Paige uncrossed her arms and held her hands in front of her, waiting until they stopped trembling while she formulated an action plan for herself. First, she had to march back to the conference room and apologize for being unprofessional, even though she had been right. She'd get through the rest of her exhausting meetings—unless Kenneth had her tracked down by security and thrown out, of course—and then she'd go home. Send him one of those bottles of wine from her bed-and-breakfast as a peace offering. Knowing she was keeping the better wine she had bought from Drew and Jessica for herself would help her feel like a little less of a sellout. Then she'd get back to work on Kassidy's research. Get through her obligations to father and daughter, and then get the hell out of their lives before they made her lose more of herself to them.

She wanted to open the bathroom door just a crack and peer out, looking for armed security officers before she crept into the hallway, but she forced herself not to hesitate and to walk out with purpose. She went back to the conference room and entered without knocking. Kenneth was sitting in the same position, staring at the wall with a startled expression on his face. He looked like a petulant child who was on the verge of a tantrum, and Paige cursed her inappropriate desire to laugh at his dumbfounded expression. He was a man who lived alone and had owned his own company for more than thirty years. He probably hadn't been yelled at by another person for decades.

She could almost hear him ticking, about to explode, and she hurried to get through the little impromptu speech she had come up with on the short walk from the bathroom.

"My outburst was inappropriate and rude. I apologize. But I won't advise Kassidy to sell her farm because I believe it has tremendous potential." Paige frowned and edited her own speech as she was giving it. "No. *She* has tremendous potential. So if you just want someone to encourage her to give up, then we can cancel my contract and I'll refund your money."

Paige had no intention of giving up on Kassidy, even if he took her offer and fired her from the job. She would do it for free as penance for shouting at a client.

Kenneth continued to watch her silently. She wasn't sure what else to say, so she gestured toward the door.

"Well. I'll just go then, I guess. To the meeting."

"Wait," he said. She paused and turned back, unsure what to expect.

"However you do it, just take care of her."

Paige nodded and left the room. She was tempted to go hide in the bathroom again, but she only allowed herself a few seconds to sag against the wall with her insides in a roiling mix of relief, discomfort, and residual anger. She pushed away after only a brief rest and headed to the accounting department. She still wasn't one hundred percent sure Kenneth wouldn't break out of his daze and decide to kick her off the premises. He couldn't fire her from the job at his firm since she'd already delivered her contracted proposal, but he could have her escorted out of the building in a way that would be embarrassing for her and possibly satisfying for him. No one stopped her in the hallway, though, and no one interrupted any of her afternoon meetings to tell her she had to go. She waited for it to happen, and her vigilance, combined with a couple of sleepless nights, left her completely worn-out by the time she got home.

❖

Home, where she found Evie sitting on her couch, watching television like they had never parted ways. Paige stood in the doorway holding Dante's leash, since she had just picked him up from his doggy daycare, until he tugged hard enough to remind her to unhook him and let him into the apartment. Her muddled mind tried to figure out what was happening. Had she misread Evie's signals, and they hadn't actually broken up? How awkward.

Evie muted the TV and came over to Paige, prying her briefcase out of her fingers and setting it on the ground.

"You look tired, babe. I take it McMinnville didn't agree with you?"

Paige lost herself in the memory of lounging on Kassidy's patio, surrounded by stillness, honeybees, and the intoxicating scent of lavender. And Kassidy coming out of her house with pages of accounts, joking with Paige about double-agent lavender plants.

"McMinnville was nice," she said vaguely, wanting to keep the fullness of it to herself. Kassidy didn't belong in the middle of this confusing scene she and Evie were playing out.

"Well, I'll bet you're glad to be back." Evie took her hand and led her toward the couch. "Sit and relax. I saw some bottles of wine on the counter. Why don't I pour us a glass?"

Paige allowed herself to be tugged halfway across the room before she mustered the strength to resist. "What happened to Seattle?" she asked.

Evie kept hold of her hand but didn't look at her. "Seattle didn't pan out."

Ah. Seattle was about a woman, not just a trip. And Paige hadn't fabricated the breakup in her mind. Even though it had been subtle—and now was apparently being revoked on Evie's side—it had been real.

"Who was she?" Paige pulled her hand free and unpinned her hair, rubbing her hands over her scalp and tousling her curls until they drifted across her cheeks.

Evie lowered her gaze, keeping it focused somewhere near the corner of the room. "We met at the design conference I went to in September. It was just the one night together, but we've been emailing since then." She turned around and put her hands on Paige's upper arms, looking at her with those wide, beautiful eyes that had always made Paige's insides turn to acquiescing mush.

"It was a mistake, Paige. A stupid, stupid mistake. You and I had never said we'd be exclusive, but I still should have told you before this. What do I need to do to make you forgive me? Please, Paige, will you forgive me?" She stepped closer with each sentence until her body was pressed against Paige's. Her full breasts, her strong thighs. Hands roaming up and down Paige's back, soothing muscles that were weary from stress and sitting all day. How easy to give in, to melt against Evie and let her erase the day's concerns, wipe away the tiredness and confusion Paige was feeling, with sex.

Paige stepped away and realized it was even easier to move away from Evie than to move closer. Questions nudged at her mind about this mystery woman, but Paige didn't care enough to make an effort to get the details. They wouldn't make a difference, anyway, because nothing Evie could say would make Paige forgive her and want her back. And, surprisingly, she realized that nothing Evie could tell her about her affair in Seattle had the power to hurt Paige, even though it might have only a week ago. She'd had enough of messed-up relationships today, with Kassidy's dysfunctional one with Kenneth, plus Paige's own melodrama with him in his conference room. She couldn't handle any more games or conflict right now. Today was not the day for subtle wordplay and vague definitions.

"I'm going to change," she said. "And then I'm going to take Dante for a walk. Leave my key and don't contact me again. Good-bye, Evie."

Paige turned away and walked down the hall toward her bedroom. Their first breakup had been too quiet and noncommittal, but this time the sounds were more pronounced and satisfying. Behind her, she heard the clink of her spare key landing with some force in the bowl on the hall table and the louder crash of the apartment door slamming behind Evie. Then the welcome sound of Dante's nails on the hardwood floor as he trotted to her side.

Chapter Ten

Kassidy pushed damp, loose soil around the roots of the young plant and pressed gently, securing the lavender in position without overtamping the ground. She put her hands on her lower back and arched against them, trying to ease the muscle twinges she was feeling after hours of kneeling. Her lower legs were plastered with mud, and the morning's perpetual drizzle had slowly soaked her hair and shoulders. She had gotten the rest of her cuttings into the ground, though, and her appearance was a small price to pay for the day's work.

She stacked the final plastic pot along with the others and groaned as she started to get up. She almost fell back in the mud when a hand appeared in front of her face.

"At least you don't have to water them, with this weather," Paige said. She motioned with her hand, and Kassidy took hold of it and was pulled to her feet.

"Thank you," she said, wiping her hands on her thighs, although all she did was smear the mud on her palms and legs. There wasn't a clean spot on her to use as a makeshift towel.

"You did all this today?" Paige asked, looking at the two long rows of freshly planted lavender. "You must be sore."

"A little," Kassidy said, stiffly bending over to pick up a bucket of gardening tools and the pots, letting the pain of movement wipe away the big goofy grin she could feel spreading over her face at Paige's arrival. Aching muscles were easier to handle than the realization that she had missed Paige this week more than was comfortable. "I didn't expect to see you until this afternoon or tomorrow. Where's Dante?"

"He's in the car." Paige took the bucket from Kassidy. "I couldn't let him see you like this, or he'd try to mimic your style. What did you do, roll on the ground to smooth it out before planting?"

"Very funny. It's hard to stay clean when you're transferring plants from pots to the ground." Plus, she had fallen a couple times, tripping over the trowel she kept forgetting to move. She decided not to share that part of her day with Paige.

"I had some free days this week, so we drove here last night." Paige followed her into the greenhouse and put the bucket against the wall. Kassidy felt a sting of disappointment that Paige hadn't called her last night to tell her she was back from the city, but the feeling disappeared when she turned away from putting the pots on a bench and got a good look at Paige's face. She was missing her usual smile, or even the hint of one about to emerge, and her skin was pale.

"Are you all right?"

Paige shrugged. "Sure. I had a migraine Thursday, and the effects linger for a few days, but I feel much better. I just needed some country air and some good company."

Kassidy grinned and jostled Paige gently as they walked back to her car. Paige opened the door for Dante, keeping hold of his collar as she led him into the house.

"I thought we could get an early start on the weekend, if you're up for it," Paige continued, letting Dante go once he was safely shut away from the muddy outdoors. He trotted over to the chair where Kipper was sleeping and tried to climb on the seat with the cat. Kipper jumped onto the back of the chair, apparently not in the mood for cuddling. "I wanted to be here for the street fair, and I thought it would be a great time for us to try out some of my ideas."

"Sounds good," Kassidy said. She was excited to show Paige her new labels, especially since a few of her customers were already using them this weekend. She pictured herself and Paige leaning close together at the computer, choosing fonts and colors for advertising the farm. Strolling through McMinnville's spring festival, bumping shoulders and brushing fingers as they walked side by side. Laughing and joking as they worked on Kassidy's website.

She put her anticipation aside for the moment and went over to the cabinet to get an eye mask. She put a few drops of essential oil on it and shook the mask to distribute the oil on the beads inside.

"Sit," she commanded, gesturing toward the couch. Paige sank wearily into the cushions and leaned her head against the backrest. Kassidy put the weighted mask over Paige's eyes.

"Relax while I take a shower," she said. Paige made a sort of moaning sound, and Kassidy assumed it was a murmur of agreement because she didn't move a muscle.

Kassidy went into her bedroom and stripped out of her dirty clothes, tossing them directly into the washer and getting in the shower. She leaned one hand against the wall and let a scalding stream of water massage the tension out of her shoulders and neck. She had to smile, thinking how such a basic act as showering—one she did every day—offered completely different sensations when her body was aware of Paige merely a room away. Shampoo slick through her fingers, lavender-scented suds sliding over her breasts and dripping onto the floor, warm water sheeting over her body and chasing away the chill from the misty morning…she turned the hot water off completely, but the shock of cold only intensified her feelings, leaving her nipples hard and her skin tingling.

She dried herself off quickly, no lingering, and dressed in a bulky sweatshirt and loose jeans, as if the baggy clothes could hide her body's response to Paige's nearness. She had to get hold of her rampant imagination if she and Paige were going to be working together all weekend. She'd showered with women in the house before, so this shouldn't be any different.

She looked at herself in the mirror, unable to lie to herself so easily. She'd had women in the shower *with* her who hadn't made her nerve endings come alive the way Paige had, when she wasn't even in the same room. Kassidy toweled some of the excess moisture out of her hair and ran her fingers through the long side, leaving it to dry in waves instead of taking time to style it.

She went back into the living room and paused in the doorway. Paige hadn't changed positions, and Kassidy could see her chest rising in slow, deep breaths as if she was asleep. Dante had moved to the couch and was lying with his head in Paige's lap. He raised his head with a soft *woof* when he noticed Kassidy, and Paige sat upright, dropping the mask.

"Hi. Oh, you're clean. I might have dozed off a little." Paige looked flustered, bending forward to put the mask on the table and tugging on her shirt when it rode slightly up her back. "That mask is wonderful. Very soothing."

Kassidy pulled her focus off the bare hip bone Paige had revealed when she moved. "It's good for headaches. I have a couple, so please take it with you, and I'll give you some lavender oil, too. You'll only need a few drops at a time. Are you hungry?"

Paige hesitated, seeming to consider the question. "Yes, I think I am," she said, sounding surprised at her own admission. "I lost my appetite for a while, but I guess the nap brought it back."

"Come in the kitchen then. I have some scones leftover from breakfast. I'll tell you the story of my trespassers while we eat."

"Trespassers? That explains the barricade across your driveway. No one dangerous, I hope, because those plastic cones are easy to move."

"Not dangerous. Just intrusive." Kassidy heated water for tea, then put scones, butter, and a jar of her marionberry, lemon balm, and lavender jam on the table while she told the tale of the Wilsons. She was glad to see Paige's laughter return, especially when Kassidy described the horrifying moment when the Wilsons threatened to swarm into her house and use her bathroom, and the last-minute salvation provided by the garden shed.

Paige managed to eat two scones even though she obviously was amused by Kassidy's recounting of the visit and several times had to wait until she finished laughing before eating more.

"That is hilarious," she said, licking some jam off her thumb. She shook her head and her laughter devolved into a guilty-looking smile. "You are so going to hate me."

Kassidy was watching Paige's tongue and the jam, and hate was about the furthest emotion from her mind. "I can't imagine why."

"Well, I could tell you were a private person and didn't open the farm like most other businesses do around here, but I didn't realize how determined you were to keep it that way." Paige picked up another scone and covered it with jam. "This stuff is amazing. It's sort of citrusy and sweet, but not too sweet. Did you can it yourself?"

Kassidy frowned, put on alert more by Paige's attempt to distract her than she had been by the *You're going to hate me* statement. "I suppose you were going to suggest I let every group of Wilsons in the country come tromp around my farm?"

"Yes. But we can come back to that idea later." Paige waved her hand dismissively. "Right now, we need to concentrate on getting ready for tomorrow's fair."

Kassidy hesitated, feeling like a dog chasing two bunnies that had just run in opposite directions. Did she follow Paige's admission that she wanted tourists coming to Kassidy's farm or stick with chasing down whatever Paige had planned for the fair? She'd follow the festival bunny for now, because it was closer in time, but she sure as hell wasn't forgetting about the other one. Out of sight was not out of mind. "Get ready, how? I've already talked to my buyers about labeling lavender products with the farm's name, like you told me to. Other than that, I need to put a sweater on in case it's chilly, and then I'm good to go."

Paige scooted her chair closer to the window until the length of the table was between them. "We need to make sure you have enough crafts to sell at your booth."

"My booth. What do you mean, my booth?" Her voice had somehow risen an octave. She hadn't realized she had such range.

"Kassidy, calm down..." Kassidy glared at her, and Paige continued. "Okay, don't calm down. Freak out if you'd rather. But either way, there's going to be a booth with the farm's name on it at the festival. It won't look good if it's empty."

Paige watched as Kassidy rubbed her hand through her hair, entranced by the silky way it feathered back into place. She needed to keep her attention on the discussion they were having, not on Kassidy's hair, or the pinkness of her skin when she had come out of her bedroom still flushed from her shower. Where she had been naked. Paige bit the inside of her lip hard enough to make her wandering imagination behave, at least until she was back in her hotel room.

Paige didn't need more than their brief acquaintance to understand how little Kassidy liked change, but until her story about the Wilsons, Paige hadn't fully comprehended how determined Kassidy was to protect her personal space. Paige was going to need all her powers of persuasion to get Kassidy to accept her full business plan, which was going to include a great deal of people like the Wilsons touching her lavender and using her bathroom. She waited patiently, giving Kassidy time to formulate questions and excuses. Paige would counter them all. She was accustomed to reluctant clients arguing against what she wanted them to do, and she wasn't afraid to fight Kassidy over this. Well, maybe a little afraid. She would feel better if Kassidy put down the butter knife she was holding, although she probably couldn't do too much damage with it.

"What did you expect me to put in this booth? And why are you laughing?"

Paige tried to scrunch her features into a frown matching Kassidy's, but the effort only made her laugh harder. She pointed at Kassidy's hand. "You look ready to stab me, but it's all so civilized with a spot of tea and some scones at the murder scene."

Kassidy put down the knife with a deliberate motion. "There. Feel safer now?"

"Not enough to turn my back on you."

"I'm waiting," Kassidy said. "Tell me about this booth." She was still scowling, but Paige thought she looked like she was trying too hard to keep her stern expression in place. Good. A return of Kassidy's sense of humor, no matter how reluctant, was a good sign.

"Well, I was originally thinking we could spend the afternoon today making crafts to sell. Even if we only have enough to make it through a couple hours of sales, you'll get some exposure. But your story about the Wilsons gave me a better idea."

Kassidy's heavy sigh implied she doubted it would be a better idea, no matter what it was.

"What if we make craft kits, instead of fully assembling them? Then people can come to the booth and we can help them make whatever they choose. Things you make on your own seem more meaningful than something you just buy, don't you think?"

"I guess," Kassidy said. "The Wilsons calmed down quite a bit when I put them to work. And the kids got less annoying."

"That's the customer service spirit I was looking for. Sort of." Paige ate the last bite of her third scone and got up, helping Kassidy clear the table. "We can talk later about how not to make your customers sound like misbehaving livestock."

"One step at a time." Kassidy quickly rinsed the dishes and put them in the dishwasher. "First, we need to get these kits started. And we'll need signs, and maybe instruction sheets in case someone wants to assemble the craft later, on their own. Oh, and I have some purple bags I use for giving gifts from the farm. We can put the kits in them, and then they'll be useful for transporting the finished crafts."

Kassidy left the kitchen, muttering to herself about extra ribbons, and Paige finished putting away the leftover food and wiping off the table. Her face was relaxed in a smile, and the last remnants of her migraine seemed to have been chased away. She felt relieved because even though Kassidy wasn't fully embracing this attempt to get publicity for her farm, she had moved from refusing to go to actively participating in the planning process. Paige wasn't ashamed to use Kassidy's pride in her farm to her advantage. Kassidy would do whatever it took to showcase her lavender well, so it didn't matter if she was internally calling Paige rude names the entire time.

Paige sighed and massaged her temples, relieved to have a respite from the pain that had plagued her since her run-ins with Kenneth and Evie. She had to admit the real reason she felt better was because of Kassidy herself, not just her acceptance of this business venture or some drops of essential oil. Even when blindsided by unexpected news, as Paige had done to her today, she was still able to see the humor in situations and was quick to adapt to new ideas as long as she was allowed to take her time processing them. And she was sexy, especially when wearing mud-covered jeans and a wet T-shirt that clung to every inch of her body. Paige had come here with lingering tension and achiness, but one look at Kassidy on her knees in the lavender field, arching her back as she stretched, had been enough to erase Paige's horrible week from her mind.

"Let's go, let's go," Kassidy said, coming through the swinging door with Dante at her heels. She sounded impatient, as if the booth was her idea and Paige was the one arguing against it. She was carrying a large cardboard box, and Paige took it from her, peering inside.

"You're bringing your laptop?"

"Yes. We can make instruction sheets while we assemble everything. Since you haven't done any of them before, we'll use you to make sure the directions are easy enough for a child or a beginner to follow."

"Gee, thanks."

"You're welcome," Kassidy said absently, digging through a drawer and adding some scissors to the box.

Paige listened to Kassidy list craft options as they walked to the drying shed. She was familiar with this stage of her job, and she loved it as much as it always saddened her. When business owners and managers first got her input, they often resisted, preferring stability over change and the familiar over the untested. But as they started to mentally weave her ideas into the passion they felt for their work, those ideas were no longer Paige's. They belonged to the people who would see them through, incorporating them into their companies. Paige still had plenty of suggestions that Kassidy would fight her over, but right now, with this project, ownership had abruptly shifted to Kassidy.

Paige set the box on one of the benches and perched on a tall stool, fiddling with the bunch of lavender Kassidy put in front of her.

"You're going to make this first. It's a lavender wand," Kassidy said, holding up a thick stem made of lavender stalks with a ribbon covered end. She opened her laptop and started typing.

"A wand? Like Harry Potter?" Paige had seen the beribboned thing during her tour but had no clue what it was for at the time. She waved it in Kassidy's direction. "Clothingus Disappearus. Hey, mine doesn't work."

Kassidy laughed. "I thought we decided to remain fully clothed during the consultation period."

"*You* decided that. At least until I either write a clothing optional clause into my proposal, or I get a more effective wand." She waved it again, but all it did was make Kassidy roll her eyes and sigh.

"Not a wand like Harry Potter," Kassidy said, taking it from her and handing her some loose pieces of lavender plants. "A wand, like something that smells good and you stick it in a drawer with your clothes. Now, I'm just going to tell you what to do without helping, so we'll be sure the instructions will work. First, gather the stems close together. No, make them even. That's right, and now tie a piece of ribbon in a knot to hold them in place."

Paige had only vague memories of doing arts and crafts while at Girl Scout camp, and she stumbled through the project while Kassidy deleted and retyped instructions until they made sense even to Paige. Eventually, Kassidy was laughing so hard she was barely able to tell Paige what she was doing wrong, let alone explain how to do it right.

"You're supposed to be weaving the ribbon through the stems, not just winding it around like you're trussing up a turkey. Weave. Like you're making a lattice piecrust."

"Seriously? A lattice piecrust? I doubt you could come up with a less useful analogy for me." Paige frowned at her bulbous wand, which had none of the elegance of Kassidy's sample.

"We'll have to include instructions with diagrams, not just words for this one. Here, let me help." Kassidy got off her stool and stood beside Paige, reaching for the jumble of lavender sticks.

Paige breathed Kassidy in, and everything else seemed to recede from her mind's grasp. All she could smell was Kassidy's scent—that blend of lavender and other notes Paige couldn't identify by name but would be able to recognize anywhere now. She had even been able to imagine it this week, when she had been alone in Portland, lying in the quiet darkness of her apartment. She had closed her eyes and let Kassidy's perfume infuse her mind, filling her with peace. Kassidy had claimed lavender was a calming herb, but Paige knew the effects on her were as much to do with the woman wearing the scent as the flower itself.

"Did you see what I did?" Kassidy asked, snapping Paige back to the present. She looked at the wand, almost convinced Kassidy had swapped it out with another. Somehow, it had been tidied into a tight cylindrical shape. Kassidy had braided a deep blue ribbon around the top, and the end was dangling down, apparently waiting for Paige to do something to it.

"Um, sort of. Can you show me once more?" Paige managed to concentrate this time and was even able to clumsily mimic Kassidy's movements.

Kassidy stepped away, bumping into the table behind her and knocking a wreath to the ground. "You're doing fine," she said, picking it up and setting it next to her laptop. "Just pull the ribbon a little tighter."

Paige continued to laboriously weave ribbon around her wand while Kassidy moved on to another craft. She moved to the far end of the table from Paige and started chatting more rapidly than usual, assembling kits and describing the food and entertainment from last year's festival. Paige wondered if Kassidy was feeling nervous about tomorrow, or if maybe—hopefully, because it wasn't fair for Paige to be the only one—she wasn't entirely immune to the zings of electricity Paige felt flash between them when they were close to each other.

"I read on the website that they're having a dog show this year, too," Paige inserted when Kassidy seemed to run out of things to say. "I've been training Dante to be an agility dog, and it would be a good experience for him to run through the course."

Kassidy made a strangling sort of sound that seemed suspiciously like a restrained laugh. "Really? I didn't realize you were training him for, well, anything."

"He's just learning," Paige said, indignantly defending either her dog or her own training skills. She wasn't sure which one. "It's the reason I got him."

"Oh?"

"Yeah. I was always very competitive in high school and college." Paige set her finished wand on the table. If she squinted when she looked at it, she could almost not notice the dividing line between Kassidy's neat work and her own questionable weaving. "Very type A, win at all costs, but I haven't had much of a chance to compete since I got out of school. I thought it might be interesting to give dog sports a try."

Paige frowned, thinking of the way she had searched for a sport that called to her and was something she could pursue as an adult in her free time, like she had tried to do with a business venture. She had come up against the same issue, though, and hadn't been able to identify a place where she really belonged. The canine agility idea had sort of been an excuse to go to the Humane Society and check out the dogs. She had always wanted a dog but had been too busy with other activities to get one. Even now, when she didn't need her parents to give their permission anymore, she had taken months to convince herself that she would be a good dog owner. Companionship hadn't been reason enough to break down and adopt a pet, but the chance to compete was a justification she could allow herself to use. She had been drawn to Dante at first sight, ensnared by his chocolate brown eyes and convincing herself that he looked fast enough to fly through an agility course. And smart enough to learn the commands she'd need to teach him. She spent more time walking him along the Willamette River and playing tug-of-war at the dog park than actually training him, but they'd get hard core about it eventually.

"He looks like a real cutthroat competitor, just like you," Kassidy said, gesturing toward the corner of the room. "What's he doing now, carbo loading for tomorrow?"

Paige looked where Kassidy was pointing and saw Dante chewing up the dried-up roots from a discarded lavender plant and dropping the gnawed pieces into a pile. Darn. She should have realized he had been too quiet to be behaving well. She sighed and took the root away from him, offering a chew toy instead, which he ignored.

"Wait until you see him on the course. He's an animal."

Kassidy laughed. "That I'll accept. I'll wait until I see him compete tomorrow to decide if I believe he's a *trained* animal."

"You're going to owe both of us an apology when we win the McMinnville Spring Festival Dog Agility trophy, if there is such a thing," Paige said, trying to sound indignant while wrestling a rake handle away from Dante. "Now let's get back to business. You still have to teach me how to make one of those wreaths."

Kassidy groaned. "It involves weaving. Why don't we switch to something easier, like the kindling logs?"

"Isn't that just a bunch of stems tied together?"

"Exactly," Kassidy said. "Don't worry, though, I'm sure you'll be able to do it. Even the littlest Wilson was able to make one."

"Gee, that's flattering," Paige mumbled.

Kassidy had moved herself out of range of Paige, but she had to come close again to hand her the pile of lavender stems. And then she needed to hover nearby and help Paige arrange the twigs so the small buds remaining on them were visible, providing small decorative spots of color.

"Turn this stem around," she said, guiding Paige's hand with hers. "You're squashing the buds on the inside."

"You're micromanaging. There are just as many flowers on the side I originally had facing out."

"They weren't as nice," Kassidy protested, perching on the bench next to Paige and typing some instructions on her laptop. Paige was right, of course, but Kassidy wasn't about to admit it. Being close to Paige calmed her nerves—something she had needed when Paige had taken her hand while they talked about Kassidy's meddlesome dad, and something she craved now when she was anxious about the festival.

The comfortable feeling of touching Paige was morphing into something decidedly less calming fairly quickly, though. Kassidy couldn't spend the entire weekend alternating between standing close to Paige like a girlfriend and running across the room from her, as if they were strangers. She moved her laptop a few inches down the table, into what she considered to be the casual acquaintance zone, far enough away so she wouldn't touch Paige if she reached out her hand.

"Why are you waving at me?" Paige asked. "Am I doing something wrong?"

"I'm just shaking out a cramp from typing so much," Kassidy said, dropping her arm back to her side. She had thought Paige was focused enough on her craft not to notice Kassidy measuring the distance between them. "And you're not doing anything wrong, although it might look nicer if you tied the ribbon into a bow instead of a square knot."

Paige held up her finished craft and studied it. "You know, this would be perfect as part of a Valentine's Day basket. What's more romantic than snuggling together on a chilly February evening, with a crackling fire and the scent of lavender filling the room?"

Kassidy propped her chin on her palm. She tried to picture the scenario in a detached way, but all she could see in her mind was her and Paige in the farmhouse's main bedroom, with its huge, rustic fireplace and cozy queen-sized bed. "And wine. A nice bottle of pinot noir."

Paige tapped the bundle of kindling against her chin. "Some food would be nice, too. Not a big meal, but small things to feed each other, like crackers and chunks of cheese. Olives and strawberries."

"Oh, yes. And chocolate," Kassidy added, closing her eyes and letting the smell of lavender transport her into the fantasy more fully. "I know it's a cliché on Valentine's Day, but it would start to melt in the warm room and we...they...whoever could lick it off each other's fingers."

"Or other parts of us...them...whomever," Paige said, barely loud enough for Kassidy to hear her.

A loud crash startled Kassidy and she opened her eyes as she swung toward the noise, nearly swiping her computer off the table. Dante was standing near a toppled pile of gardening tools and looking back over his shoulder as if searching for someone else to blame for the mess.

Kassidy laughed at his expression, relieved to have been dragged back to reality. She had been sitting an appropriate distance from Paige, but their words had managed to fill the empty space between them with something more intimate than touch.

"Well, the basket is a good idea. Be sure to write it into your proposal so I remember it next year." As if she'd be forgetting the image of Paige covered in melting chocolate anytime soon.

"I'll put it right after the naked clause," Paige said, reaching down to pick up the bundle of kindling that she had dropped. "I think I'm going to make one of those wreaths now. At least there's nothing romantic about weaving."

CHAPTER ELEVEN

Kassidy fluffed out the green bunting she had draped over the top of her booth, trying to hide the silver duct tape she had used to hold it in place. She leaned too far to one side and nearly fell off the rickety plastic chair. She flailed wildly before catching hold of the PVC pipes that framed the booth, and then held her breath as the entire structure wobbled and nearly collapsed. She was mentally cursing Paige for instigating this fiasco and almost felt disappointed when both she and the booth stabilized without any broken framework or bones. She indulged in a satisfying daydream of getting to show Paige a bandaged wrist and say *I told you this was a bad idea* before stepping gingerly off the chair, with both her body and the booth in one piece.

"I hadn't thought of including a comedic performance today, but I think it makes an entertaining addition to the booth. Do you do these shows once an hour?"

Kassidy turned to see Paige grinning at her and holding two cups of coffee. She switched her fantasy to one in which she dumped a hot cup of coffee on Paige's head.

"You try climbing on these chairs. They're not designed to support Kipper, let alone a full-grown human."

Paige handed her a coffee. "No, thanks. I'm the brains in this operation, not the brawn."

Kassidy didn't bother commenting on that statement. If anything, she agreed she wasn't acting like she had a brain, otherwise she wouldn't have agreed to go along with this plan. The only reason she had, in the end, was because she couldn't bear the thought of an empty booth with her farm's name on it sitting in the middle of the busy fair. She had too much pride in her place to allow that to happen, which was probably exactly what Paige had been gambling on when she went behind Kassidy's back and paid for this space. Kassidy had to admit they were in a perfect location, right in the heart of the festival and close enough to wine and food booths to take advantage of the crowds they always drew. And her decorations looked pretty enough to attract the attention of people passing by, even though she had arranged them under duress.

"It looks beautiful," Paige said, as if reading her mind. She stepped back and looked at the booth from a few yards away. "I didn't expect you to have decorations on hand since I knew you didn't like doing this kind of thing."

Kassidy unfurled one of the fabric pieces and showed Paige the elastic she had hidden from view. "They're my bedsheets. I couldn't think of anything else to use, and I didn't want it to be plain."

Paige made a coughing sort of noise and stepped forward, trailing one finger over the sheet. "So you were sleeping on these last night?"

Her voice hinted at an intimacy Kassidy hadn't thought of before now. She had been thinking of the sheets as fabric, but the way Paige spoke made her think of naked bodies tangled in the cool cotton and the heated scent of lavender wafting from the fireplace.

She paused for several long moments before jumping back into the conversation. She had almost forgotten how mad she was at Paige. "I would have come up with nicer decorations if someone had given me time to prepare."

Paige laughed, letting go of the sheet. "If someone had given you more than a day's notice," she said, matching Kassidy's light tone, "you would have skipped town. Someone isn't a fool."

Kassidy got a piece of thin, pale blue plastic out of one of her boxes and spread it over the table, securing the corners with more tape.

"What's this?" Paige asked. "Your shower curtain? Are you going to tape up your underwear next?"

Kassidy smacked her in the arm. "It's an outdoor tablecloth. I had an extra from a barbecue last year. But the underwear is a fitting metaphor because I really do feel exposed out here. I'm not comfortable dealing with the public like this."

Paige seemed to naturally understand when Kassidy finished joking and was being serious. "I know, Kass. A lot of what I suggest for your farm is going to push you out of your comfort zone. I've researched this industry over the past week, and the businesses with longevity and financial success share several traits in common. You offer an outstanding, unique product, but otherwise you're falling short in a few key areas. One of them is public access."

Kassidy dropped into a chair, nearly tipping over on the uneven ground. Paige scooted the other chair over and sat close to her, not even making a single teasing comment about Kassidy's second episode of flailing.

"You're blunt," Kassidy said. Part of her wanted to ignore Paige's dire warning. What did she know about owning a lavender farm in McMinnville, anyway? But Kassidy had studied the market, too. As much as she wanted to preserve her farm sanctuary, and even though she was making decent money right now, she wasn't confident about her future.

"I guess I've known I should make the farm public, but I hoped I could find another way."

Paige jostled Kassidy's shoulder with her own. "Most of my clients already suspect they're making mistakes, but they don't want to admit to them. They're too stubborn, too frightened, or too resistant to change. Sometimes all three. They bring me in, hoping I'll give them an easier answer, or the one they really want to hear, instead of the truth they're trying to ignore."

"I had myself convinced you were going to be satisfied if I updated my website and put some labels on olive oil soap and candles," Kassidy said, admitting to her fantasy without adding the part about her and Paige working side by side. Touching. And kissing. Yeah. Paige didn't need to know the details.

"Well, you need to do both of those things, but they're small steps that won't make too much difference in the long run. The bigger steps are ones like opening a small shop on your farm where you'll sell those labeled products, plus some of your own."

Kassidy made herself picture the Wilsons' visit again, trying not to cringe, and imagined what they would have liked to find on her farm. "Or like turning the field between the house and drying shed into a U-pick area."

Paige reached over and took Kassidy's hand with a surprising gentleness. Kassidy sighed, knowing she wasn't going to like hearing whatever Paige said next, if she felt the need to soften it with this kind of comfort. She was almost too worried about what she was going to hear to notice how warm Paige's hand felt in hers, or how easily Paige's fingers fit when twined around her own. Almost.

"One more step I'd like you to take today. When people ask about lavender, even if you think their questions are dumb, please answer them politely, and don't leave the party and run home."

Kassidy laughed and shoved at Paige, almost upending them in the process. "I can't believe you brought that up again. You insulted my food."

Paige grinned. "Sometimes the public is rude and insulting. Maybe I was just getting you prepared for this."

"You didn't even know who I was," Kassidy said with a snort. The burst of laughter had felt good, loosening something tight inside her belly. She didn't bother going into her list of excuses from the night she had first seen Paige. She had just come out of hiding after a long winter and a breakup. She had thought Paige was beautiful, like someone who had an amazing secret to share, and she hadn't handled it well when some of the first words out of her mouth were negative ones about Kassidy's food.

"All right, point taken. I've been to enough tasting rooms and have watched people like Drew and Jessica, and Everett and Brian talk to customers. I know how to act."

Paige shook her head. "No. Don't act. Be yourself. Share your passion." She hesitated, as if trying to find the right words. "Think about walking out of your house on a summer day. You look at the fields around you and see a hundred shades of purples and pinks, grays and greens. The scent of lavender warming in the morning sun makes the air feel heavy with perfume. And you feel like the luckiest person in the world because you get to experience it. Share that feeling and that gratitude when you talk to people who are here for a short time, taking a break from the work and stress and responsibilities of daily life."

If Kassidy hadn't been staring intently at Paige's face when she spoke, she might have missed the wistfulness, the longing that showed in her expression for a heartbeat.

Paige cleared her throat and stood up. "Speaking of the public, they'll be here soon. Are the craft kits ready to go?"

Kassidy nodded and got up as well, hauling a box full of lavender bundles out from under the booth's table. "What's yours?" she asked.

Paige was arranging sample crafts on one side of the table and she gave Kassidy a quizzical look. "My what?"

"You described my ideal morning, when I feel connected to my farm and happy to be there. What's your passion?"

Paige laughed, but without any of the humor and joy Kassidy had come to expect from her. "I don't have one of my own. I guess my ideal life is helping people figure out how to have theirs without going bankrupt."

"That's a good reason to feel proud," Kassidy said, but Paige merely shrugged without taking her eyes off the table in front of her.

❖

After three hours of sharing her passion for lavender and helping visitors at the booth fumble through their crafts, Kassidy felt a renewed sense of irritation toward Paige for making her come to the fair. Maybe Paige was wrong, and Kassidy could just hide out on her farm, avoiding all contact with the public. Who cared if she went broke after a couple years? It would probably take that long before the muscles in her face—unused to forcing a smile for hours at a time—finally healed.

Paige, on the other hand, had annoyingly gotten more cheerful as the day wore on. Whenever someone got frustrated with their craft, unable to recreate Kassidy's elegant examples, Paige would bring out the wand she had made last night and would soon have the child or adult joining in her laughter. They walked away from the booth in love with their imperfect creations.

"Where are the doughnuts?" Kassidy asked, getting on her hands and knees and looking through the empty boxes under the table.

"You've had four," Paige said, putting the last few craft bags out on display. "You're going to have a massive sugar crash any minute now."

"That's why I need another one," Kassidy snapped, letting her public mask slip a little. Or maybe a lot, since Paige raised her eyebrows at the surly tone. "Sorry. You seem to thrive on this. It's draining me."

"I have more experience being in situations where I need to behave a certain way. You'll build up your stamina for it."

"So this is an act? You're not having fun, you're just better at hiding your aggravation than I am?"

"Yes," Paige said, looking like she was trying to force a serious expression on her face. She laughed. "Well, no. I'm having a blast. This is a vacation for me, though. You're still trying to come to terms with a change in lifestyle. It's understandable that you aren't enjoying this as much as I am."

Somehow, being understood only made Kassidy feel more annoyed. Paige merely grinned and handed her a bottle of water, which was an unacceptable substitution for a glazed doughnut.

"I gave the rest of the box to Jessica and asked her to either eat them or hide them from you. Were you planning to inhale the entire dozen?"

"I thought you might want one or two, but otherwise, yes." Kassidy took a drink of water and nearly choked on it. She grabbed Paige's shirt and pulled at her until she was standing between Kassidy and the public front of the booth. "Hide me. Here come the Wilsons, and they've multiplied."

❖

Even though Kassidy had initially agreed with Paige's description of a summer morning as her favorite place to be, she discovered a new, better version of heaven later that afternoon, sitting on her flimsy plastic chair next to Drew and Jessica, with a glass of wine in her hand and absolutely no need to smile unless she felt like it.

She had survived, though. Her farm had made its first steps toward being a public commodity, and she had made it through with nothing worse than sore cheekbones and a torn bedsheet from when she had tripped over one end of it. She even had a newfound love for the Wilsons since, between their kids and the friends they had brought with them, they had purchased the last of her crafts, allowing her to close the booth and Paige to go back to her inn and get Dante.

"Ouch," Kassidy said under her breath, massaging her jaw when a small, real smile escaped. She'd never tell Paige, but she had enjoyed talking to the Wilsons again, especially since they seemed so appreciative of her lavender. And while she was keeping secrets from Paige, she'd also definitely hide the fact that she had been slightly disappointed when they were finished working in the booth together. They had been in close quarters all day, touching each other with brief flashes of heat, although Kassidy was sure she was the only one who had felt the warmth of Paige's touch. Paige's hand on her waist when she had to move around her to the other side of the booth. Her fingers brushing against Kassidy's, leaving a trail of sparks with the tiniest of touches when one of them handed a craft to the other.

Kassidy had needed to remind herself that Paige was here for a month or so, not forever. Next year—if Kassidy managed to follow Paige's business plan and didn't give up—Kassidy would be working at the festival on her own. Paige was a temporary business partner, not a life partner. Kassidy frowned and took a sip of her wine. How had Paige become a fixture in her life when they hadn't spent more than a handful of days together? She could already imagine how quiet the booth—and her life—would be without Paige's laughter filling in the empty spaces. But Kassidy didn't want someone stepping permanently into her life. She'd lost confidence in herself with Audrey, and now she wasn't sure she could ever be in a relationship without reverting to the frightened six-year-old whose father had disappeared into the city and her mother into the confines of her dark bedroom.

Nothing was stopping Kassidy from seeking pleasure though, when she could control how close she got to someone and let them go when she felt herself getting too deeply involved. That's all she would want from Paige—a chance to explore the currents between them and an opportunity to gather some memories that would keep her warm during the nights when she was alone. An opportunity to beta test the Valentine's Day basket before offering it to the public. Knowing Paige had her life in the city and wouldn't stay in McMinnville made it even more tempting to think of being with her. If only the pesky fact of their professional relationship wasn't an issue…

Kassidy needed to stop thinking of Paige in personal terms and pay more attention to her as a consultant because, truthfully, Paige was much better at marketing Kassidy's business than she was. When someone had mentioned how good their hands smelled after working with the lavender, Paige had vanished, reappearing seconds later with a bottle of appropriately, yet cumbersomely, labeled Lavender Lane Farm Goat's Milk Lotion to give to the visitor. And somehow, while Kassidy was helping a child make a wreath, Paige hurried around the festival and returned with an armful of lavender products to display and business cards from the vendors who sold them. She saw the big picture and was working on establishing relationships with these strangers who came to the booth. Kassidy had barely been able to concentrate on the person in front of her at the time, willing them to hurry through their crafts and leave her alone so she could eat another doughnut.

Kassidy laughed to herself. In her heart, she was proud of how she had done. She would get better as she adjusted to a new way of living and selling her lavender. She might be slow to accept change, but she was aware enough to see the necessity of it. She'd adapt.

Kassidy had been slouching wearily in her chair, but she sat up when the first entrant in the dog agility class came into the ring. The events so far had included wiener dog races and a costume contest. Not exactly the high stakes type of competition Paige claimed to crave. Kassidy could see them standing among the other dogs and owners, and Paige appeared to be giving Dante a pep talk, probably similar to the one she had given Kassidy today.

"Are they any good?" Drew asked, leaning across Jessica's lap toward her. "I saw her walking him around town last weekend and I'd be surprised if she didn't have rope burns."

"Paige says speed and independence are desirable qualities for an agility dog," Kassidy said, repeating what Paige had told her before she left the fair to get her dog. "Actually, though, she seems to think he'd win the Tour de France if he could just reach the bike pedals, so I'm not sure if her expectations are realistic."

The dog events were a recent addition to the fair, but the turnout was impressive, with a mix of owners with well-trained, speedy dogs and ones that looked like they decided to enter on a whim and had never actually seen an agility course before.

Kassidy shouted her encouragement when it was Paige's turn, and Dante promptly galloped over to visit her on the sidelines.

"Oops," Kassidy said when Paige came to herd him back toward the obstacles. "At least the timer hasn't started yet."

Paige winked at her. "You're quite a distraction for us."

Kassidy pressed her lips together to hide her smile, pretending she didn't see Jessica and Drew nudging each other, and wondering if Paige had really meant to include herself when she said *us*.

Dante's obedience didn't improve when the whistle blew, and he and Paige started the course. He apparently wasn't only interested in Kassidy, because he stopped by the sideline for a pat every time he passed a child among the spectators. He followed Paige around most of the obstacles instead of going over or through them, and at one point he disappeared into the tunnel and didn't emerge again for an unusually long time. By the end, Paige was laughing as hard as the audience. Dante got the loudest cheers of any of the dogs when he sailed over a jump at the end of the course, heading in the wrong direction, but leaping with exuberance.

Paige clapped, too, and praised him as she snapped on his leash and led him out of the ring. Kassidy watched with curiosity. She didn't doubt that Paige had believed her own words when she talked about her competitive drive, but she looked far too happy for someone who had claimed to have adopted Dante solely for his agility championship potential. She had made a comment about wearing a mask to hide her true nature when she was around clients, and Kassidy wondered if Paige had been wearing it so long that she'd started to believe it was real, too.

CHAPTER TWELVE

Paige was glad to have Dante to care for during the rest of their stay at the fair. He was enthralled by all the people and the permeating smell of food, and he kept her busy so she didn't have to face the temptation of touching Kassidy. She had given in to the desire to reach for her too often while they were in the farm's booth, sometimes out of necessity when Paige needed to get by her, but usually just because she wanted to.

Kassidy was filled with contrasts, and Paige wanted to explore them all. She was a talented chef who made exquisite dishes, yet had a serious junk food addiction. Her hands were as soft and scented as if she had just gotten an expensive manicure, but when Paige had held her hand this morning, she had felt calluses at the base of her fingers and had seen the short, rough fingernails of a person who spent most of her days digging in the dirt. She was fiercely private, but willing to hang her sheets out in public because the color was pretty, and the booth needed decoration.

Oh, those sheets. Paige had thought the green material nice enough when she first saw it. When Kassidy told her where they had come from, however, Paige hadn't been able to stop her imagination from zooming directly to the bed itself, with Kassidy naked and warm and reaching for Paige...

A steady pull on the leash brought her back to the present. Dante was aiming toward another food booth, of course.

"Maybe you should train him as a retriever, instead. Find the pizza, Dante. Good boy!" Kassidy grinned and patted his head as she walked to the counter and bought two slices.

"Thank you," Paige said, accepting the piece of pizza when Kassidy handed it to her. "He showed great promise today on the course. We need to work on going in the right direction, but he was really fast."

"Fast? He sat inside the tunnel for two minutes." Kassidy shook her head and took a big bite of pizza.

"She's exaggerating. Don't listen to her," Paige told Dante, giving him a tiny bite of her cheese.

They started walking again, bumping shoulders whenever they were in a crowded area. Paige knew she could have moved a few inches over and avoided any contact whatsoever, but Kassidy could have moved just as easily, so Paige stayed where she was. It was innocent touching, just like this morning's hand-holding had only been a way to get Kassidy's attention and to offer support.

Yeah, right. Paige hadn't made any effort to hold Kenneth's hand during her consulting job with his firm. She needed to be honest with herself and admit she was attracted to Kassidy. Then she had to be on guard against any attempt her damned body made to ignore their business relationship and explore the options for something more.

Paige took a deep breath and altered her steps enough to keep their shoulders well apart. Kassidy didn't seem to notice, and she made no effort to get close to Paige again. Kassidy seemed lost in thought and content to meander through the festival with Paige and Dante.

At least the lack of physical contact helped Paige focus a little better on doing her job. She had been pleased with the way the festival had gone. She had veered away from her usual consulting process with Kassidy by introducing parts of her proposal before she had finished her evaluation phase. Usually, she provided a complete business plan all at once, instead of piecemeal, but she couldn't treat Kassidy's business like one of her corporations. The fair had been a perfect way to push Kassidy to make a change, and the rest of

Paige's ideas would follow organically from this one. Plus, she was entranced by this community, with its artisanal, collaborative feel. She wanted to be part of it for a short time, and she had a chance to be in Kassidy's world when they tried out Paige's plans together instead of Paige telling her what to do and moving on to the next job while she did it. Most of all, though, she simply liked spending time with Kassidy. More than she wanted to admit.

Most of her reasons for sharing the day with Kassidy were sound, but even putting her personal attraction aside, she saw the day as a professional success. She was aware of Kassidy's discomfort and how much the effort to remain upbeat and polite had wearied her, but Paige doubted anyone else had seen the strain on Kassidy's face and in her posture. She was naturally a quiet person and would never be the boisterous type of host someone like Drew could be, but her gentleness and grace were perfectly suited to the delicate lavender she grew. She fit the role of lavender keeper perfectly. She probably would never be totally comfortable in a public role, and the heavy tourist season would be draining for her, but once she realized it was okay to be herself with her customers, she was going to make the farm even more of a success than it already was and keep it that way for the long haul.

Paige handed Dante's leash to Kassidy when they got to another food stand, and she threw away their greasy paper plates before buying them each a lemonade. When she got back to Kassidy, she was kneeling on the ground and scratching Dante's belly.

"You both seemed to be having fun in the ring today," Kassidy said. She stood up and accepted the lemonade. "After all your talk about being competitive, I thought you'd be disappointed about not winning."

Paige smiled. She'd had a great time out there, and her stomach still hurt from laughing so hard. "Winning? We were disqualified at the first obstacle when he tried to chew on the hoop instead of jumping through it. I'm sure the judge only let us continue for entertainment value since everyone seemed to like watching us plow through the course. Winning wasn't an option after the first beat of the timer."

"He showed promise," Kassidy said. She angled Dante away from the thinning crowds until they were aiming for the street where they had parked. "As a canine comedian, if nothing else. I take it you were accustomed to being in first place in your other sports?"

Paige tossed her empty lemonade cup in an ornate garbage can like she was dunking a basketball. "My teams usually did well, and I was always first string. But Dad practiced with me all the time when I was little. We'd spend evenings and weekends playing basketball or softball. Starting in about first grade, my mom would take me to the high school track, too, and I was running hurdles by the time I was ten."

Paige leaned against the passenger door of her car once they reached it. "It was pretty intense at times, but it was okay. Those were the sports they had played, and it's like they were sharing them with me. It was something we could do together."

"That's nice," Kassidy said, her attention focused on the leash she was twisting around her wrist. "So they played those sports in school, and you did, too?"

Paige shrugged even though Kassidy wasn't looking at her to see the movement. She was accustomed to talking about the activities she had been pushed toward in school, but no one ever asked *why*. Something that didn't need to be a private thing had inadvertently become one by accident and habit, and as a result she felt strange talking about her childhood out loud. "Sort of. I mean, I think they had regrets about missing stuff in high school, and they didn't want me to feel the same way. They pushed a little, but only to help me get the most out of my time at school."

"And did you?"

Kassidy looked up when Paige laughed in response. The sound was a little harsh, and not as free as most of her laughter, but Paige attributed it to being uncomfortable talking about herself. She talked about business owners, about their employees, about her clients' lives—but not her own.

"I did," Paige said, controlling her features again. "Sports, yearbook committee, even chairperson for prom. Student council, debate club, choir. I was in band for a while, but it interfered with my teams."

"That sounds exhausting," Kassidy said quietly. "And your parents had done all of those activities, too?"

Paige shook her head. "They were too busy taking care of a little present they got after a sophomore dance." She pointed at herself.

"Oh." Kassidy stared into the distance without seeming to see anything, as if she was looking at a memory instead. She met Paige's gaze again, with a sort of sad smile. "What was your favorite, of all those sports and committees?"

Paige struggled for a moment, wanting to grab Dante's leash and get in the car. Or close the distance between them and kiss Kassidy until she forgot what she had just asked. Her question was treading in an area Paige didn't even like to think about, let alone share with other people, but Kassidy had put her faith in Paige today. She had stepped out of her comfortable, isolated world because of Paige's advice. The least Paige could do was to expose a part of herself as well.

"None of them," she said. She could have stopped there, with the enigmatic, but true answer, but she didn't. "I had fun in some, others were a bore, but nothing really felt like mine. I always hoped I'd discover a great passion, like you have with your lavender and your home, or even a strong preference for a hobby or business idea. But I guess I'm destined to facilitate other people's dreams, not to have any of my own."

Kassidy smiled, with a shake of her head. "Don't give up too easily, Paige," she said. She handed back Dante's leash and stroked her fingers along Paige's cheek, almost too quickly and softly to be noticeable, although Paige's skin felt permanently marked by her touch.

Kassidy stepped back, and Paige emphasized the distance between them by a shift in voice and topic. "I still have more to discuss with you about our business plan," she said, relieved when she sounded more like a professional adult than a confused teenager. "I have to go back to Portland tomorrow night, but we could get together in the morning or afternoon, if you want."

"What about tonight?" Kassidy asked. "I can make us some dinner and we can go over your notes while we eat."

Say no. Make up an excuse. "Sure," Paige said, ignoring the clamoring voices in her head. "I'll stop by the inn and get my notebook, and we'll meet you back at the farm."

Paige got in the car and fiddled with her keys before driving away. She was feeling close to Kassidy after today, and it wasn't a good idea to be around her at night, when Paige had been feeling vulnerable. So close to the bed Paige had been daydreaming about far too much today.

"It's just a business dinner," she told Dante as she put the keys in the ignition and started the car. "Besides, it will be a good time to make more suggestions about the farm, following up after today's positive experiences." It also would help that Kassidy was worn-out after her hours in the booth. She might be less resistant to Paige's suggestions.

"Suggestions about the farm," Paige said. "Nothing else."

Dante flopped on the back seat, tongue lolling and ears sticking out to the sides, looking completely unconvinced by Paige's justifications.

"Fine," she said, glaring at him in her rearview mirror. "I just want to spend more time with her. Are you happy now?"

Dante's doggy grin let her know he was.

Chapter Thirteen

Kassidy was searching through her fridge for some reasonably fresh ingredients for dinner when the headlights from Paige's car slashed across her window, momentarily illuminating the back wall of the kitchen. Kassidy wanted to head outside and meet Paige, but she made herself wait, continuing her exploration of the vegetable crisper's contents instead.

She shouldn't feel this excited to see Paige. Well, if she was going to be critical, she also shouldn't have invited her over for dinner tonight. The fair had been emotionally refreshing and draining at various times, and Kassidy's defenses were low. She would have been better off meeting with Paige tomorrow when she was rested and in control again. God only knew what she'd agree to tonight when her carefully positioned barriers were chipped and shaken.

Kassidy tossed a wilted bunch of kale in her composting bin. What was she even worried about? That she'd agree to turn her farm into a site for a traveling circus, or that she'd sleep with Paige? She'd obviously prefer the latter, but she wasn't weak enough to allow either to happen. As much as she was tempted every time Paige showed any indication of wanting her, she wasn't about to jeopardize their working relationship. Her libido was going to have to take a back seat right now, along with her pride, because she was going to give common sense control of the steering.

Paige had been right about this festival. The booth had been a success, and Kassidy had made some great new contacts with tourists and with some local business owners she hadn't met before. She had gone to the fair on her own for the past few years, but she had always been a spectator, keeping to herself and chatting only with her close friends. Without Paige's prompting, Kassidy would never have made the effort to give her farm such a noticeable presence.

So Kassidy would keep her clothes on and listen to what Paige suggested. She'd say no to anything crazy, like the three-ring circus, but she'd follow Paige's advice when it seemed to be logical and not too drastic.

She didn't have to keep business and pleasure completely separate, though. She could give in to her desire to know more about Paige. To hear more about her overwhelming list of school achievements and to try to understand why she seemed so sad about not particularly loving any of them. Curiosity wasn't a crime. It was a poor substitution for sex, but a friendship was all Kassidy would allow herself to have while they worked together. Once they were done, Paige would be back in Portland, and Kassidy would be facing the most challenging tourist season of her life. Mayhem and distance would keep her safe from Paige's charms.

And until then, Kassidy could let a little friendship worm its way into their relationship. She slit open a package of steaks she had bought two days before and gave them a sniff. Yes, still good. She was thinking about side dishes when she realized she had been mentally dissecting her relationship with Paige for quite a while, but the woman herself had yet to make an appearance.

Kassidy put the steaks back in the fridge in case Kipper came to investigate the counters and went out her back door. When she came around the side of her house, she saw Paige poking around in the garden shed, with the doors wide open and the lights on. Dante stopped rummaging through some discarded cardboard boxes and trotted over to greet her.

"Oh, hi," Paige said when she saw Kassidy in the doorway. "I got sidetracked."

"I can see that," Kassidy said. Most of the shed's front wall was made up of double Dutch doors, revealing almost the entirety of the interior when they were open. She stepped inside. "It's wonderful, isn't it? I had thought of making it into a guest room for my family, but I suppose you're devising evil plans to turn it into a shop for tourists."

"Maybe," Paige said with a shrug, turning away from Kassidy and peering inside the tiny bathroom.

Her evasive posture wasn't reassuring to Kassidy. She was reluctant enough to open a store here on the property. What could Paige possibly have in mind that she knew Kassidy would hate even more?

"I'd noticed it here but didn't really think much about it until you were telling me about the Wilsons and your bathroom." Paige came back into the center of the space. "What is it, about twelve by twelve? And these doors, can you open the top half of them like windows and leave the bottoms closed?"

"Yes. I'll show you." Kassidy started to unhook one side of the Dutch doors when another set of headlights beamed across Paige's car. She was imagining the gate she would buy for her driveway, complete with concertina wire, to replace the flimsy cone barricade, when the car moved into the light enough for her to recognize it.

Shit. Apparently a family reunion had been planned without her knowledge. She looked at Paige, wondering briefly if she could get her to leave somehow. She couldn't come up with a polite way to say *Get out*, so she'd have to settle for trusting the twins not to talk about any of their personal family business—namely her dad—in front of company.

"It seems you're about to meet my brother and sister," she said.

Paige gestured over to where Dante was bounding around Kyle's legs. "Looks like it's just your brother."

Kassidy shook her head with a deep sigh. "They're a matched set. If one is here, the other isn't far behind."

"Hey, K," Kyle said, wading past Dante and coming over to give her a kiss on the cheek. He smiled at Paige. "Is this your dog? He's awesome."

"Kyle, this is Paige. And you've met Dante. Paige, this is my brother, here on a surprise visit from Corvallis. With no advance notice."

He cheerfully ignored her comments and hopped onto the plywood floor of the shed to shake hands with Paige.

"So, what are the two of you doing out here in the dark?"

His voice sounded casual, but Kassidy noticed the way he moved between her and Paige, as if he was prepared to protect her. Kassidy was afraid to look at Paige because she felt on the verge of laughter and figured Paige was, too. But when she looked her way, Paige was watching the two of them with one of her more serious expressions. Kassidy had noticed those looks appearing now and again, and she was hoping to piece together the pattern behind Paige's rare descents into melancholy if given the chance.

Kassidy turned back to her brother, who seemed to be waiting for an answer. She wanted to avoid the topic of her father, which made it difficult to explain anything she and Paige did together. Or anything she imagined doing with Paige—that was definitely not a subject to discuss tonight. "Oh, I was just showing Paige where I store extra rakes. She was wondering."

"I was," Paige said, with the return of a familiar quirk of her lips. "I can't decide where to keep mine, and Kassidy was showing me her system."

"Which is to toss them on the floor of a cluttered shed?" Kyle asked.

"Yes. Brilliant. I don't know why I didn't think of it before."

Kyle kept smiling, as though the conversation made perfect sense to him. "Well, Kayla's here."

Paige looked at Kassidy with a confused expression on her face. "The other twin," Kassidy explained. She waved her hand toward the driveway a few seconds before the next set of car lights appeared. She would make sure her new gate was electrified.

Like most experiences with the twins, Kayla's entrance practically mirrored Kyle's, from Dante's greeting to Kayla's determined smile and to the inevitable question about why they were all standing outside by the shed.

Kassidy eventually managed to close the doors on the brilliantly arranged rake display and usher everyone into the house. The twins sat together on the sofa, and Dante and Kipper clustered around Kayla, like all animals tended to do.

"Do you live in Corvallis, too?" Paige asked Kayla.

"We're not conjoined," Kayla snapped.

"Kayla!" Although Kassidy usually acted like just another sibling, she had raised these two since infancy. She wasn't above scolding them when one—or usually both—of them acted like an ass.

The result was satisfyingly abrupt. "I'm sorry," Kayla said immediately. "People assume we live the same lives just because we're twins."

"Kyle is a teacher in Corvallis, and Kayla is a vet in Albany," Kassidy said.

Paige laughed. Kassidy sighed. Of course, she did. She was Paige.

"Wow, so you live in cities ten whole minutes apart. You're really bucking the twin stereotype."

"We're going to make dinner. You two stay out here." Kassidy grabbed Paige's sleeve and pulled her into the kitchen.

"What? You have to admit that was funny." Paige leaned against the counter, grinning.

"You're right. She's always talked like she's the independent one, but for most of her childhood, she'd cry if I didn't buy them matching outfits." Kassidy pulled the package of steak out again. The two pieces had been plenty for her and Paige, but now she had double the company. She grabbed some tomatoes, onions, and peppers plus a package of fresh tortillas and dumped everything on the counter. "Start chopping, please."

"I won't tease them if it makes you uncomfortable," Paige said, accepting the knife from Kassidy and slicing a tomato in half. "I don't know why you seem tense, though. They're related to you, so they're clearly nice people. I didn't have siblings, even though I really wanted a huge family, so it's fun for me to watch brothers and sisters interact."

"Yeah. Fun." Except Paige wasn't aware of the subtext involved tonight. "They're protective of me sometimes, especially where my..." Kassidy hesitated, not wanting to bring up her dad.

If she kept the conversation off the farm and Paige's job here, then maybe they'd make it through the evening in a civil way. "Especially where my business is concerned. Let's just talk about other things, like Dante's big show today. And I can ask about their patients and students. They'll both talk about those subjects all night."

"Deal," Paige said as she massacred a red pepper.

Kassidy put a skillet on the stove to heat and cut the steak into narrow strips. She glanced at Paige as she worked, finally able to relax a little about the evening ahead. Paige would stay off the topic of work. The twins would be polite and grill her after Paige left. Nothing Kassidy couldn't handle.

She seasoned the meat and let her thoughts linger on Paige's comment about wanting a big family. She was starting to get a better picture of Paige's childhood, and she guessed that even one brother or sister would have eased Paige's sense of responsibility for living out each one of her parents' failed dreams. Giving her a chance to follow her own desires for a change, exploring her own interests instead of repeating theirs. Kassidy's twins must represent an abundance of riches to Paige.

Paige was obviously following her own train of thought about Kassidy's life, because she brought up the comment Kassidy had accidentally let slip.

"You said Kayla wanted *you* to buy them matching outfits. Weren't you just a kid then, too? You can't be much more than five years older than they are."

"Six." Kassidy dropped the steak into the hot pan, and the scent of the chili peppers and herbs she had used was released with the sizzling oil. "My dad left soon after they were born, and my mom had some issues with postpartum depression. I took over some of the responsibility of caring for them."

If Kassidy had substituted *a severe case of* for *some issues with*, and changed *some responsibility* to *almost all*, then the statement would have been closer to fact, but this version was the more acceptable public one. Paige looked at her for a silent moment before returning to her chopping job, and Kassidy had a feeling that her imagined words had been heard rather than the spoken ones.

Paige was someone who looked beneath the surface for meaning, not someone who took what she saw at face value. Kassidy hadn't meant to confide too much information, and she waited for a feeling of panic, a need to flee, to come to her, but it didn't. She felt oddly safe knowing Paige understood something about her, and that very sense of security frightened her more than anything. She had felt safe with Audrey, too. And with her mom and dad, before they vanished emotionally, leaving her with only shells of parents.

"I need cilantro," she said, scraping the cooked steak onto a serving plate. "I'll just run to the greenhouse and cut some."

Paige nodded, keeping her attention focused on the knife in her hand and trying not to accidentally cut herself when she was almost shaking in anger. Even if she imagined Kassidy's experience in its mildest form, it was infuriating. She had been a child of six. She shouldn't have had to step in as both mother and father to newborns, not even for a brief time. And Paige had a feeling the reality was even more extreme than Kassidy let on. She wanted to go back to Kenneth's office and yell at him some more. And take back her apology for her initial outburst, too. If he had been the only emotionally functioning parent, he should have stayed. Or taken the kids with him. Not left Kassidy on her own.

She heard the swinging door open behind her, and she quickly got control of her expression. She didn't want Kassidy to see her anger and mistake it for pity.

"Did you forget some...Aaugh!"

Paige turned to find the twins standing close behind her, wearing identical scowls and both standing with the same posture, arms crossed over their chests. Like the twins in every horror movie ever.

"So, you're Dad's minion," Kayla said.

"Well, I prefer *business consultant*, but as they say, tomato, tomahto." Paige realized she was holding the knife out in front of her and she lowered it to her side. She didn't put it down, but she lowered it.

"What's your game?" Kyle asked. "Talk Kassidy into some poor investments so she has to sell the farm? Sabotage her business with a bunch of suggestions that cost her a fortune?"

"Or are you trying to convince her that Dad's a great guy? Get her to give him control of the farm?"

Paige set the knife on the counter and crossed her arms, mirroring their positions. "First of all, Kassidy is not an idiot. She's an excellent business manager, and even if I tried to get her to make stupid choices, she'd never fall for it." Paige took a deep breath, looking past the creepy twin act and seeing the same protective drive she had been feeling toward Kassidy since the moment Kenneth had suggested she come here.

"Second, you're right, in a way. Kenneth implied that he hired me because I was supposed to talk Kassidy into selling. Pretend to be helping but tell her I didn't see any way to save the business."

She held up her hand before they could attack. "I told Kassidy about his true agenda. I also told her—and your dad—that I was going to ignore him and do everything I could to help her keep the farm."

"You told him? I didn't know that."

Paige turned and saw Kassidy standing by the back door with a handful of green leaves.

"I technically yelled it at him when I was in his office this week. It was humiliating. I've never lost control like that during my entire career as a minion...I mean, consultant."

"And he didn't fire you?"

"No, he said he wanted me to take care of you, even if I did it my way and not his."

Kassidy nodded slowly. "Give him his money back." She walked over to the sink and put the cilantro in a colander to rinse it.

Paige felt a strange sense of panic rise in her. She didn't want to leave. "Don't refuse my help just because you're mad at him, Kassidy. I want to be here, and I think we can do—"

Kassidy held up her hand to stop Paige. "I'm not asking you to go, but I'm doing what I should have done at the beginning of this. *I'll* pay you to help with *my* farm. That way no one"—she pointed at the twins—"will think Dad has any influence over the decisions we make together. Plus, I can fire you if you annoy me too much. All right?"

Paige grinned. She'd have offered to finish the work here for free, just as she'd been prepared to do after her outburst with Kenneth, but she knew this arrangement would be best for all of them. "I'll send him a refund Monday."

"Are we all right now?" Kassidy aimed this question at the twins, using a voice Paige could only describe as parental. When they nodded, she snapped her fingers at them. "Good. Now go set the dining room table."

"They're a little scary," Paige said once they had left the kitchen.

Kassidy laughed as she filled a bowl with cilantro and set it on a tray with the platter of meat. "Would you believe they got kicked out of their first daycare place because they were freaking out the other kids? Speaking in unison, that sort of thing."

Paige could absolutely believe it. She walked over to Kassidy and took the tray from her. "I like our new arrangement. I have to warn you, though, I'm an expensive minion."

"I know. I saw the prices on your website. I was kind of hoping I could pay you in lavender wands instead of cash."

Paige laughed and nudged Kassidy gently with the edge of the tray. "Only if they're ones you've made and not the DIY version. I don't think ribbon weaving is one of my true talents."

CHAPTER FOURTEEN

I still don't understand why you invited her," Kassidy complained, her voice muffled as she pulled a pale yellow cashmere sweater over her head. She tugged the hem down and smoothed it over her jeans-clad hips. "I don't see the two of you often enough as it is, and I would have liked some private family time."

"Oh, please," Kayla said with a snort of derision. She was sprawled in Kassidy's bed with Kipper purring on her stomach. "Last time we were here you kept leaving brochures around the house for vacation places. In other states."

"You stayed for two weeks," Kassidy teased. They both knew her hints at getting the twins to take a trip hadn't been serious. She would let them live with her full time if she could. Maybe not in her house, but at least in the same town. She ran a brush through her hair and grabbed her keys and wallet from the top of the dresser. "And neither one of you seems to know how to push a vacuum."

"We were here because we love our sister and wanted to spend quality time with her."

Kassidy mimicked Kayla's snort. "You were here because you're both too cheap to go on a real holiday and pay for a hotel and food."

Kayla shrugged, not bothering to deny Kassidy's claim. "Well, we like Paige. She's funny and she has a great dog. It'll be nice to have her come with us today."

Kassidy had no doubt the twins liked Dante, but she was less convinced that they adored Paige enough to want to spend an entire day with her. She was sure they were still in protective mode and wanted to run interference in case she tried to bully Kassidy into giving up her farm. The four of them had managed to have a civil dinner the night before, mainly because Kassidy had steered them toward safe subjects like animals and the twins' jobs with an exhausting tenacity.

"I just wish you had asked me first." There. Kassidy had put up her token resistance to having Paige join them for a day of wine tasting. Now she could let herself enjoy Paige's company without worrying about crossing any professional lines. She had second-guessed her decision to invite Paige to dinner last night because she had been afraid of letting their professional relationship get entangled with her personal feelings. Today, the full responsibility for Paige's presence was on Kyle and Kayla. What could be less romantic than having the twins as chaperones?

Kyle was putting the breakfast dishes into the dishwasher when Kassidy and her sister came out of the bedroom. Kayla had cooked for them this morning, and now Kyle was cleaning. Kassidy shook her head. She must have been more noticeably upset lately about her dad and his intrusion into her farm than she had realized. The twins' defensive mode extended to household chores when they thought she needed to be protected and cared for. It wasn't consistent, but she appreciated the effort because she knew it was something they did just for her. She had seen their messy apartments and fridges packed with take-out containers. Cooking and cleaning were the ways they showed their love for her, just as she had done when they were children, and not things they did for themselves.

"Have you picked a winery yet?" Kassidy asked as they piled into Kayla's SUV. "Drew and Jessica have some wonderful wines this year."

"You taste their wines all the time," Kyle said from the seat behind her. "We're going to do something different today."

"Did Paige tell you to say that?" Kassidy sighed. What was wrong with letting things remain the same? Her favorite winery, her best friends, her private farm. Those were good and comfortable and didn't need to be replaced by new wineries and annoying tourists. "Just make sure it's not Alexandra's. Jessica would never forgive me, unless I'm going as a spy to report back to her."

❖

"I've heard this place does wonderful picnic lunches," Kassidy said when they pulled up in front of the inn where Paige was staying. "We could just do a tasting here."

The twins ignored her suggestion and Kayla rolled down her window when Paige came out of the front door with Dante. She looked gorgeous in a black turtleneck and dark blue jeans, and Kassidy's remaining doubts about having Paige spend the day with her and her family vanished. She would give herself a day off being in control—just one day—and let the twins pick the activities. And let Paige's humor and lightness spread to her.

"Hey," Paige called. "Just give me a sec to put him in the dog run."

"You can bring him with us," Kayla said, waving toward the back of her SUV. "He'll love where we're going."

Kyle got out to open the rear door for her, and then he and Paige got in the middle seats.

"Are you sure?" Paige asked, peering into the back where Dante was snuffling around. "He can be a little destructive."

Kassidy laughed at the understatement of the day, and Kayla playfully punched her in the leg.

"Of course, we're sure," Kayla said. "I've had lots of animals in here, so don't worry. He can't hurt anything back there."

Paige leaned forward and tugged on a lock of Kassidy's hair. "Hi," she said quietly. "You look happy."

"I am," Kassidy said. "Because it's not my car that's about to be destroyed."

Paige laughed and squeezed Kassidy's shoulder before she sat back. "Darn. I thought you were just glad to see me."

Kassidy stared straight ahead and ignored the laser-like stares she could feel coming from both twins, not wanting to let them know that Paige was right and she was the reason for Kassidy's smile. Paige didn't seem to be as immune to their glares as Kassidy was.

"Yikes," she yelped from the back seat. "You two need to audition for the next Stephen King movie. So where are we going today? A creepy mansion? Haunted cemetery?"

"No need to be scared of us unless you have a guilty conscience," Kyle said. "We're doing the Diamond."

Kassidy let out her breath. She had been prepared to be annoyed by whatever choice the twins made, for no reason other than her penchant for staying in her comfort zone, and she realized she didn't like that tendency in herself. Wanting to build a comfortable and fairly predictable life was fine. Being afraid to try new experiences was not. "I've always wanted to do that," she admitted.

"We should stay dry, at least," Kayla said. "It's not supposed to rain today."

"What's the Diamond?" Paige asked, still sounding wary.

Kassidy turned in her seat to face her, grinning at her skeptical expression. "It's a group of four wineries. They have bikes you can rent to do a circuit of about two miles to visit all four of them, and you can start at whichever one you want."

"So you keep tasting until you fall off your bike?"

"You three do," Kyle said. "I'm not drinking, so I can drive us home."

"Besides, they keep the samples really small since they know people will be biking," Kassidy added. "I don't remember the last time I was on a bike, so I might fall over even without the help of wine. Although I won't be the one trying to pedal while holding on to Dante, so at least I won't look as foolish as that person."

"Yeah, I think I'll be walking instead of biking," Paige said.

"He'll be great," Kayla said with as much misguided optimism as she had shown when Dante got in the back of her car. "The bike paths aren't on the main roads, so there isn't any car traffic. Plus, we'll be stopping a few times at the wineries, so he won't get tired."

Kassidy shrugged at Paige. "Good luck."

Kayla parked in the lot of the first winery, and the twins went inside to rent the bikes and order a picnic lunch for when they had completed the circuit. Kassidy held Dante while Paige made sure the back of the SUV was still in decent shape.

"It looks okay, I guess," Paige said, climbing out again. She took Dante's leash from Kassidy and leaned against the side of the car next to her, so their shoulders were nearly touching. "There are a couple of chewed areas, but I'm pretty sure they were like that before he got in. You should join with some other farms and do something like this Diamond. It's a great idea, and you can just change the shape."

Kassidy shifted until she was facing Paige, breathing in the piney scent of her that called to mind a morning stroll along a dewy forest path. Preferably after a night of chocolate-licking in front of a lavender fire. Kassidy exhaled quietly. When Paige looked like this, with darkened eyes and wind-tousled hair, Kassidy was in danger of agreeing to anything she suggested, whether it had to do with her farm or with the two of them together. At least she wasn't foolish enough to give Paige that information, or the next thing she knew the Wilsons would be moving into her spare room. "What did you have in mind? An Herb Octagon?"

"Perfume Pentagon?" Paige suggested, ducking playfully as if she thought Kassidy might punch her.

"I'll be sure to serve lavender chicken in the picnic lunches," Kassidy said, trying to sound mocking and dismissive of the idea even as she mentally mapped out the farms nearest hers. There were four within easy walking distance of her place, and each could contribute something made with their produce or herbs for the lunch boxes. The thought of all those tourists sprawled on her fields eating lunches made her cringe, though. Maybe she could confine them to the driveway?

"God, you're not going to start kissing, are you?" Kassidy and Paige simultaneously jumped away from each other at the sound of Kayla's voice. "I don't want to lose my appetite for lunch."

"We're talking about the farm," Kassidy said, although she figured the twins could easily guess the real reason for her flushed cheeks. "We have to whisper because other lavender farmers might be trying to overhear our plans."

"You never know which of these flowers has been genetically modified with a recording device inside," Paige said, peering into one of the pink-and-white daylilies bordering the parking lot.

Kassidy laughed, ignoring the twins' confused expressions. "I'll bet those ornamental grasses are really clusters of antennae. Herb farmers will stop at nothing to steal trade secrets. We're a competitive bunch."

The twins rolled their eyes with mirror-image dismissive expressions and headed toward a rack full of mountain bikes.

"It's eerie," Paige said with a playful shiver. "They move as one."

"They speak the same way, too, although not as often as they used to," Kassidy said as they followed the twins. "They were in a perpetual state of jinx from ages four to seven."

Kassidy picked the first bike that looked tall enough for her, while Paige spent some time looking over each one before making her choice. The twins rode on ahead, shouting challenges about racing each other to the next winery.

"What's taking you so long?" Kassidy asked, resting with one foot on the ground and her hip balanced on the bike's seat. "Are you trying to find one that matches your outfit?"

Paige shook her head and finally wheeled a bike onto the path. "I wanted to get the one with the most dents and scratches because I have a feeling it'll be spending most of its time on the ground. Dante drags me when I'm on my feet. Just imagine what he'll do when I'm on wheels and easier to pull."

She came close to Kassidy, fiddling with Dante's leash and straddling the bike without actually getting on it.

"You're stalling," Kassidy said.

Paige grinned. "Maybe I'm just letting the twins get farther ahead so I can be alone with you."

"I'd be more inclined to believe that if you weren't trembling with fear."

Paige held her hand out in front of her. "Steady as can be," she said, reaching over to put her hand on top of Kassidy's, linking their fingers together. "I was kidding about being nervous. A ride like this is easy for a dog as well trained as Dante."

Kassidy felt a rush of warmth spread from the point where she had contact with Paige's skin until even the air between them felt heated. She wasn't fooled by Paige's confident tone, and she figured the hand-holding gesture was another way to avoid getting on the bike and careening down the path behind Dante. Still, she let herself enjoy touching Paige. Even more, she reveled in the signs that Paige wasn't unaffected by their closeness. Like the way she bit her bottom lip and glanced at Kassidy's mouth. And the way she leaned a little closer until Kassidy was certain they were about to kiss—

"Come on, you two," Kyle yelled from the entrance to the bike path. "We already made it up that hill and back."

Paige startled away from Kassidy again, tripping over the bike as it dropped beneath her and onto its side. Dante barked, adding his voice to Kyle's rallying cry and straining at his leash.

Damn. Paige wound the leash around her wrist and resolutely picked up the bike. Kassidy had been correct about her stalling, but as soon as she had felt Kassidy's fingers wrap around hers, the scenery around them had seemed to fade out of focus as if someone had thrown a bucket of water on a painting. Colors blended, sounds muted, until Kassidy was the only point of focus in the world. For too brief a moment.

"I'm guessing you didn't do much dating when you were younger, with the two of them underfoot," Paige joked, belatedly realizing how insensitive her words sounded. "Hey, I'm sorry. I shouldn't tease about that, since you did so much to take care of them."

Kassidy reached over and stroked Paige's arm. "Don't be sorry because you're right. They were more effective than a chastity belt." Kassidy grinned, putting Paige at ease. "I tried to date a few times in high school, when they were old enough to stay home without me, but they always managed to find out where I had gone. They'd show up and ask my dates the most humiliating questions. Even when I started going out in college, I was always looking over my shoulder because I half expected them to appear at any time."

Paige still felt the aftershocks of Kassidy's touch on her arm, even though she had already moved away. Maybe it was a good thing the twins had shown up last night and stayed until today. Paige was annoyed at their intrusions, but once she was back in Portland, alone in her city life and apartment, she'd probably be thankful they had been around to keep her and Kassidy in check. Missed opportunities were romantic fantasies, while broken hearts were painful realities.

"We should start riding," Kassidy said, and Paige thought she heard a note of regret in her voice. "They'll be back any minute if we don't catch up."

"So I have to choose between a humiliating interrogation about my intentions toward you, or the likelihood that I'll face-plant along the trail?" Paige asked.

"Exactly. The second option would be much less painful."

"Says the person who isn't leading Dante," Paige muttered, slowly starting to pedal down the path. "Come on, boy. It's just like heeling, but I'm on wheels."

"Does he know how to heel?" Kassidy asked with a note of disbelief in her voice.

"He's heard the word before, but he hasn't quite grasped the concept yet. We're a work in progress," Paige said as she wove tentatively down the tidy gravel path while Kassidy rode slowly alongside her, calling out encouragement to Dante and swerving every once in a while to keep from being hit by Paige. Most of Paige's attention was devoted to remaining upright—how in the hell was she supposed to do this after having some wine?—but every brain cell she had to spare was still focused on Kassidy. How she had leaned slightly toward Paige when their hands touched. How little effort it would have taken to move forward and kiss her.

All she seemed to have with Kassidy were these isolated moments. The ones that fell in between interruptions by other people or discussions about the farm or revelations about their family lives. Moments that seemed uncomplicated and pure, amidst the complexity of their working relationship. Paige's logical side—the part of her that realized how she would feel if she got too close to Kassidy and then had to leave—knew she shouldn't be encouraging these brief brushes with intimacy. Still, her irrational side didn't have the desire or willpower to give them up, and Kassidy didn't seem inclined to, either.

They weren't much—and they were never enough—but they were worth the frustration and yearning they evoked. Paige felt more alive and happier here with Kassidy than she had felt in a long time, and as long as she was in McMinnville, she wasn't going to reject the moments of shared laughter and intimacy that life doled out to her, piece by piece.

Chapter Fifteen

Paige took a deep breath as they got close to their first destination and let out some more leash for Dante, pedaling faster to keep up with his surge of speed. At least he was going straight now, barreling along toward the twins who were yards ahead. Paige heard Kassidy's laughter behind her as she raced to catch up. Paige saw the winery sign marking the turn off the bike path at the end of a row of tall rhododendron bushes, and she watched the twins veer to the right and off the bike path. She relaxed, assuming Dante would continue along the path and follow them through the entrance, but instead he made a hard right turn at exactly the same moment they did, plowing through the shrubs.

"Are you broken?" Kassidy asked from the path behind her, sounding far more amused than concerned.

"No, but this rhododendron will never be the same." Paige stood up and pried the bike out of the branches. Dante wiggled under the shrub to the other side, where the twins were apparently waiting because Paige heard dual cries of *Got him!*

Kassidy walked her bike over and brushed at the loose soil on Paige's thigh, still laughing. "I wish I had been able to see your face, but it looked pretty funny from behind. Good thing you're wearing dark colors."

"I've learned I need to dress in mud-colored clothes when I take Dante anywhere," Paige said, leaning into Kassidy's touch. She pointed at her rear. "There's more dirt back here. Can you get that, too?"

Kassidy gave her a swat instead and wiped tears of laughter from the corners of her eyes with the back of her hand, leaving a smudge. Paige used her thumb to clean it off, wanting to linger but moving away instead when she saw more tourists coming down the path. She bumped Kassidy with her shoulder as they walked their bikes onto the winery's property.

They parked their bikes and wandered over to the outdoor bar where Kyle and Kayla were waiting for them with Dante. Paige felt a slight twinge in her hip from where she had landed, and Dante had an orange rhododendron flower caught in his collar, but otherwise they were in better shape than she had anticipated.

"Welcome to Misty Hills Winery." The winery owner greeted them and splashed biker-sized samples into their glasses. Paige raised her eyebrows at Kassidy, who was swirling the wine around her glass.

"Notice how the owner welcomed us to her winery instead of yelling at us to get off her property? That's a good way to greet visitors."

"Don't start, or I'll sic the twins on you," Kassidy said, taking a sip of her wine. "And I said the word *welcome* to the Wilsons. I told them they were welcome to leave by the same way they came onto the farm. That's sort of the same thing."

"Well..." Paige drew the word out for several seconds. "Not really. And look, she's smiling at everyone."

"I smiled when they left. I can't promise more than that."

Paige laughed as they took their glasses over to where the twins were sitting at a picnic table where some board games and puzzles had been set out. She changed the subject away from Kassidy's farm, gesturing instead toward the twins who seemed to be embroiled in a heated game of Boggle while Dante looked on, ready to snatch a letter cube if given the chance.

"Is everything a competition with them?"

Kassidy sighed with the indulgence of a doting parent. Or a long-suffering one. Paige wasn't sure.

"They've always been that way. They'll compete and fight and scream at each other, but the second there's an outside threat they'll stick so close together they seem like one person."

"A threat, like the arrival of your dad's minion?"

"Exactly." Kassidy paused, and then added, "The fact that they're racing each other and playing games today means they like you. They're being themselves around you."

Paige felt a surprising rush of pleasure at Kassidy's words. She was the outsider here, not part of Kassidy's family and only temporarily part of her farm. That was the way she spent most of her life, dipping into businesses and relationships for short periods and stepping out of them again without hesitation. She was shocked to find out how great it felt to get close enough to someone to feel like an insider in their lives. She enjoyed spending time with Kassidy and was already dreading the time when they would inevitably part ways, but this was different. Right now—just for today—she was part of Kassidy's whole world, not just one corner of it.

"So I can let my guard down now that they aren't mirroring each other's posture and speaking in unison?" Paige asked, reverting to jokes because she wasn't ready to face the mix of emotions Kassidy's confession had raised in her.

"Those are the danger signs," Kassidy said, nodding with mock solemnity. "If you see them, get on your bike and ride for the hills."

As soon as they sat down, Kyle and Kayla set their pencils down and turned to Paige.

"Uh-oh." Kassidy leaned close to her and whispered in her ear. "Run!"

As if Paige had a chance of moving with Kassidy's breath warm against her neck and her hand resting on the bench next to Paige's thigh. She didn't feel capable of standing up, let alone running away.

"So, Paige. Tell us more about your business," Kayla said.

"Um, what do you want to know?" Paige asked, unable to think much beyond her physical reaction to Kassidy. They had been near each other before and had held hands. Paige should be getting used to her presence and becoming less affected by her, not more.

"Do you have some sort of nickname in Portland's corporate world?" Kyle asked. "Something like the Terminator or the Battle-ax?"

"Because all the employees know that when you show up, they're about to be fired to save the company some money?" Kayla added, as if Kyle's nicknames needed an explanation.

"Stop it, you two," Kassidy said in a stern voice. "Don't be rude."

Paige burst out laughing, relieved to have been released—at least temporarily—from the spell cast by having Kassidy's lips so close to her neck.

"You asked me something quite similar the first day I came to your farm, Kass. Remember?"

"All I remember from that weekend is someone calling someone else's chicken perfume-y," Kassidy said, waving her hand vaguely through the air. "The rest is hazy."

Paige grinned and pushed at Kassidy's shoulder. She turned back to the twins who were laughing along with them.

"Kidding aside, it's a legitimate question," she said, hearing the laughter fade from her own voice, replaced with a more serious tone. The topic was one that mattered to her personally, and she found herself wanting to reassure the twins that she wasn't a monster and Kassidy was safe with her. "I hate knowing I'm the cause of anyone losing a job, and I do my best to focus on retraining and a reallocation of duties rather than firing anyone. It's a different matter with upper management in top-heavy companies, though. They're less likely to accept a change in title or responsibilities, and often choose to leave a company instead."

She smiled at Kassidy. "It'd be like suggesting we demote you from lavender keeper to lavender bystander. That conversation wouldn't go well."

"I'm sure I would handle it with dignity if I believed it was best for my farm," Kassidy said, kicking Kayla's leg under the table when she laughed so hard she choked on her wine.

"My turn to ask a question," Paige said. She was enjoying the chance to see this different side of Kassidy as she interacted with her siblings, fluidly changing from sister to parent to friend with the twins. The controlled, private lavender farmer gave way to a softer, more complex woman when she was with them. "What was Kassidy like when she was young?"

"K was never young," Kyle said.

"I mean, has she always been such a good cook?" Paige quickly changed the tone of her original question when she felt Kassidy grow tense beside her and saw Kayla frown at her brother.

"As long as we can remember, she was," Kyle said, easily accepting the revised question. "She talks about how bad she was at first, but we were too young to care that we were guinea pigs while she was learning. She always was good at the basic things like macaroni and cheese, but after a while she was creating her own recipes and making fancier meals."

"Baking was another story, though. Remember the first time she made brownies?" Kayla asked. She and Kyle made identical grimaces.

Kassidy groaned. "Please don't tell this story."

She was sitting close enough to Paige for their arms and shoulders to be in contact, and Paige was relieved to feel when Kassidy relaxed again. "Please *do* tell the story," Paige said.

"It was our first bake sale at school, when we were in kindergarten," Kayla said. "She sent a package of store-bought cookies with us, and I came home crying because all the other parents had sent homemade treats."

Kyle laughed and continued the story. "So for the next sale she made brownies. They were too hard to cut, so she had to break them into pieces with a hammer. Kayla came home from school crying again, begging her to go back to store-bought the next time."

Kassidy poked Paige in the side with her elbow to get her attention. "To be fair, Kayla was prone to overdramatizing everything that happened at school, so her criticism of my baking was probably exaggerated." She paused, and then grinned at Paige. "The part about the hammer was true, though."

Kyle smiled at his sister with obvious fondness. "By the time we were in first grade, she had taught herself to bake really well. Her shortbread cookies were famous and always sold out before anything else."

"They were amazing," Kayla agreed. "And I was never overdramatic."

"*I wanted to use the red crayon, but Robbie wouldn't let me,*" Kyle said in a high-pitched whine.

"Enough of this. Come on," Kassidy said, laughing as she got up and tugged on Paige's sleeve. "Let's get to our next stop. I'll take Dante for this leg, if only to spare the poor bushes along the way."

The twins jostled each other as they raced toward their bikes, while Kassidy and Paige walked more slowly, sticking close together.

Paige reached for Kassidy's hand and gave it a squeeze. "The brownie story was funny, but I can't imagine what it was like for you to face those kinds of responsibilities when you were eleven. I was concerned about doing homework and playing sports, while you were doing so much more. I really admire you for the way you took care of the twins."

Kassidy tugged on their joined hands, pulling Paige against her. "You were doing more than homework and sports, Paige. You were living out your parents' unmet dreams. We both had expectations to fulfill, but I wouldn't change mine even if I could because my relationship with the twins is so much more than it would have been if circumstances had been different."

Paige leaned into the contact between them while she considered Kassidy's statement. Would Paige change the way she had been raised if she had the chance? Who would she be right now if the pressure to perform had been removed, allowing her to follow her own path? Maybe she would have discovered some cherished passion in life, or maybe she just wasn't the type of person who had one. Still, her past had brought her here, to McMinnville and Kassidy. She was grateful for that and didn't want to imagine a life in which they hadn't met.

"I guess you're right," she said. "An easier road might not have been as rewarding."

Kassidy let go of Paige's hand when they got to the trail. "I'll keep chanting that to myself when I listen to your business proposal."

Paige laughed as she got on her bike and watched Kassidy and Dante maneuver around a group of tourists. "Are you sure you can handle him? We're going to see plenty more rhododendrons along the way, and he might run under any one of them."

"We'll be fine," Kassidy said, waving off her protests. She started pedaling down the trail, and Dante—just like he had during Paige's tour of the first farm—trotted obediently at her side.

"He's only behaving because I already tired him out," Paige called to Kassidy, hurrying to catch up to the pair. Her wrist still had red bands around it where Dante's leash had embedded itself into her skin, but now he was jogging along with a slack line. The ride to the first winery certainly hadn't been long enough to wear him out, but she had to save face somehow. Hard to do when she still had dirt stains from hip to ankle.

Paige was glad to be riding again. She enjoyed being included in some of Kassidy's family camaraderie and she loved being close to Kassidy, but neither of those had any impact on the work she was here to do. They were distractions. Wonderful ones, but irrelevant to her job. For one quarter of a mile, though, she was going to do nothing more than lag behind and admire the view of Kassidy on her bike. Completely and unabashedly unprofessional.

Before they reached the winery, Kassidy stopped by a small trail leading off the bike path. Dante stood beside her, tongue lolling in a happy grin as they waited for Paige.

"Beautiful, isn't it?" Kassidy asked, gesturing toward the valley next to them. "Should we take this path for a little while and see where it goes?"

"I'm game," said Paige, following her onto the narrow track. They wound along the edge of a small hill, and the downward-sloping meadow on the opposite side of the path was blanketed with green grass, bright pink foxglove, and deep purple lupine. When Paige had first come to McMinnville, spring had been visible in small spots of color against a rainy gray backdrop. On this sunny weekend, the season was bursting out and the area looked more like the fertile farming region shown in Oregon travel brochures.

"Gorgeous," Paige said, although she was still contemplating the view she had of Kassidy as much as the scenery.

They came around a corner and halted when the slope grew steeper and the path disappeared into the thick grass. This side of the hill was dotted with dozens of tiny but vivid wildflowers, like multicolored fairy lights.

"Wow," Paige said, putting down the kickstand on her bike and coming to stand next to Kassidy and Dante. "Look at all those colors. Could you plant something like this in a corner of one of your empty fields? It would be a great spot for picnics."

Kassidy put her hand on Paige's arm. "That's a good idea, Paige," she said. "And I'm sure you have a million of them. But can you be off duty for the rest of the day?"

"I'll try," Paige said. She wasn't about to ignore her personal interest in Kassidy or stop grasping for those moments when she felt compelled to let her feelings show, especially since Kassidy seemed to invite them as often as she did. But she was working very hard to convince herself that as long as she balanced those connections with times of focus on Kassidy's business, she could keep them from developing into something deeper. She was afraid that if she shut off the work side of her brain and let Kassidy have free rein over all her thoughts, she'd lose herself in wanting what she couldn't have. "Unless I notice something that would be perfect for your farm, then—"

Kassidy leaned forward and kissed her far too briefly before pulling away again. "Then…what?"

Paige exhaled slowly. "Then I'll write it down and bring it up later?"

Kassidy nodded. "Much later," she said, covering Paige's mouth with hers again. Lingering this time. Hovering in the space between new romance and full-blown passion.

Paige loved the feel of Kassidy's lips moving slowly against hers as she pressed her body closer. It was the perfect kiss for a long, sensual evening in front of a lavender-scented fire, with chocolate melting on fingers and tongues. But she and Kassidy didn't have that luxury, and probably never would. They just had this moment, like all the others before it, until the twins came around the corner and interrupted them, or Dante got restless and pulled Paige out of reach. Paige wasn't about to waste a single nanosecond with Kassidy when she only had a handful of them to savor.

She wrapped her free arm around Kassidy's waist and pulled them flush against each other. A determined nip from her teeth, and Kassidy's mouth opened to her, deepening the kiss as their tongues met. Paige felt desire coil inside her belly as tightly as Kassidy's hand twisting in her hair. Subtlety was shoved to the side, and suddenly the kiss that had merely promised passion delivered it in abundance.

As if they had reached an agreed upon moment, both Kassidy and Paige broke away from the kiss at the same time. Kassidy felt rather than heard Paige's sigh as she leaned briefly against her before standing upright again.

"That was..." Kassidy started, but she had no idea how to finish the sentence. Amazing. Arousing. Far too short. A mistake? No, she couldn't say that.

"Not exactly professional," Paige finished for her. "I'm sorry." She raked her fingers roughly through her hair, and Kassidy clenched her hands into fists to keep from reaching out to straighten her tangled curls.

Kassidy struggled to figure out the direction to take with this awkward conversation. *We shouldn't have done this* vied with *Please kiss me again*, but neither option would bring them back to the innocent moment before she had given in to the desire she had felt for too long and kissed Paige. Kassidy didn't regret the kiss— absolutely not—but she was afraid of the emotions that had led to it. She had spent her life excluding people from her home life. Friends and girlfriends were allowed to be close to her, but not to her family. Even the little she had shared with Audrey had been used against her, reinforcing her need to keep her past private. Today, Paige had been included in her relationship with the twins, delving beyond the polite facade Kassidy and her siblings showed in public, to the fights, embarrassing stories, and love underneath.

I let you get too close, and I don't want to get hurt.

Kassidy smiled at Paige, touching her fingertips to Paige's cheek. "Don't be sorry," she said, wanting to put them both at ease and get back to being friends. "This was a completely professional kiss. You're constantly telling me to improve my customer service skills, so I was just practicing a new way to greet tourists."

Paige burst out laughing, and Kassidy smiled in return, relieved to see Paige's humor replace her obvious concern. Right now Kassidy was more prepared to handle jokes and lightness than to take a serious look at her growing feelings for Paige.

"I'm sure this new approach would increase your lavender sales a thousandfold," Paige said. "But maybe we can find some middle ground between kissing people and telling them to get the hell off your farm."

Kassidy shrugged. "If you say so. You're the fancy consultant, so I suppose you know what's best."

"For the general public, at least," Paige said. She bumped Kassidy with her shoulder as they turned their bikes to face the way they'd come. "Feel free to greet me that way any time you want."

Kassidy laughed off the suggestion as if it didn't make her heart beat faster. She got on her bike and readjusted Dante's leash in her hand. "We'd better get back there before the twins come shouting for us."

Paige laughed. "They're probably at the winery already, challenging each other to see who can balance an empty wine bottle on their head the longest."

Kassidy groaned. "Don't say things like that around them. They love a good dare." She paused, studying Paige's face, unsure of what she wanted to see reflected there. The kiss had been intense, but Paige's expression was unreadable. Was she relieved that Kassidy had turned their kiss into a playful joke? Disappointed?

Paige had honestly sounded willing to kiss her again, and Kassidy hesitated, tempted to try. But if they kissed once more, she might lose herself in it and never be found again. She stepped out of reach, back to the casual acquaintance zone, and started down the trail.

Chapter Sixteen

Paige sat in a seat by the window of a downtown Portland café on Tuesday, waiting for Kassidy to arrive. She felt strange meeting her out of context since the two aspects of her life had been well-defined until now. Portland Paige wore business clothes and, with one outburst exception, maintained a distance from her clients even as she worked to help their businesses. McMinnville Paige was different. She looked different. She acted differently, too, taking an almost personal role in her client's life. Well, an overly personal one at times.

Like having dinner with Kassidy and her siblings. Or meandering around a fair together even after the day's work had been concluded.

Or kissing her in the middle of a meadow, as if nothing else in the world mattered besides the two of them.

Paige sighed and took a drink of her ice water. Aside from the kissing part, she was doing okay. She had made it her life's work to study businesses and determine how best to transform them. Everything she had learned about the community in which Kassidy's farm functioned convinced her that a more hands-on role was a requirement. She needed to dig in the dirt and create items in the drying shed until her nails were jagged and the skin of her hands was permanently saturated with lavender if she really wanted to understand how the farm worked and know how to improve it.

The trouble was, in getting involved enough to understand the lavender business, she had gotten too close to Kassidy herself. Her heart was saturated with the smell of Kassidy's perfume, with the memory of her lips and skin and breath. When she returned to her normal life, her nails would grow back, and the smell of lavender would eventually fade, but those deeper impressions might never heal.

Kassidy had managed to move them past their unexpected—but much anticipated—kiss with her funny comments about greeting tourists, but she had clearly been as affected by the encounter as Paige had been. Paige wasn't comfortable looking too closely at her feelings for Kassidy, or her growing desire for her, and she had been more than willing to follow Kassidy's lead and return to their familiar habit of joking together. Once she finished her proposal, though, and her relationship with Kassidy became open for renegotiation, she might be ready to face the deeper current of emotions she felt moving under the professional, friendly surface of their interactions. Maybe.

She looked up and saw Kassidy approaching. She was wearing a loosely knit white sweater and jeans, and she managed to look sophisticated enough to be wandering the streets of Paris, yet still fresh enough to belong to her country farm. Paige wanted nothing more than to kiss her again, but right now they needed to leave that experience behind them in the secluded meadow. Hands-on with the business, Paige thought. Hands-off with Kassidy herself.

Paige repeated her mantra, smiling and waving Kassidy over to the booth as if she was completely unaffected by the sight of her.

"Thanks for meeting me here," Paige said.

Kassidy smiled. "I had an errand to do in the city, anyway. Otherwise, I might have said no since you were very mysterious about why we're here."

Paige knew Kassidy would definitely have said *hell, no* if Paige had told her the reason ahead of time. She and Kassidy hadn't had much of a chance to discuss business after Saturday's dinner with the twins and Sunday's winery tour, but Paige wasn't at all sorry to have had more time with Kassidy. She would extend the timeline for this project over the next forty years of weekends if she could, but she had enough information for her proposal now.

Still, the delay of one more week was acceptable, and more than welcome since it had resulted in an amazing kiss. Paige had been hesitant to bring up any controversial issues about the farm with the twins around in case Kassidy got upset, and they slipped back into creepy twin mode. She had set aside her plan to talk about ways Kassidy could open the farm for more public exposure. Now, they were alone again, and Paige could bring up the touchier topics like smiling at people and letting them actually touch the lavender plants.

"What was your errand?" she asked as they looked over the menu. She wasn't trying to pry, but she was avoiding bringing up the plan for today's outing. Casual conversation about Kassidy's shopping trips or lavender deliveries was preferable to confrontation.

"I was, um, well, visiting someone," Kassidy said, keeping her eyes lowered and sounding awkward and evasive.

Oh. Paige had never asked about Kassidy's romantic life. No one's name had been mentioned around Paige, and she had assumed Kassidy was single, especially after sharing the kiss with her. Not that it mattered to her, because that kiss had belonged to a day that had been set apart from reality. She was just surprised. Great, now she was sounding awkward in her own mind.

"My mom," Kassidy said, watching Paige with an indecipherable expression. Had Paige's reaction been evident on her face?

"Oh, good. I mean, good that you had a chance to visit." Paige stared at the menu with determination. "I didn't know she lived in Portland."

"In the suburbs. Tigard." Kassidy paused, as if she was making up her mind about something. "She's in an assisted living facility there."

Paige looked at Kassidy in surprise. Her mom shouldn't be old enough to need professional care, so it was likely related to an illness. She latched on to one of the few things Kassidy had shared about her life. "The depression?" she asked. "Is it still bad?"

Kassidy nodded. "She was diagnosed with severe depression after I was born. She seemed to be managing it okay, until after the twins. She's never fully recovered, but the staff there takes good care of her and makes sure she gets her meds. Sometimes we can shop, or she'll want to come see the farm."

Kassidy shrugged in the silence after she stopped speaking, and Paige figured those good days were few and far between. "The redacted lines in your accounts. Oh, Kassidy, I'm sorry I laughed."

Kassidy reached across the table and grabbed her hand. "No. I love your laugh and I liked joking about the secret agent plants. You had no idea what the expenses were. I didn't trust you enough to tell you the truth, and you had no way of guessing what it was."

Paige smiled and twined her fingers with Kassidy's, holding her tight and letting go reluctantly when the waiter came over and they ordered sandwiches and Cokes.

"So, you trust me now?"

"I'm still taking it on a case by case basis. I'll need to hear about today's plan before I decide."

Paige laughed. "Fair enough. Here goes. I want us to pick out furniture and paint for the garden shed."

Kassidy visibly relaxed. "All right. I'm kind of resigned to the idea of using it as a store, so it'll be fun to redecorate it."

"Not a store. You'll need more space for the crafts and plants you're going to sell, so the drying shed or greenhouse will be better choices. I think you should make a guest cottage that's available to rent out. There's plenty of space for one person, a couple, or even a small family. They'll have their own bathroom, so all you'll need to provide is a continental breakfast. Muffins, coffee, that sort of thing. Maybe afternoon tea, but I'd charge for that to make it a special occasion meal and not something you're expected to do every day. Since there isn't a kitchen, the guests will be responsible for getting their other meals off site."

Once Paige had started talking, she kept going until their food arrived. Kassidy looked ready to mount a violent protest during the entire speech, but Paige didn't let her get a word in until she stopped for a breath and a bite of her BLT.

"I am not...no way..." Kassidy sputtered to a halt, as if she didn't have the vocabulary to express how much she hated the idea.

Paige swallowed a mouthful of sandwich, completely calm because she hadn't expected anything less than mutiny from Kassidy about this.

"Here's the plan. We decorate the shed and I'll be your first customer when I come next weekend. I'll even pay premium, high season rates. I spoke to a rental broker in McMinnville, and you can select the dates you'll make the place available. Try it for a few days a month at first and add more if you want. Just know that in order to make a significant income from it, you'll need to have it fully booked for most of the tourist season, so don't try it for just one weekend in June and say it wasn't worth the money you made. If you hate it, worst case is you have a nice place for Kyle or Kayla to stay when they visit."

Kassidy picked at her grilled cheese, eating it in small angry bites instead of responding to the plan.

"I like orange-cranberry muffins, but I'm sure whatever you make for me next weekend will be fine. Can you make anything breakfast-like with lavender?"

"Really? You want perfume first thing in the morning?"

Paige laughed. A joking Kassidy was much better than the silent one.

Kassidy mumbled something indistinctly, and Paige leaned forward.

"What? I couldn't hear you."

"I said I make a really good blueberry lavender bread," Kassidy enunciated loudly, as if furious with herself for admitting it and abetting the enemy.

"Perfect," Paige said. "Now finish your potato chips because we have shopping to do."

❖

Kassidy lagged behind Paige as she entered a downtown department store. This was definitely not the type of store she would choose for this redecorating project, but she didn't want it to happen in the first place, so she wasn't going to worry about doing it the right way.

Paige wandered over to the store directory. "I think we should start by finding some throw pillows. Those are standard in bed and breakfasts, aren't they? They're decorations for a house, so I guess we want to go to housewares."

"It's not going to work, Paige."

"Throw pillows won't work? I'm sure they'll be fine."

Kassidy rolled her eyes. She wasn't sure how Paige was keeping a straight face, but she was certain this was all an act. "No, I meant you pretending to make bad decisions isn't going to make me jump in and tell you the way I'd do it. You're just trying to get me involved enough to forget I don't want to be here, like you did with the crafts for the booth."

Paige merely gave her a look of wide-eyed innocence and headed toward housewares, where she roamed among stacks of blenders and coffeemakers. "Huh. This isn't what we need. Oh, look. Bedding. C'mon."

"If you want to wander aimlessly through the store for the next few hours, it's fine with me," Kassidy said, as Paige searched through a bin full of discounted sheet sets. "I've got nowhere else to be."

Paige shrugged. "Fine. I'm sure I can pick out some great stuff. This screams country living, doesn't it?" She handed Kassidy a plastic sleeve containing a set of beige sheets decorated with crowing roosters and baby chicks. "Your guests will love it. Oh, and you can get some real chickens to wander through the garden. They'll tie the whole theme together."

Kassidy tossed the sheets back on the sale pile, and Paige shrugged.

"You don't like them? How about something daintier, like these?" She held up a set of baby pink sheets, edged in eyelet lace. "These are so cute, like sleeping on a pink cloud. Oh, and we need a fairly small bed, so it doesn't overwhelm the space. Something from the children's section ought to do. Over here."

Kassidy reluctantly went across the aisle with her and stopped next to the child's green plastic dinosaur bed Paige was admiring. "You're not giving up, are you?" she asked.

Paige took out a credit card and held it up. Her expression changed from clueless to calculating in a heartbeat. "If you don't give me other options, I'll buy this right now and have it delivered to your farm. And I'll expect to be sleeping in it this weekend."

"You're manipulative."

"Charmingly determined."

Kassidy sighed. She had a feeling Paige would get this bed to her house even if she had to strap it on top of her Tercel, just to prove her point. Kassidy could give in now, and at the very least come through this ordeal with a beautifully—and tastefully—furnished guest cottage, or she could hold her ground and wait in dread for this green monstrosity, complete with frilly pink sheets and probably a rooster throw pillow, to arrive on her doorstep.

She swatted Paige's credit card away. "Paint first. Once we pick colors, we can choose the rest to match."

"Are you sure you don't want to get these sheets, just in case we don't find anything better? They're on clearance."

❖

Kassidy placed an afghan over the back of the couch so its tassels draped at an angle. She had to admit—not to Paige, but in her own mind—she was thrilled with the results of their shopping spree. She looked around the cottage and imagined herself sitting in here and having a cup of tea after a busy summer morning spent harvesting lavender. No matter how hard she tried, although she really didn't put much effort into the exercise, she couldn't imagine strangers staying here.

Unfortunately, she could easily imagine Paige sleeping in here, with her bare legs uncovered because of the sultry summer heat. Of course, Paige was going to be here this weekend when they were expecting cool, spring rain, and Kassidy didn't know if she slept in the nude or in a pair of old sweats, but it was her fantasy. She was going to create any setting she wanted, and she wanted sweaty nakedness. She sat on the sofa, hugging one of the throw pillows Paige had insisted on buying to her chest. She seemed to have been fixated on them as a requirement for a bed-and-breakfast room. At least it was a solid blue color and not chicken-themed.

Kassidy had painted the walls blue, too, but in such a soft powdery hue they almost looked white. The couch was a neutral, easy-to-clean tweed, and when the folding bed was extended, it was covered with plain green sheets, similar to the ones Kassidy had hung on the booth at the fair. Paige had been determined to get those, too. Most of the room was in pale shades of blue, green, and yellow to give the small space an open, airy feel, but the occasional flash of brightness in matching tones kept it from seeming washed out.

She reached over and adjusted the lamp on the nightstand, moving it a little closer to her. The stand was her favorite find, located in the cluttered backyard of a local antiques dealer. It was an old wooden step stool, chipped and worn, that managed to look elegant once it was placed in the room and topped with a vase full of dried lavender. She and Paige had picked out paint colors and the sofa bed together, as well as some of the bedding items, but Kassidy had selected the more decorative finishing pieces on her own at shops near McMinnville, and she was excited for Paige to see them. They had bought the furniture together, but Kassidy had sanded away the dark stain after she got everything home, revealing the light honey-blond oak underneath. Then she had used more saturated versions of green, blue, and yellow paints to give the wood a distressed, well-used look.

Paige had offered to come over this week to help paint and decorate the room, but a last-minute call to interview with a prospective new client had gotten in the way. Kassidy had been secretly glad, because then she had been able to work on her own with the furniture and other unique decorations. The tiny space had been easy enough to paint and decorate once she had cleared out the clutter and hidden it away in the large greenhouse. She couldn't wait to see Paige's expression when she saw the finished product.

The beauty of the room would likely get Paige even more excited about the potential of renting it out, though. Kassidy had briefly considered making it uninhabitable by following all of Paige's original suggestions for décor, but she hadn't been able to insult the poor, unsuspecting shed in such an awful way. Now it was a pretty space, and tourists would probably love to stay here. That didn't mean Kassidy had to let them, of course.

Kassidy got up and shut the wide doors to the cottage. As much as she wanted to hang out in here and make it her retreat, with only Paige, nakedness, and summer heat to keep her company, she had work to do. Naked Paige could come with her, though, in Kassidy's imagination. She was never far from Kassidy's mind.

Chapter Seventeen

Paige stood in front of the tiny bathroom mirror and pulled her hair back, fastening it with a plain bronze clip. She set her comb back on the small shelf Kassidy had hung on the wall for guests to use and fixed the collar of her pressed white shirt. She was amazed by the way Kassidy had transformed the guest cottage, including the miniature bathroom. Kassidy had installed a new pedestal sink and a toilet and had painted the walls in a light shade of lavender. A few matching towels and some guest soaps were about all that she could fit in this room and still expect a person to get inside, too, but the effect was clean and pleasant.

The main room was where Kassidy had really put her eye for design to its best use. Paige wanted to sublet the place and have it waiting for her whenever she needed to leave the city. Although, as long as she was planning to drive to McMinnville, she'd much rather stay in the main house with Kassidy and not out here, only steps away from her front door. Last night had been the first time Paige had spent the night in a place where Kassidy's bedroom was within walking distance, and her fantasies about traversing the distance had kept her awake long after midnight.

She slipped her feet into a pair of polished black flats and picked up the bound copies of her final proposal. She had changed the wording of her usual contract before sending it to Kassidy when they had transferred the responsibility for Paige's fees from Kenneth to her. Instead of remaining on call during an extended transition period, Paige's job as business consultant for Lavender Lane Farm ended the moment her presentation did. Tonight, she'd be sleeping on the farm as a guest, and not in a professional capacity.

Maybe she'd take that midnight stroll after all.

She picked up a gift bag and an ice chest that was just big enough to hold a six-pack of pop and went over to Kassidy's porch, leaving the cottage doors open behind her because Dante was settled on the couch and didn't look prepared to move anytime soon. She sat at the table where she had first pitched her idea for branding labels on lavender products. She figured it was as close to a conference room as Kassidy ever wanted to get.

"I hope you have beer in that cooler. I have a feeling I'm going to need one," Kassidy said, coming out of her back door and settling into her chair. "Or two, or three, depending on what words come out of your mouth during this presentation."

Paige laughed. "Not beer, although you just gave me another great idea. There are bars in Portland dedicated to using fancy botanicals and local ingredients in the cocktails they make. You should come up with some fancy drink concepts and pitch them to the bar managers, like a Lavender Lane Farmopolitan or a Lavender Lane Farmartini. Check with the local microbreweries, too, because they usually offer small batch seasonal beers."

"How about a Lavender Lane Farmimosa?" Kassidy suggested.

"Now you're getting in the spirit." Paige already had the microbrew idea in her proposal, so she flipped through until she found the right page and put a small check mark next to the bullet point. She added a note about the cocktail bars, too.

"As long as all your suggestions include alcohol, we're going to have an easy time of it today."

Paige flipped open the minicooler and took out an old-fashioned glass bottle.

"Milk?" asked Kassidy. "Definitely losing interest here."

"This is an addendum to the proposal and not vital in any way, but I think you should get goats."

"To help with the harvest? I'd like the extra help, but I think they might eat all the profits."

Paige ignored the sarcasm. She had a feeling she was going to need to do that a lot during this presentation. "For fun."

"Fun for me? Or the goats?"

Paige waved off Kassidy's skeptical tone. "Fun for your visitors. I've been noticing that a lot of the local farms have goats, as sort of a petting zoo kind of attraction for kids. Dante loved the one they had at our bed and breakfast. What do you think of serving lavender flavored goat's milk for breakfast?"

"Do you really want to know what I think, or was that a rhetorical question?"

Paige sighed and opened the bag next to her and took out two small wineglasses she had got while on one of her tastings. She had thought the glasses would add an elegant touch to the sampling, but she started to have serious doubts as she poured the thick liquid into them. She had lost some of Kassidy's already questionable confidence in her as a consultant. She couldn't let her own doubts show, but she really did want to make sure it was supposed to look this way before she drank it.

"Shouldn't he have pasteurized it or whatever you do to milk to make it less..." She was going to say mucus-like but thought Kassidy might see her hesitation about drinking the stuff as a sign of weakness. "Less viscous?"

Kassidy covered her mouth to hide her snort of laughter. "You need to research exactly what pasteurization is. Let me guess, you usually buy skim milk from the grocery store, not whole milk directly from a farm."

Paige nodded.

"Oh, this is going to be good."

Paige was concerned by how happy Kassidy looked at the thought of her tasting the goat's milk, but she pressed on with her speech. "Anyway, back to business. I read that goat's milk takes on the flavor of whatever they eat, so I asked the guy who makes the lavender hand lotion to feed some lavender to a goat and give us a sample of the milk."

"And this is the result?" Kassidy sniffed at her glass and made a face.

"Well, not exactly. He said the goat wouldn't eat it, so he infused the lavender in the milk instead. But don't worry. I used the kind you cook with, not the kind you give him for soap. And why don't you save some of the eye rolling for the rest of my presentation. You don't want to wear yourself out before we even open the folder."

"You first. This was your idea."

Paige raised the glass in a mock salute, hoping Kassidy didn't realize that the gesture was meant more to stall for time than anything else.

"Are you composing a five-page toast in your mind, or are you trying to get out of drinking this stuff?"

Paige took a deep breath and held it as she took a sip. She very carefully set the glass on the table, putting all her concentration into not throwing up.

"I'm always willing to admit when I'm wrong," she said when she thought it was safe to open her mouth and speak again. "This is one of those times. Actually, I think this is the most wrong I've ever been."

Kassidy laughed happily. "Darn. Now I have to taste it, too, just to find out how bad it is. I'll bet Ralph told you it wouldn't be good."

"Maybe," Paige said, watching as Kassidy sampled the milk and grimaced. "So let's get on with the real presentation."

"This was just the warm-up act? I'm afraid to find out what the main event is going to be."

Paige moved the glasses and milk bottle to the far side of the table. Usually, she'd give her clients their copy of the proposal and go through it step-by-step with them reading along, but she decided to keep both copies in front of her for now. She figured Kassidy would read ahead if she had her own, arguing over Paige's ideas before she had a chance to get to them in order. Besides, Kassidy had brought some paper and a pen with her, in case she needed to take notes about how awful Paige's suggestions were.

"I've identified three general areas in which you're not taking full advantage of the farm's potential. We've already discussed several aspects of them over the past two weeks, such as branding products and opening the farm to the public, and now I want to cover the three themes in more detail."

Paige felt herself seamlessly slipping into presentation mode. The setting might be pastoral, but from her clothes to the sound of her voice, she was boardroom ready. She hoped that her professional attitude—now that the horrid milk tasting was over—would help Kassidy see the benefits of listening to her and trying some new things.

"Let's cover making the farm more accessible, first." Might as well get the most contentious issue over with as soon as possible. Paige turned to the right page in her proposal, although she didn't need to look at her bullet points to remind herself of what she had written. She had absorbed Kassidy's farm, and the directions Kassidy needed to take were clear in Paige's mind, as if she could see two farms at once. The way it was now, and the thriving business it had the potential to be.

"We've talked about why it's important to invite tourists here, and you've agreed with my assessment," Paige stated with conviction. Kassidy gave her a sort of nod, sort of shrug that leaned toward noncommittal. "A store and U-pick area on the farm, a booth at next year's street fair, at least a trial period for renting out the cottage. Most important, a friendly face for the tourists to associate with the farm."

Kassidy sighed. "Yes, I'll do those things. I already said I would."

"Fine, but you need to do more. Right now, you're unenthusiastic about this. Once I'm no longer pushing you to make crafts or talk to people, I worry you're going to revert to a...let's say passive state. You'll take down your driveway barricade and be nice to the people who happen to drive by and stumble in, but you won't make an effort to attract them to the farm as a planned destination."

"What do you know?" Kassidy's surly tone told Paige she was correct, as if she'd needed proof.

"You need to actively look for ways to interact with the public. The farm should have a presence at farmers markets and festivals, but you need to go a step further. You could have an open house or lavender festival on the farm and invite local businesses to come here. Make it an annual event. I also have a detailed marketing plan for the store, website, and the guest cottage, but you can read through those later."

"I guess I don't hate the idea of my own lavender festival," Kassidy said with an elaborate shrug, but Paige wasn't fooled by her casual attitude. She could already see Kassidy's expression change as plans started coming to mind, and she wasn't surprised when Kassidy surreptitiously jotted down some notes.

"The second area I want you to address relates to farm products. Getting your name on everything made with your lavender is a good first step, but you should also think about developing some products that are proprietary to the farm. It makes more sense financially, of course, but I also see it as a way to develop the first step in my plan more fully. Develop a brand and a loyal following. Open your farm to the public and give them plenty of things to buy while they're here."

"My own products…" Kassidy said, tapping her lip with her pen. "I like it. Do you mean crafts, or did you have other things in mind?"

Paige lost her professional self for a moment as her attention was drawn to Kassidy's mouth by her fidgeting movement. She made an effort to remember how to think and speak, and eventually remembered the types of products she had meant to recommend.

After experiencing Kassidy's reaction to the flavored goat's milk plan, Paige had a feeling her next suggestion would be met with equal disdain, but she had to say it. It was written in the proposal Kassidy would eventually read, anyway. "I had originally planned to mention putting beehives on the property and selling lavender honey. You'd need to coordinate the honey harvest with the times when the lavender is in full bloom. You could probably work with a local bee farmer to have them bring a hive here and take care of it, if you weren't interested in doing it yourself."

"I've had lavender honey before, and it's delicious. I could handle bees." Kassidy wrote notes as she mumbled. "Let's see, the small barn behind the greenhouse would make a good workspace for extracting and bottling. I'd need to get a suit, and a smoker. And bees." She looked at Paige again. "Okay, what's next?"

Paige held up her hand. "Wait. You acted like I was ridiculous for suggesting you get some cute little goats, but you're fine with a swarm of insects?"

"Yes. Honeybees are important, and I don't know why I hadn't thought of this before. That's what I'm paying you for, though, isn't it?"

"I suppose so." Paige realized she was arguing against Kassidy's acceptance of her idea, and she decided to stop. Somewhere along the way, Kassidy had gotten excited about the possibilities Paige had seen in the farm from day one. She had stopped looking for limits and was open to what was possible. Paige felt a responding tingle of excitement inside her belly. The feeling wasn't one she usually got during a presentation, even if her clients were thrilled with her plans for change. At this point, she tended to emotionally withdraw from the project, if anything, and she wasn't sure why she felt different in Kassidy's case. Maybe because she had a dream stirring inside about being a part of some of these changes. Standing alongside Kassidy and cheering her on. Close enough to touch, to smell, to taste her…

"Your perfume," Paige said, abruptly returning to her presentation. "It's lavender, isn't it? Do you make it or buy it?"

Kassidy sniffed her wrist, as if she'd forgotten how good she smelled. Paige never forgot. This aspect of the proposal was both a real suggestion and a personal indulgence. Paige wanted to either find out the name of what Kassidy used or have Kassidy make it and give Paige a bottle. She planned to sprinkle it liberally through her apartment, starting with the pillows on her bed, as if the scent would conjure Kassidy into her bedroom.

"I make it myself. I have a home distilling machine, so I can make small batches. It's a blend of five lavenders, sweet pea, and a few other herbs. It was just okay until I added a tiny amount of mint. That neutralized some of the heavy floral notes and freshened it up."

"Patent it. Bottle it. Whatever you need to do. You'll sell out every year." As much as Paige preferred the thought of the scent being uniquely Kassidy's, she wasn't going to miss the opportunity to help her make money.

"Perfume..." Kassidy flipped her paper over and wrote more notes. "What else?"

"Well, it's my fault for bringing this next one up right after I mentioned perfume, so feel free to share your snide comments. As if you ever needed approval for that. So, I loved your chicken hors d'oeuvres. And whenever your name came up when I was talking to locals, they would always mention some amazing dish you'd brought to a party, or the cookies you sent to the school bake sale that sold out in the first half hour. I think you should write a cookbook."

Kassidy looked as if she'd been about to protest if the plan was for her to bake cookies all day, but she stopped with her mouth partway open. Then closed it.

Paige wasn't sure if she was excited or appalled by the recommendation, so she kept selling it. "I'm picturing a full-color hardback, with pictures from around the farm and of all the food. You can add information about lavender in between recipes."

"Oh," Kassidy said quietly. "Yes, I can imagine writing a book like that."

"I have no doubt about it." Paige would have preferred to give Kassidy some time to explore this new possibility in her mind, but she pressed on. Her third area of concentration would be needed to make the first two work.

"The last item on my list is more of an attitude than a project," she said, closing the proposal and resting her hands on it. "You hesitate too much when it comes to the farm, taking steps that are too cautious and small. Like the lavender for crafts. Your sales have been strong, but instead of expanding into the market, you've taken baby steps for three years by selling some dried flowers to the local craft store and adding a few dozen plants each year. Think bigger. You have two acres of unplanted fields on the farm, and you have an untapped market in Portland where there are dozens of florists and upscale grocery stores and craft fairs. And the empty greenhouse with your two tables of pots? It should be full. What you don't plant in your fields, you can sell to nurseries as a wholesale product."

Paige leaned forward. "There's too much empty space, Kassidy. Fill this place with plants and people and products. Treat this like a high-end, diversified artisanal venture and not like it's a hobby farm."

Kassidy was stunned into silence by Paige's vehement tone. She was beginning to understand what made Paige so good at her job. She seemed to have developed a personal stake in the farm, and she spoke as if she was determined to convince Kassidy about how great it could be.

"You'd be a great motivational speaker," she said, finally able to express what she was thinking. "I felt like standing up and cheering after that speech, even though most of it was about what I'm doing wrong."

"I'm not trying to—"

Kassidy stopped her by putting her hand on Paige's arm. "I'm not complaining. You're being honest, and as much as I want to, I can't argue with what you're saying." She pushed at Paige's arm playfully before releasing her contact. "I'm overwhelmed right now, partly because I can't wait to get started on some of the ideas, but also because I dread others. I guess I've always been worried that if I turn the farm into something bigger and more productive, I'll lose the best parts of it."

Paige nodded. "I understand. You've created a peaceful haven here, and this proposal will change that in some ways. But I want you to be able to afford to live here as long as you want, selling when and if you choose." She handed Kassidy one of the proposals. "You can start with the projects that electrify you, as long as you don't ignore for too long the ones that will be more challenging, yet still beneficial for the farm."

Kassidy flipped through nearly one hundred pages filled with print. "There's quite a lot more here than what you talked about today."

"Yes. I put more detailed information in the proposal and just covered the three main themes today. Everything connects to them, though."

Kassidy ticked them off on her fingers. "Smile. Make something. Go big or go home."

Paige laughed, suddenly looking like herself again, even though she had reverted to the same style of clothes and demeanor she had worn on her first day on the farm. Her untouchable business uniform.

"Thank you for summing up hours of painstaking research and contemplation so succinctly." She stood up and carefully poured the milk remaining in their glasses back into the bottle. "This is going down the drain, although it's thick enough to clog it. Are you satisfied with what we've discussed today?"

Satisfied? Try terrified, elated, and ready to hide under the bedcovers. Kassidy just nodded, though. Eventually she'd come to terms with what she needed to do, so she'd consider that as satisfied.

"Great. I'm officially off the clock, so I'm going to relax and enjoy my weekend. My contract only extended through this presentation, but if you have questions about anything in the proposal, you can send an email. My business's contact information is on the cover."

She put her hand out and Kassidy stared at it in confusion for a moment before she reached out and shook Paige's hand. She got a small, professional smile in return, and then Paige went back to the guest cottage and closed the Dutch doors fully behind her.

"Um…" Kassidy wasn't sure how to respond to Paige's sudden dismissal of their relationship, but Paige was no longer there to hear the response, so Kassidy stopped talking and sat in a stunned silence. She had really thought they were developing a connection, but maybe it had all been designed to make Kassidy comfortable enough with Paige to listen to her advice.

She'd thought Paige really cared about the farm, but maybe her enthusiasm for it had been an act, too, like the mask she said she wore when doing business. What had she been expecting? A hug? A kiss? Probably not the usual ways Paige concluded her presentations in the corporate world. Kassidy had been a fool to think she was different.

She was about to get up and go back inside when Paige came out again, followed by Dante and wearing khakis and a burgundy T-shirt. Her hair was loose and mussed, just the way Kassidy liked it.

She dropped heavily into the chair on the other side of the table from where she had just been sitting.

"Hi, I'm Paige. I'm renting your cottage for the weekend." She leaned back and closed her eyes. "I definitely needed to get away. You would not believe the demanding client I had this month. She was tyrannical."

Kassidy grinned, all her confusion fading away as she realized that Paige had made the end of their business arrangement as formal and obvious as possible. Which left the rest of the weekend open for something new.

"I'm glad to meet you, Paige, and delighted to be opening my home to random strangers. I'm Kassidy, by the way. Your host. The one who will be making your breakfast tomorrow."

Paige sat up. "Did I say tyrannical? I meant delightful. A candidate for Client of the Year."

Kassidy shook her head, laughing as she pushed her notepaper and Paige's proposal to one side. She would get to these projects, wholeheartedly and not timidly, starting next week. This weekend was going to be devoted to something else entirely.

Paige smiled at her with the expression of someone with a wonderful secret to share. "I hope you don't have a policy about not dating houseguests, Kassidy, because I would love to take you out to dinner."

Chapter Eighteen

Kassidy went into the house to change for dinner while Paige took Dante for a walk along the paths through her lavender fields. Once she was alone, with the door closed behind her, she sat on the bed in her room without taking off her clothes or picking something for tonight. She felt shaky, and she worked through her mixed-up emotions until she could unravel the separate strands.

Hearing Paige's evaluation of her business had been intense, as Kassidy had expected it would be. After last weekend when she had thought Paige's only advice would be to make some labels and fix her website, but instead had involved dragging her to the town fair, Kassidy had realized that Paige was going to expect her to stretch her boundaries for her farm. And she hadn't been disappointed in the proposal, either in its scary attempts to push her out of her comfort zone or in the enticing possibilities it encouraged her to acknowledge. But even the really great aspects, like the thought of creating a beautiful farm-inspired cookbook, triggered nervousness because of the amount of effort and skill they would require from her. She was feeling worn-out from the process of hearing Paige's presentation, but her present state of discomfort stemmed from more than that.

Five minutes. Paige had gone into the guest cottage for five minutes after ending her presentation, and Kassidy had responded like a helpless child facing abandonment. Wondering what she had done wrong, questioning their entire relationship. How long would it have been before she had reacted like she had with Audrey and gone seeking Paige's attention again?

Paige hadn't been more than a dozen yards away from her as she had acted out her playful separation of their work and personal lives. Kassidy had no doubt that Paige's intentions had not been harmful. She liked Kassidy. Wanted to take her out. Kassidy was angry with herself for reacting the way she had, not with Paige for being a trigger, albeit a charming and funny one.

Kassidy got up and smoothed out the covers on the bed. She felt better after analyzing her behavior and the way she had talked to herself after Paige had walked away. As long as she understood why she responded the way she did, she could get control over it. The only way she knew how to control her reaction to Paige was to stay away from her. As much as she loved spending time with Paige and laughing with her, Kassidy wasn't looking for a serious relationship. She had her farm to worry about, with all the upcoming work, tourists, and risks it now entailed. Paige had spent a few weekends here, and now the job that had brought her to McMinnville was at an end. They both knew this when Paige asked Kassidy out and she accepted. The date was for tonight. Dinner. Sex, hopefully. Laughter, most assuredly, if Paige was involved.

Kassidy changed from jeans to a nice pair of slacks and a blouse. She could ignore her concerns about how she had reacted since the problem wasn't a long-term one. She would make the most of this one, wonderful night.

They left Dante in the house with Kipper, and Kassidy drove them to Sarai's restaurant. Paige had offered, but getting stranded on the side of the road in a nonfunctioning Tercel would put a definite crimp in Kassidy's plans for the evening. She felt an almost desperate sense of freedom as she reached over and took Paige's hand while she drove. She was free to be with Paige tonight even though she was concerned about how hard and fast she had fallen for her. But at the same time, the freedom came at a price she didn't even want to consider right now. Paige would go back to Portland.

Paige squeezed her hand and let go while Kassidy parked on the street around the corner from the restaurant. "You're quiet," she said. "Is everything okay? Are you upset about the proposal that jerk of a consultant gave you?"

"Oh, she wasn't so bad. And it's not like I'm actually going to do any of those things she told me to do."

Paige smiled, but she seemed uncharacteristically quiet, too. Kassidy turned in her seat to face her. "You gave me a lot to think about, and it's not easy to switch it off completely. I'm happy to be here with you, though."

"Me, too." Paige lifted her hand, hesitated as if still accustomed to having a work relationship in the way, and then put her palm against Kassidy's cheek. The touch was gentle, questioning, and Kassidy answered by covering Paige's hand with hers, taking hold of it, and tugging Paige closer.

Paige had been clear about the change in their relationship, and Kassidy wanted to respond with a clarity of her own. She leaned forward and kissed Paige, expecting her lips to be soft against Kassidy's and her hair to feel silky when Kassidy wrapped her fingers in her curls. But she wasn't anticipating the way her heart would respond, even though the kiss was tentative at first and chaste throughout, unlike the first one they had shared.

Kassidy was familiar with desire, or at least with some mild variations of attraction, but this was something too far beyond to classify with the same word. Kassidy was perfectly happy to let her body have its way tonight, but she had planned to keep the rest of herself at a distance. She pulled back and looked in Paige's eyes and thought she saw promises of shared afternoons, secret laughter, and something building toward a future in them. But were the promises truly there or just projections of what she wanted to find?

Either way, she was in big trouble. Those weren't things she should want from Paige, or from anyone else. Still, she could barely get through an innocent kiss without falling into something sort of resembling love. What would she be like after a night together? She would survive, no doubt, but she wouldn't be the same after Paige left. She clasped on to the knowledge that Paige certainly wasn't interested in exchanging her career and life in the city for a tourist-infested rural farm.

"We should go in and eat," Paige said, trailing her fingertips over Kassidy's cheek and jawline. "Have you had anything besides doughnuts today?"

"I didn't eat any doughnuts today," Kassidy said, laughing even as she tried to sound affronted. "Although I did eat the bigger half of the loaf of blueberry lavender bread I made for you this morning."

"I should have expanded the customer service section of my proposal, but I was running out of paper."

"What? At least you got some of it. Most of my guests will be lucky if they get day-old coffee and a frozen waffle."

"Toasted?"

Kassidy shrugged. "If I'm in a good mood."

She smiled as she got out of the car. Paige's teasing always seemed to come at the perfect time, letting her know to lighten up and enjoy their time together. The kiss had caught her off guard, but she was prepared for the rest of the night now. Probably.

Maybe.

Paige had eaten at Sarai's restaurant almost every night she had stayed in McMinnville, so she and Kassidy were led directly to Paige's favorite booth by the front window. The rest of the dining room was packed with people, and Paige figured the table had been saved for her since she had told Sarai they would be here tonight, taking a chance Kassidy would say yes to dinner. The interior was decorated in dark earth tones with gold accents, creating a cozy, den-like atmosphere, and the air was permeated with the warm, spicy scents emanating from the kitchen. The place had become as familiar to her as her own apartment kitchen.

She already knew what she was going to order—the vegetable biryani was one of the dishes Sarai used to make when they were in college, and it was still her favorite—but she pretended to read the menu because it gave her a chance to stare over the top of it at Kassidy. In the dark room with candles as the main source of light, Kassidy's hair glowed with an amber hue, and the play of shadows on her face emphasized her serious expression. Paige wasn't worried, though. She could always make Kassidy laugh, and she was anxious to try coaxing some new sounds and feelings out of her tonight.

She wasn't in a hurry, although she had expected to be. Usually, she felt a need to rush relationships past the awkward courting stage and into the bedroom. She had never been comfortable with the getting-to-know-you phase, with all its generic questions and carefully phrased answers. What kind of music do you like? What are your hobbies? She preferred moving quickly to sex—after all, if she was dating someone, she obviously found them attractive. Once there, in what she considered to be the mildly boring phase of a relationship, conversations usually became less intense. Small talk, to fill the time until the sexual tension was played out and they were ready to move on.

She felt like such a different person with Kassidy that those past relationships seemed like someone else's memories. She and Kassidy had already shared details about their childhoods. She had already been involved in Kassidy's life in a way she knew Kassidy considered to be intimate. She had seen Kassidy's vulnerabilities and her desire for privacy. She had met her family members.

Instead of making her want to get away or hurry forward to avoid more revelations, her friendship with Kassidy made her want more. To tell her more, to hear more, to share more.

And to kiss more, obviously. She reveled in the knowledge she now had about the perfect way Kassidy's mouth felt against hers. The way her hands felt strong and sure, pulling her closer as if she felt the same yearning Paige did. The kiss had been innocent, though. On her part, because as much as she wanted to devour Kassidy, she was amazed by the stillness she felt inside when she was with her. She had spent her life rushing from one activity to the next, one woman to the next. She looked at Kassidy now and had no desire to be anywhere else or doing anything else.

Kassidy seemed tense, though, and Paige didn't think it had anything to do with her business proposal. Rather, she had seemed excited about some of the prospects and accepting of the others. Her change in mood had happened after Paige had asked her out. If she had been uncertain about Kassidy's attraction to her, the kiss would have reassured her. Something else was on Kassidy's mind, and Paige had a feeling she knew what it was. Anyone who had been through the emotional neglect Kassidy had faced as child would be determined to protect themselves from having it happen again. As far as Kassidy knew, Paige was leaving McMinnville tomorrow and never returning. Paige had to do her best to make sure Kassidy understood what she would do to keep them in contact until they decided where their relationship was heading.

Sarai came over to the table with a woven plate of warm chapatis. She gave them each a hug and sat down next to Kassidy.

"The kitchen is crazy tonight, so I'll only stay a minute. I'm not trying to barge in on your date."

"It's great to see such a big crowd already, so early in the season," Kassidy said, reaching for a chapati and smearing it with Sarai's fig and lemon chutney.

"I know. Paige has been doing her part to keep me in business by eating here all the time, but it's a relief to have more than one table filled. Maybe some of them will be better tippers than she is."

"Maybe they will be, if the food you serve them is better than what you've given me," Paige joked.

"Oh, now you're a food critic?" Sarai leaned toward Kassidy. "I used to cook my own food when we were roommates in college. She used to sit on her bed and watch me with those big Dickensian eyes until I offered her some. I believe she graduated without knowing where the dining hall was located."

Kassidy laughed. "She is a mooch, isn't she?"

Paige nudged her ankle under the table. "Says the woman who just admitted she ate most of my breakfast this morning."

"I hope all my guests won't be so demanding." Kassidy shook her head at Sarai. "I think calling the place a bed-and-breakfast leads to too many expectations. I'm going to rent out the cottage as a Bed Only."

"Oh, that reminds me," Sarai said. "My parents will be visiting in June, and I'll want to rent your cottage for a week for them. I'll get the dates and a deposit to you this week."

"I'd love to have them."

Sarai disappeared into the kitchen again after a brief visit, and once they were alone, Paige reached across the table and squeezed Kassidy's hand.

"Good for you. You got your first reservation. Besides me, of course."

Kassidy took a big gulp of water. "I know. It's already getting out of hand. Do you think they'll mind a bag of potato chips for breakfast?"

"That's what all the fanciest B and Bs serve." Paige smiled, glad to see Kassidy kidding around again. Well, she hoped she was kidding.

"What were you like in college? Aside from begging for food?"

Paige put her elbows on the table and rested her chin on her hands, for once in her life not minding when the conversation turned to her. "Busy. I only had a chance to spend time with Sarai at meals. If she hadn't been cooking such great smelling dishes, I'd probably have barely known her. I'd have grabbed something from the cafeteria on my way to class or practice or the library."

Kassidy paused while the waiter set their dishes on the table. "Did you do all the same activities in college as high school?"

Paige shrugged. Her parents had seemed both thrilled and jealous when she had gotten accepted to Reed. They had been raising a toddler when their friends went off to college. She had privately wondered why they never made the effort to go back to school or join a sports team instead of expecting her to continue to live out their dreams, but she never spoke the questions out loud. She had heard the *We would have done this if we hadn't gotten pregnant* story since before she was old enough to grasp the concepts involved and she had always understood what her role was in the family, even though she hadn't had time to figure out what her purpose was in the outside world.

"I did most of the same things in college, but it was more difficult. Everything required more from me, whether it was practicing to get to first string or doing homework to get good grades." Paige paused, thinking back to the fair when she had first told Kassidy about her school experiences. "You asked before if my parents had actually done all these things, and I said they hadn't because of me. Part of me always suspected that they wouldn't have been involved in those activities even if they hadn't had me. I think that made it harder, because I was trying to live up to their fantasies, not their realities."

She took a bite of her food before continuing. "I shouldn't complain, though. My parents had a kind of self-centered agenda, but they were there for me. Playing ball or making class projects. I sometimes felt smothered, but I imagine it would have been much harder to be left alone."

Kassidy shook her head. "Don't downplay your experiences because they were different from mine. I'm not going to say my life was easy when I was little, but the twins were always there for me, too. And once they were in school, I had more opportunities to take part in school activities. Not at your cutthroat level, though. I suppose I was more of a Dante when it came to sports."

"A Dante is a good thing to be," Paige said, feeling the unaccustomed sensation of being content. She had never been able to share like this, whether it was laughter or painful memories, and she didn't want her time with Kassidy to end. She'd do her best to make sure it didn't.

❖

Kassidy parked her car in the driveway and shut off the ignition. Her earlier concerns had vanished, unable to withstand the force of Paige's presence. She made Kassidy laugh and think and care too much to remain down for long.

Paige was leaving soon. The heartache Kassidy would surely feel once she left would be awful, but manageable, and was a price she was willing to pay for this time with her.

She had expected things to happen more quickly between them tonight, but Paige had seemed content to inch toward the bedroom, seemingly unconcerned by the time limit on their relationship. Kassidy couldn't get the ticking clock out of her mind, both loving and hating it because it was the reason she was able to be with Paige. Relationships always had ends, people always left, but at least Kassidy knew precisely when it would happen. She could find some comfort in that.

She wanted more than comfort from Paige, though. They had been in nearly constant contact tonight, but only in delicate ways. Small touches, more intimate than those they had shared at the festival or on the farm, had permeated her skin until it felt like a shell of glass, ready to shatter at any moment. An ankle, a hand, fingertips…Paige could do amazing things to Kassidy's body with only those innocent parts. Who knew what would happen once the rest of their bodies were involved.

They got out of the car and walked to Kassidy's house without needing to discuss it. Kassidy opened the door, and once they got Dante and Kipper settled down, she took Paige's hand and led her toward the bedroom.

"Wait," Paige said. "Can we talk first?"

Kassidy sighed dramatically. "More waiting? We've been waiting all night."

Paige laughed, clearly finding pleasure in Kassidy's impatience. She sat on the couch and tugged Kassidy onto the cushions next to her.

"Okay. What do you want to talk about? If it's something to do with a new idea you had for getting people to overrun my farm, then I'm going to send you back to the guest cottage."

"It's nothing to do with the farm," Paige said. She held Kassidy's hand gently in hers and used the other to play with Kassidy's hair. "It's about us."

"Us?" Kassidy sighed, loving the sensation of Paige's fingers in her hair and on her temples. Now on her neck. Even better. "I would think the bedroom would be the best place for that discussion."

Paige shook her head. "I've had a couple job offers in the area, Kass. I might have a new client in Portland, too, but two of the farmers I've met while I've been here asked for my help with their businesses. I can help them on weekends, like we were doing, and go back to the city during the week. I know you'll be busy with tourist season, but I thought you could get away for a night in Portland with me sometimes."

Kassidy caught hold of Paige's hand, which had continued on its meandering path and was tracing the open V at the neck of her shirt. Kassidy didn't really want to stop Paige's progression, but the touch was too distracting, and she needed to figure out what Paige was really saying.

"Wait, Paige. Are you talking about this being more than one night?"

"Well, yes. I thought...That's not what you want?"

Was it? No. Kassidy stood up, as desperate to get distance as she had been to get close only moments before.

"I didn't expect forever, Paige."

Paige stood, too, but didn't make a move to close the gap between them. "I'm not offering forever. I'm offering the possibility, the chance to find out how far we can go together. I thought you wanted me, too, for more than one night." She rubbed her fingers through her hair, mussing it in the way that drove Kassidy mad with longing to touch it.

Paige walked a few steps away, and then came back, as if the emotions inside her couldn't remain still.

"You know, I actually thought I was doing something you'd appreciate," Paige said, with a forced laugh that wasn't anything like her usual joyful one. "I wanted to reassure you. To let you know I had plans to stick around and be close to you because you meant more to me than a one-night stand. What do I mean to you, Kassidy?"

Kassidy closed her eyes. Paige meant everything to her. More than anyone should. Kassidy couldn't trust herself to care this much about someone and still remain strong enough to survive when she eventually withdrew, physically or mentally. If Kassidy had cared less than this, she would have been thrilled to know Paige was interested in a real relationship. How could she explain what it was like to love someone too much to be with her?

She didn't need to explain. She just needed to get back to the security of being alone.

"I'm sorry, Paige. All I wanted was this one night."

Paige nodded, either unable or unwilling to say anything more. She called for Dante and left the house. Ten minutes later, when the Tercel started up and Paige left, Kassidy was still standing in the same spot, unable to move.

CHAPTER NINETEEN

Paige walked into the foyer of Portland Connect, the city's newest—and soon to be most successful, if she had any say in it—telecom service provider. The carpet was plush under her feet and the fixtures and upholstery were coordinated in bright silver and pale shades of blue. She had been watching the redecorating process with interest, especially since it had been her suggestion to do something different from the sea of green-logoed competitors, and this was the first time she was seeing the finished product. She thought it was perfect for the company because most of her proposal had been aimed at getting them to set themselves apart instead of trying to act, look, and do business like the more established, bigger corporations.

The transformation was nice, but certainly not on par with what Kassidy had done with her guest cottage. What could compete with the renovated garden shed where Paige had spent a fitful night dreaming about Kassidy and hoping the next night would find them tangled together on the pullout bed, with the Dutch doors wide open to the fragrant lavender fields?

Paige stopped for a moment, gathering herself together and banishing all thoughts of Kassidy out of her mind, or at least to the back corner of it, while she was doing her job. Kassidy never really left her thoughts completely, not when Paige was commuting, researching, or discussing plans with executives. Hopefully, one day Paige would look up at a clock and realize she had gone ten whole minutes without daydreaming about Kassidy. Then she could try for fifteen.

At this rate, when she turned fifty, she might be able to go an entire day without thinking of her.

She started walking again, smiling a greeting at the receptionist who was on the phone, and he waved her back to the conference room. She had been working with the company since leaving Kassidy and McMinnville behind, and she had already presented her proposal. Today was a chance for her to meet with upper-level management and catch up on their progress so far. Paige loved the job since everyone had been on board with the need for change right from the start. She found it refreshing to work with a new company, free from entrenched bad habits. She had managed to maneuver through the salary allotments and job descriptions until she was able to restructure personnel without needing to fire a single person. The work was pleasant and rewarding, and promised to be one of the highlights of her career in terms of increased revenue and client base.

And she would have traded all of it to be back at work on an eight-acre lavender farm with a woman who was, at times, violently opposed to her ideas, and who fought her every step of the way.

Paige sighed and made one last effort to scoot Kassidy away from the forefront of her thoughts. It devolved into a shoving match, and Paige finally gave up and let Kassidy take center stage where she was best able to make Paige feel the ache of longing and the frustration of unmet desire. At least Paige was dressed in her usual work garb and had every hair in place. She would look composed on the outside, by God, no matter how off-kilter she felt inside.

Paige and Dante got back to her apartment where she stripped out of her business clothes and put on a pair of cargo shorts and a heathered gray T-shirt. He lounged on the couch next to her, chewing on a dog toy shaped like a rubber chicken, while she did some research for her most recent Willamette Valley client. A chocolatier.

She would have paid for the chance to work on this project, with all its accompanying taste testing, but she was actually making money on the job.

She had been tempted to refuse the work she had been offered in McMinnville after Kassidy rejected her, but she had already given her word to the people involved. She had slipped in and out of town, sticking close to either her familiar winery-slash-bed-and-breakfast or the farms where she was working in an attempt to avoid any contact with Kassidy. She hadn't seen Kassidy herself, but over the weeks following their last day together, she began to see the farm's presence growing in the town. Window displays now featured her collaborative products complete with a newly designed Lavender Lane Farm logo on them. The rental broker had a photo advertising the guest cottage—Paige still thought of it as *her* cottage—along with rental rates far higher than she had anticipated. As much as she felt the humiliation of Kassidy's withdrawal from her life, Paige blossomed inside with pride because Kassidy was taking care of her farm the way she needed to. And that meant Kassidy herself would be protected in the future.

She had intuitively changed her working style with Kassidy, partly because she wanted to hang out with her, but also because the unique nature of her farm demanded it. She had been adjusting her approach as she got more and more clients from the Willamette Valley—something Evie had scoffed at, and Paige had been certain she didn't want. Now Leighton Consulting offered different plans for each customer. The corporate clients still got her professionally dressed self, along with continuing services for an extended restructuring period. With the local farmers and artisans, she took a more hands-on approach, like she had done with Kassidy. She came into the business and worked alongside the owners and staff, exploring the individual characteristics of the specific store or farm and making changes on the spot, cutting out the need for much involvement after the short time she was on-site.

And she loved every moment of it. Even the times, like now, when she got sidetracked by searching online for distracting things such as recipes for lavender truffles. Because of the quick turnover of jobs, she was almost constantly learning and exploring. She had felt more alive and creative when she had been working with Kassidy, and most of the feeling carried with her to these new jobs. She was able to commute to outlying Willamette Valley suburbs and towns on weekends and keep her bill-paying corporate work in Portland during the week.

She had designed this new type of life with Kassidy in mind, to give them time together, but Paige still felt she had found some sort of niche for herself, even though the discovery was lessened without Kassidy there to share in it.

Paige printed out a recipe using lavender oil and dark chocolate, complete with a photo of a candy with a tiny crystallized lavender bud on top. If Kassidy could invent some new variation on it, the confection would be a beautiful addition to her cookbook. She folded the picture and stuck it in her book on candy-making techniques. Maybe she'd send it to Kassidy anonymously, although she'd likely be the prime suspect. Or she could give it to Jessica next time she was in McMinnville and have her pass it along. It was a business item, after all, and not an embarrassing plea for a second chance.

Even though the flashes of inspiration connected to Kassidy's farm made her uncomfortable because she couldn't share them, the exploding sense of creativity she was feeling as she helped artisanal businesses find their distinctive markets was unexpected and heartwarming. She hadn't seen the appeal before, being just as happy to shop at a big box store or mega-chain to get the products she needed and prices she had come to expect. She thought back to the time when Kassidy had jokingly called her an artiste, and how she had denied any connection between her work and creative expression. She had accepted those big box stores, with their bland and mass-produced selections, because she saw herself the same way. Nothing special, nothing unique. Jack-of-all-trades, without caring about any of them.

Thanks to her time with Kassidy, Paige was starting to see herself in a new light. The job she had fallen into because she didn't know what else to do might just prove to be the calling she had never thought she'd hear. She was thankful for what she had learned on Kassidy's farm. Gratitude didn't keep her warm on lonely nights, but it was something.

Another lesson Kassidy had taught her was to have fun with her dog. The problem with recognizing all the effects Kassidy had on her life was that they made her even harder to forget. She was everywhere with Paige. At work, in her daily routines, and now in her newfound hobbies. She got off the couch and picked up Dante's leash, and he ran over and sat obediently by the door. Then he started disobediently scratching it. Paige sighed. One step at a time. She hooked the leash onto his collar and grabbed her car keys out of the bowl on the way out.

Paige got them both into the car and started driving north, toward Vancouver. She had used the dog agility excuse as a reason to get Dante because the need to compete had been too ingrained in her to ignore. She had put off training him, though, because it was more enjoyable to play fetch or go for walks, without imposing the stress of winning trials and meets. She was slowly finding it less important to have a frenzy of activity in her life than to cultivate a few hobbies she did for their own sakes, and she had found out that training Dante didn't have to turn into yet another high-stakes need to prove herself.

She hadn't talked about her parents and their expectations to anyone before, preferring to claim she was hyperinvolved because of her personal drive and determination, but Kassidy had laughed her way through Paige's claims of being a type A, cutthroat competitor. Paige had believed her own assertions until Kassidy called her out on them, pointing out how Paige hadn't cared one iota whether she and Dante won the McMinnville agility class, or even whether they got through the course in the correct order. Paige had spent a lot of time since then having imaginary conversations with Kassidy in her mind about her upbringing. She had come back again and again to the question she had never asked, about why her parents hadn't done those million activities themselves once Paige was no longer a baby and they had a good income coming in from their two jobs, rather than prodding her to do them.

In her mind, Kassidy turned the question around and aimed it at Paige, asking why she still felt the need to filter her life through their standards of approval when she was now an adult and able to make her own choices. Paige hadn't been able to find an answer. She had been using her parents as a crutch to keep herself from exploring interests that meant something personal to her, even if she wasn't particularly outstanding at them or if they didn't offer a defined set of steps, achievements, and awards.

She parked in front of Crystal's dog training school and captured Dante before he launched himself through the closed window of the car. This new venture was a case in point. She and Dante loved it even though they really did suck at it. There might be trophies to win in the sport, but if they wanted one, they'd need to buy it and pay to have it engraved because they weren't going to earn one the old-fashioned way anytime soon.

"It's my favorite student!" Crystal exclaimed when they came through the door, and Dante bolted toward her, dragging Paige along with him. Crystal bent down to pet him before smiling up at Paige. She was pretty, with short red-gold hair and green eyes and a hint of the accent she had brought with her from Dublin when her family came to the States as a child. Paige had slowly been getting to know her, even though an image of Kassidy was always present in her thoughts, mocking her attempts to find someone new who could fill the void in her life. Still, Paige did her best to ignore any sarcastic comments in her head and concentrate on forming a bond with a woman without trying to hurry along to the sex and breakup highlights. She didn't feel much of anything for Crystal except for an appreciation of her beauty and the occasional laughter Paige experienced in her company, but maybe a deeper attraction would develop over time.

Please. You wanted me the second you saw me.

Paige shook her head, trying to dislodge Kassidy's voice and concentrate on what Crystal was saying.

"Let's go through some of the basics, and then we'll let him run through the course."

Crystal had initially told her she expected her canine students to have their obedience skills firmly in place before they moved to the course and started working through the agility obstacles. She had eventually given in and allowed Paige and Dante to skip ahead even though they hadn't mastered the basics. Paige had, at first, thought her willingness to give them special treatment was a sign of Crystal's interest in her, but as the sessions went on she realized Crystal probably didn't think Dante would get to see the agility course in the next decade if she didn't make allowances for his lack of trainability.

Paige was determined to prove them both wrong, though. Both Crystal and Kassidy, whose shimmering laughter as she watched Dante at the fair still echoed through her head and her heart.

"We've practiced this week," she said, adding her usual warning. "You might not be able to tell, but we worked every day."

"I believe you, don't worry. Let's start with getting him to sit," Crystal said with a laugh. It was a nice laugh, but it didn't resonate through Paige's body like Kassidy's had.

You still want me.

"Do not," Paige muttered to herself. She pointed at Dante's hind end and commanded him to sit. He twisted around and looked over his shoulder as if he thought she was pointing out a treat he had missed that was somewhere on the ground behind him.

"Maybe we should try with the clicker again," Crystal said. "Just be sure to keep it out of reach this time."

Twenty minutes later, Crystal gave in and let them loose on the course. Dante seemed to have the terms *over* and *under* confused in his mind, because he usually tried to do the opposite of what was required. Finally, he ran into the tunnel and didn't come out the other side.

"He's like a kid in a blanket fort," Crystal said as they stood at either end of the tunnel and called for him to come out. "He seems to value his alone time."

Hey, just like me!

Paige rubbed her temples and pushed her hands through her hair. How was she ever going to get her imaginary Kassidy to leave her alone like the real woman had been so damned eager to do? She looked up and saw Crystal watching her mess up her hair.

"I don't suppose you'd want to meet for coffee sometime?" Crystal asked. "Or maybe lunch?"

No!

Paige ignored Kassidy's voice and smiled at Crystal. Maybe she was the answer to the question Paige had just been asking herself.

"I'd love to," she said.

Chapter Twenty

I can't believe you left without me."

"We weren't even supposed to leave Corvallis until an hour from now, yet somehow you're already here. Seems you were planning to leave without me, too. You're just mad because I got here first."

Kassidy sighed, trying to ignore the bickering twins. She had thought they were planning to drive to the farm together this afternoon, but apparently each of them had tried to get an early start. Kyle had won, with the prize being the guest cottage for the weekend. Kassidy didn't think the cottage was enough of an upgrade from the comfortable guest rooms in the main house, so she chalked it up to twin rivalry. Kyle had arrived not long after dawn, which meant Kayla would try to be even earlier the next time they came for a visit.

"Well, you're both here now, so stop fighting and help me."

Kassidy handed each of them a roll of barricade tape. "We need to string these along all the paths. I've already put stakes in the ground, so wrap the tape around each one to make a barrier."

"Did you steal this from a hunter?" Kyle pulled on the end of the bright orange tape.

"Why does it say CRIME SCENE on it?" Kayla asked.

"I wanted it to be noticeable, and this is all I could find. It will be easy to see, even when it starts to get dark."

She pushed them toward the west field and headed in the opposite direction. Their continued argument receded into the background as she put her house between them, and suddenly she was alone in the middle of a quiet field. She couldn't remember the last time she had been this isolated on the farm, surrounded by plants and no people. The farm was closed to give her time to prepare for the next day's festival, and she had left the cottage unrented during the event for one of the twins to use, although she could easily have tripled her usual rates this weekend.

She sighed again. It seemed to have become her expression of choice. Sighs of irritation when tourists annoyed her, yet she had to keep smiling at them. Sighs of relief when the farm was closed for the night, and whoever was staying in the guest cottage had finally gone to bed.

And sighs of heartsickness whenever she thought of Paige. Those sighs seemed to occur at an alarming rate of one per minute. She worried she might hyperventilate from them. It had been two months since Kassidy had driven Paige away, and she wasn't showing any signs of forgetting her.

The tourists and houseguests were challenging for her, but they kept her busy enough to get through the days without wallowing. Nights were another matter, especially when Kassidy knew she could have had Paige with her right now, helping her get ready for tomorrow's first annual Lavender Lane Farm Festival.

She tied the end of her orange tape to a stake and started walking along the edge of the path, clearly separating her rows of plants from careless feet and grubby hands. She smiled when she imagined what Paige would say to her right now when she, on the eve of her first festival, was spending more time barricading her lavender than decorating the booths for the fair.

Once she finished her row, she wandered back to the area between the house and the drying shed where most of the festivities would take place. Her shop would be open, even though she still mainly had craft items for sale, as well as some baked goods and packets of culinary items she had made, all featuring her lavender. She had powdered lemonade that just needed water added, a homemade Herbes de Provence blend, and jars of lavender sugar for baking. She let herself see the future through Paige's eyes and pictured her store full of other things, too, including her own honey and perfume, and a display of her very own cookbook.

The future store would be well stocked, but the present one was a little sparse. Luckily, the fifty local vendors she had invited would more than fill the empty spaces. Her friends had been supportive of all her recent projects, and they had enthusiastically accepted the invitation to be part of her new event. There were also craft tables and carnival games for the kids. A temporary pen housed a small petting zoo consisting of three goats and a miniature donkey, because Kassidy wasn't missing Paige enough and needed to torture herself with reminders of Paige's recommendation that she get goats. Kayla had brought the little menagerie with her, and Kassidy liked having them here as long as it wasn't on a permanent basis. They looked ready to do more damage than Dante if they happened to break out of the pen.

Kassidy went over to her porch and rested her hand on the back of the chair where Paige had been sitting when she asked her out to dinner. Most likely, Paige was dating someone else by now. She was too wonderful and vivacious to be alone for long, especially when she had a city full of women at her fingertips. Kassidy had eaten at Sarai's a few times since their night together, braving the pain of memories for the chance of getting information about Paige. Sarai didn't say much, except for the brief mention of an Irish dog trainer the last time Kassidy had been at the restaurant. Kassidy had barely made it to the privacy of her bedroom before she was crying and raging about the blasted woman who was probably bribing Dante with treats and using his affection to snare Paige.

Kassidy shook off the memories and hauled her patio furniture to the back of the cottage. Some local musicians would set up here, entertaining the crowds as they wandered through the one area Kassidy hadn't cordoned off and picked their own lavender.

The twins got back to the house soon after, and Kyle held up the empty spools from the tape.

"We ran out at the top of the hill, but there aren't many rows beyond where we stopped. Those plants should be fine."

Kassidy put her hands on her hips and looked at the orange line stretching from near the greenhouse to the hill. "Do you think it's too late to hire armed guards to patrol the paths? I wasn't thinking, Kayla. I should have had you bring some guard dogs to protect the fields instead of animals that might eat them if they get loose."

Kyle and Kayla exchanged the look they shared when they were worried about the way she was acting. Did they think she didn't notice?

"I'm fine," she said, emphasizing the word. "I'm just nervous."

"You've done amazing things with the farm, K," Kyle said. "You're allowed to be a little paranoid about the plants after coming this far, from living here on your own to hosting a festival this big."

"Thank you," Kassidy said. She felt the ache of tears in the back of her eyes just for a moment. Not because of his praise, which was nice to hear, but because every damned thing she did on the farm was connected to Paige. Kassidy had spent several days determined to find other options besides the ones Paige had presented. She had even tried to keep the same themes Paige had used but change the details. She hadn't been able to come up with better options, and she wasn't going to let the farm down because she missed Paige. So she had implemented every step of the proposal, even though each one made a jagged cut on her barely healing heart. Now she saw Paige in every corner of her farm. She couldn't go anywhere without seeing a reminder of Paige and hearing a voice-over in her head about why the improvement in question was necessary.

"What do you want us to do now?"

Kassidy looked across the yard. Tomorrow it would be full of color and noise and people, set against the deep purple and pink blooms of the summer lavender. She was surprised to realize the thought of it was no longer giving her the dry heaves. Paige would have been proud.

"We still need to hang decorations on the booths, and set up the craft tables, but we can finish later. Let's go get dinner first."

❖

Kassidy sank onto her living room couch. She kept running through a checklist in her mind, but everything seemed to be in order. The twins had helped her get the last of the decorations put up, and the only thing left to do was wait until the chaos of arriving vendors descended on them in the morning. And then her fair would be open for business.

She felt a thrill of excitement, tempered by the desire to get in her car and drive through the night until she found more barricade tape for the upper hill. Next year, she was buying a dozen extra rolls, just in case.

Kayla came into the room with two cups of tea and handed her one. Kassidy thanked her sister and breathed in the soothing blend of chamomile and lavender before taking a sip of the scalding liquid.

"Are you going to tell me what happened?" Kayla asked, settling beside her on the couch, near enough for their shoulders to touch. Kayla was the least demonstrative of the three siblings, and Kassidy knew she was worried if she was sitting this close.

"With what?" she asked, even though she had a feeling this was connected to Paige somehow. She wanted to change the subject, or go hide in her room, but she didn't. The desire to talk about Paige was far too tempting to ignore. She had come up obliquely in conversations with Sarai, Jessica, and Drew, but otherwise Kassidy didn't have anyone she could confide in about how awful she'd felt since Paige left.

"What happened with Paige," Kayla clarified, as Kassidy had expected. "After we spent the weekend with the two of you, Kyle and I were saying how we'd never seen you laugh and smile as much as you did with her. Now, you seem sad without her. Did she do something to hurt you? Because we can—"

Kassidy patted Kayla's thigh to stop her from issuing whatever threat she and Kyle had dreamed up for Paige. "It wasn't her fault. She told me she wanted to give our relationship a chance to work. She even scheduled some jobs around us, so she'd be in McMinnville more often. I told her I was fine with a one-night stand, but I didn't want more."

Kayla choked on her tea.

"Are you laughing? I just poured out my confession, and you're *laughing* at me?"

"I'm sorry. It's just…" Kayla set down her mug and wiped her eyes. "You're the last person on earth I'd pick as one-night stand material. You sound awkward saying the phrase, let alone doing the deed."

Kassidy shoved Kayla's shoulder in mock anger, but she was holding back laughter because Kayla was right about her. "It's not an option I normally would choose," she admitted. "I just wanted her enough to take what I could get."

"But not enough to give a relationship with her a chance? Even when she was making such an effort to be with you?"

"I wanted her too much for that." Kassidy shook her head, frustrated by her inability to explain the emotions she had been keeping inside for too long. "You don't know what happened with Audrey. She'd heard the stories about what it was like living with Mom, how she'd be talking to me one minute, then withdraw the next, often for days. How hard I tried to draw her pictures and show her my good report cards and take care of the house, hoping she'd look out of her prison and actually see me. Audrey did the same thing whenever we fought. She used that pain against me, and after hours or days of it, I'd turn into that little girl again, begging for her to come back to me."

"Wow." Kayla wrapped her arm over Kassidy's shoulders and leaned back on the couch, holding Kassidy close. "I didn't know what had happened with you and Audrey, but the breakup wasn't a surprise to either of us. I'm sorry she treated you like that, but I'm proud of you for figuring out what was wrong and getting out of the relationship."

"Thank you," Kassidy said. She put her head on Kayla's shoulder, and then raised it again. "Wait, why did you think we'd break up? I thought you liked Audrey."

Kayla shrugged and made a *meh* sort of sound. "She was okay, but you didn't seem to like her. To be honest, I thought you were the one who withdrew from her. You do that with a lot of people, until you get to know and trust them. That's why it seemed so different with Paige. You were present with her, and you had just met."

Kassidy sat upright. "*I* withdrew?" She searched desperately through her memories of prolonged fights with Audrey, wondering if it was possible that Audrey had sometimes shut down because Kassidy already had. As a response instead of an intended punishment. "I have to protect myself," she said, explaining herself even though she wasn't convinced that Kayla's assessment was accurate. She needed to think about this more, to force herself to relive some of those fights and understand if she had been partly to blame and not the innocent victim she had always thought she was.

"No, you don't," said Kayla. "You have to love, and hurt, and laugh, and cry. If you spend your life protecting yourself, you'll never feel anything, either good or bad."

Kassidy curled up against Kayla again. She had tried to protect herself from loving Paige, and all she had gotten was the hurt and the tears, with none of the laughter and joy Paige seemed to spread around her. Kassidy and the twins had often talked about how different their perceptions of their family life were, since the two of them had never known a life other than the one in which Kassidy was their tiny parent, while their real Mom and Dad were rarely emotionally present, even on the rare occasions when they were physically so.

It was easy for Kayla to tell Kassidy to stop shutting down and allow herself to face the potential of being hurt, but it was much more difficult for Kassidy to let go of the past and follow the advice. She had managed to open her life to Paige, allowing her onto the farm and into her personal and business affairs. Her life had definitely become fuller and richer because of it. Maybe it was worthwhile for Kassidy to open her heart to Paige, as well.

Unless, of course, the mysterious dog trainer had beat her to it.

CHAPTER TWENTY-ONE

Paige had to park almost a quarter mile from the place where she had stopped and gotten her first glimpse of Lavender Lane Farm. Now, the border shrubs along the road were full of extravagant blooms and had grown nearly as tall as her. Two large garden flags with the farm's logo and a sheaf of lavender woven on them flanked the farm's sign, and a dozen placards advertising the festival were placed along the main road, pointing tourists in the direction of the farm. She had seen the signs advertising Kassidy's festival around McMinnville—and, if she was being honest, on the farm's website where she had established herself as a pathetic lurker.

She hadn't planned on coming, but Kassidy had sent her an email about it last night. Nothing personal or swoon-inducing. Just a link to the festival's web page. Before she could stop herself, Paige had inferred a lifetime of love from the single line of the email.

She had never considered herself to be a romantic, hopeless or otherwise, so her willingness to pack Dante in the car and drive to the farm because of a non-invite was another example of how much she had changed because of Kassidy.

Paige kept Dante carefully under control as she joined several groups of people walking from the distant parking spots to the farm's entrance. The turnout was even better than she had imagined when she had suggested the annual festival in her proposal, and she found herself scanning the area for better parking options for next year, unable to fully disconnect the consultant part of her brain.

She was about to deliver a mental lecture to herself about not having high expectations from the day, or any expectations at all, when she and Dante turned onto the driveway, just past the last of the high shrubs, and she saw the farm laid out in front of her. She heard her own gasp echoed in the crowds around her. The plants that had seemed beautiful and serene in the spring had transformed into lavender with attitude. With a capital *A*. Vibrant shades spanning from pale pink to rich indigo spread across the acreage in tidy rows, bordered by glimpses of silver-green leaves and lines of black from the landscape fabric. Paige understood Kassidy's love for this place more profoundly now, and she was glad Kassidy had opened the farm to tourists. This place was too glorious not to share.

People were wandering along the farm's paths, the same ones Kassidy and Paige had followed during her tour, and once Paige's eyes recovered from being drunk on color, she noticed strips of garish orange on the trails. Instead of heading to the heart of the festival, she veered off toward the greenhouse and found a wooden stake at the start of the trail, with a ribbon of crime scene tape tied around it.

Paige put her hands on her knees and laughed until she could barely breathe. Of all the decorative choices anyone could have made, this one was the most perfectly *Kassidy*. Paige was certain that if so much as a petal was damaged during the festival, Kassidy would be in full CSI mode, dusting for fingerprints and searching for clues with a large magnifying glass.

She brushed her fingers across her cheeks, wiping away the tears. She had been nervous about coming here, and the past two months had been hell, but damn if Kassidy didn't still have the power to make her laugh.

Paige led Dante past a bluegrass band playing on Kassidy's patio and toward the main booths. She was pleased to see the Dutch doors of the cottage standing wide open, with advertisements for the rental on a folding table. She wandered through the crowd, recognizing all the vendor names and chatting with some of her new friends. The smell of lavender was thick in the air, in a way it hadn't been during the spring.

She was walking past the craft tables, where Kyle was helping some children make lavender wands—better than hers, of course, the little brats—when she felt a hand on her arm. She closed her eyes briefly, drinking in the feel of Kassidy's touch, before she turned around. Dante went ballistic, and Paige was grateful for the chance to collect herself while Kassidy played with him.

"You came," Kassidy stated. Paige wasn't sure if she seemed happy or not about her presence.

She gestured around them. "You took my advice," she said. She shook her head and smiled, not able to keep a stiff demeanor around Kassidy for long. "It's more than I ever imagined, even when I was telling you to—how did you rephrase it?—go big or go home."

Kassidy smiled and looked around the drying shed full of people, and once her face lost its closed expression, Paige could see more of what she was feeling. Weariness, stress over all those potentially destructive hands and feet. Good things, too, like pride in her farm and a charmed surprise to see so many people who wanted to visit it.

"So I heard you've been dating a dog trainer." Kassidy's voice was casual, and she kept her gaze focused on the craft table next to her, but the comment was obviously not one that an uninterested person would make. Or was it?

"So," Paige mimicked Kassidy's inflection. "You've been keeping track of my social life."

Kassidy shrugged. "It's a small town. You hear things."

"Hm, okay. Sarai told me that she mentioned it when you were at her restaurant. She said you seemed devastated by the news."

Actually, Sarai had told Paige she'd dropped the information as a way to gauge Kassidy's reaction, which had been minimal. Paige wasn't going to give up her chance to embellish, though.

Kassidy faced her. "Devastated? Please. I'll admit I was shocked that a dog trainer who had worked with you and Dante wasn't locked away in a straitjacket after the experience, but that's about all I felt."

"Hey. He's top of his class in both obedience and agility." Kassidy didn't need to know they were taking private lessons.

"Really," Kassidy said. "Then where'd he get that shoe?"

Paige followed her gesture and saw Dante chewing on a tiny white sneaker. She tugged it out of his mouth and returned it to the woman with the stroller who had just passed by them.

"Is she someone special?" Kassidy asked, her voice suddenly almost too quiet to hear in the noisy shed.

Paige hesitated before answering. Here was her chance to get back at Kassidy for hurting her. To pretend she hadn't cared, that she hadn't worried about how she'd survive the pain of losing her. Paige shook her head, finished with her teasing. "She's nice, but not the one for me. I wanted to forget about you, Kassidy. Crystal and I went to lunch a couple of times, but nothing more, because she just wasn't...she wasn't you."

Kassidy grabbed Paige's arm with a shaking hand and pulled her and Dante through the hordes of people, not slowing down until she had reached her back door. She only let go of Paige to fish her key out of her jeans pocket and unlock the door. She was fairly sure she hadn't shown any alteration in her expression when Sarai had talked about the dog trainer, so she guessed Paige had been kidding about Sarai saying she was devastated. She really had been, though, and the long nights after hearing the news had been the worst of this whole ordeal. The ordeal she had caused when she rejected Paige. But she had asked about the woman and Paige hadn't played games with her. She hadn't tried to hide how she felt about Kassidy even though she had turned her away once and could easily have done it again.

Kassidy shut and locked the door behind them once they were inside.

"Why didn't I trust you, Paige? Why did I pull away?"

Paige smiled, although it was merely a movement of her mouth. Kassidy saw sadness and tension in her cheeks and forehead. "I don't know, Kass. I wanted to be up front with you and let you know I wasn't going to have sex with you and then disappear back to Portland the next day. I didn't realize my reassurances were the last thing you wanted to hear, and that you wanted me to go away."

Kassidy shook her head, reaching toward Paige and using the pad of her thumb to trace her frown lines, smoothing them away with her touch.

"I wanted more, but I was afraid. In the past, I've been in relationships that bring out the worst in me. The scared little girl who can't understand why her mother won't get out of bed and make dinner. I was starting to fall in love with you, and I was afraid of turning into her again."

"Oh, Kassidy. That little girl you used to be is not the worst part of you at all." Paige put her hands on Kassidy's shoulders, squeezing her gently as if determined to make her hear the words she was saying. "She's the best of who you are. Strong and determined. Dedicated to her family. Brave enough to grow up early and accept the responsibilities of an adult. I love those aspects of you."

Kassidy paused, startled because she had never felt honored this way by another person. She was *seen* by Paige, but she hadn't believed it until now. She shook her head. She didn't deserve it. "I withdraw. I push people away. I pushed you away."

Paige nodded. "You did, and it hurt. I understand why, but I also know there are better ways for us to manage our relationship when one of us gets scared. It's not something I can handle if it happens every time we argue, or you get upset."

Kassidy nodded. She had been doing a lot of soul searching after her talk with Kayla, and she wanted to share it with Paige. Later. Right now, she had something more pressing on her mind.

"When we argue," she repeated. "Does that mean you're willing to give me another chance? Do you want to stick around long enough for us to find something to argue about?"

Paige smiled. "You mean something like orange crime scene tape marring the beauty of your idyllic farm?"

Kassidy tilted her head. "Something like that. Of course, we could also have an argument about something else entirely, if you want to have any chance in hell of winning."

Paige grinned. Her hands still on Kassidy's shoulders, she pushed her backward until Kassidy was pressed to the door, feeling the grooves of the carved panels against her hips. Paige leaned close and kissed her.

Kassidy gasped in surprise as Paige kissed her with all the force and passion they had been missing before. She had been awed by their quieter kiss in the car, but too much of her mind had been devoted to her fears. Now there was nothing to her or for her besides Paige. Kassidy opened her mouth, responding to the insistent pressure of Paige's tongue. Paige's hand slipped from her shoulder to her waist, anchoring them together as her fingers gently stroked and dipped below the top of her jeans.

Nerve endings made connections Kassidy had never felt before, and her entire body from the top of her head to her toes seemed to explode with pleasure, and then the feeling flowed through her, concentrating deep in her core when Paige's fingers unbuttoned her jeans and rested against her belly.

She fumbled for the hem of Paige's T-shirt and then her bra, finally managing to get them off, and she tossed them aside with a growl of frustration because they had taken too long to remove. She wanted skin. Now. She curled one hand around the back of Paige's neck and kissed her way to Paige's ear, then down to her collarbone. Her other hand explored Paige's breasts, teasing them until Paige's breath turned rapid and shallow. Kassidy brushed the lightly callused part of her palm over Paige's nipple and squirmed in response when the touch made Paige moan and push her hand deeper down the front of Kassidy's jeans.

Kassidy pushed her thigh between Paige's legs, pressing against her until she felt Paige's warmth soak through the denim between them. Paige rocked against her, mirroring the movement with her fingers as they moved lower and finally slid through Kassidy's wetness. The rhythm overpowered any residual thought Kassidy might have had about protecting herself until she was fully open and ready for Paige to enter her. She felt Paige's climax building as surely as her own, until they thrust toward each other and came together.

Kassidy sagged against the door, hoping her legs would continue to support her and not give up entirely, sending them both crashing to the floor. The sounds of a festival in full swing eventually entered her mind again.

She laughed weakly as Paige tipped her head and placed light kisses along the side of her neck. "You made me forget about all those people out there, laying siege to my farm," she said with a sigh. A blissful sigh, this time. "If that isn't love, I don't know what is."

Paige wrapped her arms around Kassidy's waist and hugged her. "You're right, Kass. This is love," she whispered in Kassidy's ear, her breath soft as a downy feather. "And I'm never letting you go again."

Chapter Twenty-two

Paige drove along the tree-encroached highway to McMinnville with the temptation to pull over and take photos of the colorful foliage vying with her desire to get to Kassidy as soon as possible. Years of city living had numbed her senses to the changing seasons, but now she was falling into the rhythm of the year.

Portland had a significant number of trees, especially when compared to other cities in which she'd lived, and she hadn't been immune to the ones that changed to vibrant reds and yellows in the fall. Still, most of her time had been spent inside buildings, apartments, and cars, where heaters and air conditioners regulated the temperature and gave a false impression of similarity to all four seasons. Now the majority of her days were connected to the current mood of the natural world around her. She ate hazelnuts and asparagus when nature decided she should. She scheduled her weeks around the seasonal needs of the farm, making sure she had extra time off when Kassidy was expecting large numbers of tourists, or when the lavender plants needed to be pruned before winter.

Winter. Cold weather meant for snuggling indoors in front of the fire. Sleepy fields bare of blooms and empty of visitors. Time for her and Kassidy to catch their breath after an insanely busy summer and fall and focus solely on each other. Paige had a feeling winter was going to be her favorite season of all.

She noticed a strange car in the driveway when she got home, so she let herself into the farmhouse, bracing for Dante's frenzied greeting. He spun in circles around her as she walked to the back door to look outside for Kassidy.

Paige sighed happily when she spotted her in one of the lavender fields behind the house with an older couple. She considered going out to rescue her, but Kassidy was smiling and gesturing with one hand full of lavender fronds while her other hand rested on the handle of the pitchfork she had probably been using to spread protective straw over her plants, so Paige leaned against the doorjamb and just gazed at her. She liked to cover some of the tourist wrangling when she was in McMinnville on her long weekends—partly because she enjoyed it, but mostly to give Kassidy a break from the near-constant stream of tourists who wanted to see her farm. Despite Kassidy's initial reluctance to open her sanctuary to visitors, she had fully embraced Paige's advice and seemed pleased by the response from the public. Lavender Lane Farm was thriving, and Paige knew that even though her efforts as a consultant had played a part in its success, most of the credit belonged to Kassidy who had stepped out of her comfort zone and turned the farm's potential into reality.

Another reason Paige decided to wait inside for Kassidy and not go outside to see her right away was because she doubted she'd be able to limit herself to a quick kiss hello, whether or not Kassidy was alone. Paige's three days in Portland had been lonely ones, even though her new job with a struggling tech company had kept her very busy. Every hour had been filled with reading how-to manuals to familiarize herself with the company's software products, doing some tricky restructuring with the staff, and overhauling the business's marketing plan, but she had still managed to spend a ridiculous amount of time staring into space and missing Kassidy.

Once Kassidy and her visitors started walking toward the driveway, Paige went into the living room to wait for her. She sat on the couch with Dante beside her and Kipper perched on the armrest at her side, remembering the first time she had seen this room with its beautiful furnishings marred by muddy paw prints. Now, of course, it was clean, but there were signs everywhere that she and

Dante lived here now. His dog toys were strewn across the carpet, and books related to Paige's latest local consulting job with a new art gallery were stacked on the dining room table, next to a chair with one of her sweaters draped over the back. It felt like home to her now, more than her apartment in the city where she stayed as little as possible, and more than any other place she had ever lived. Not because it was where she kept her favorite books and most of her clothes, but because of Kassidy.

Finally, Paige heard an engine start, and Kassidy came through the front door looking as glad to see Paige as she felt in return.

"You were spying on me," Kassidy said, grinning despite her mock scolding tone.

"I was not. I just got here." Paige stood up, gesturing around innocently, as if her position on the couch was proof she hadn't been standing by the back door only minutes before.

Kassidy shrugged out of her heavy jacket and hung it up. "Were, too. I could see your silhouette through the screen door." She laughed. "It looked kind of creepy, with just the shadow of a person visible, so I told those people they were getting a rare sighting of the Lavender Lane Farm ghost. I said they should tell all their friends."

Paige's answering laugh faded and she squinted at Kassidy, trying to deduce her motive. "Wait…were you trying to scare them off or to create interest in the farm?"

Kassidy shrugged noncommittally, meeting Paige in the middle of the living room and giving her one of the dreamy, lavender-scented kisses Paige had been pining for all week. "You're the one who told me to brand everything associated with this place," Kassidy continued when she pulled away again. "You didn't say I couldn't have Lavender Lane Farm ghosts. Or zombies that like to feast on the brains of tourists."

"I guess I need to be more specific in my proposals from now on," Paige said, wrapping her arms around Kassidy and holding her close. "And I'll admit I was watching you, but only because the past three days were unbearable without you. Not because I was spying."

"Oh, please," Kassidy said with a laugh. "You were making sure I wasn't about to chase those people off the farm with my pitchfork."

"The thought never crossed my mind," Paige said, with as much indignation as she could cram into the words. Kassidy looked at her steadily until Paige smiled and gave up the pretense. "Okay, it may have momentarily crossed my mind, but it didn't linger for long."

"Despite your insulting suspicions, they left without any puncture wounds," Kassidy said, brushing her nose against Paige's. "I almost stabbed the guy in the foot once, but it was purely an accident. And he had much better reflexes than I was expecting."

Paige laughed and nuzzled closer to Kassidy, kissing the base of her neck. "However you got rid of them, I'm glad they're gone, and we're alone."

"Mm." Kassidy tipped her head to give Paige better access, but her soft moan turned into a sigh. "Alone for about ten more minutes. Sarai is coming over to help me with some new recipes for my book, and you, Drew, and Jessica are our tasters."

Paige echoed Kassidy's sigh, resting their foreheads together. Her social life had been sporadic in the past, with whirlwind dates at the beginning of her relationships followed by long periods of solo nights spent reading with Dante at her side. Until the next round of dates. As much as she preferred being alone with Kassidy, long evenings spent with friends or the twins were a revelation for her. Being part of a couple filled her life in unexpected ways—with more laughter and fun than she had known before. "I forgot," she admitted. Her sole focus had been on getting home to Kassidy. "I had other plans in mind for us, but they were contingent on us being alone, without any guests. I suppose they can be delayed for a few hours. Or less, if you get the pitchfork out right after we eat."

Kassidy pressed closer to Paige, even though she had been the one to remind her about their plans for the evening. "I'll serve all the courses at once. That'll get them out of here sooner."

She kissed Paige again, melting under the pressure of Paige's tongue against hers and responding to Paige's obvious arousal with a growing urgency. Over the past months she had learned that Paige's openness to humor and new experiences was indicative of her personality in all areas of her life. She seemed as comfortable expressing herself when something bothered her as she was laughing at most situations, and Kassidy had discovered a level of trust with Paige that she had never encountered before. She knew exactly where she stood with Paige all the time.

Luckily for Kassidy, the feeling Paige expressed most often with her was a desire that matched hers. She nudged Paige with her knee, encouraging her to back up until they tumbled onto the couch together.

"We have eight minutes," Kassidy said, sifting her fingers through Paige's hair. "If we make the most of them, we can manage to get through a few hours with company, and then we'll have—"

She was going to say *all weekend*, but Paige kissed her, stopping her midsentence.

Paige settled herself between Kassidy's thighs and smiled at her, her expression echoing the sense of wonder and love Kassidy was feeling inside. "And then, we'll have a lifetime."

About the Author

Karis Walsh lives in the Pacific Northwest, where she finds inspiration for the settings of her contemporary romances and romantic intrigues. She was a Golden Crown Literary Award winner with *Tales from Sea Glass Inn*, and her novels have been shortlisted for a Lambda Literary award and a Forward INDIES award. She can usually be found reading with a cat curled on her lap, hiking with a dog at her side, or playing her viola with both animals hiding under the bed. Contact her at kariswalsh@gmail.com.

Books Available from Bold Strokes Books

Comrade Cowgirl by Yolanda Wallace. When cattle rancher Laramie Bowman accepts a lucrative job offer far from home, will her heart end up getting lost in translation? (978-1-63555-375-8)

Double Vision by Ellie Hart. When her cell phone rings, Giselle Cutler answers it—and finds herself speaking to a dead woman. (978-1-63555-385-7)

Inheritors of Chaos by Barbara Ann Wright. As factions splinter and reunite, will anyone survive the final showdown between gods and mortals on an alien world? (978-1-63555-294-2)

Love on Lavender Lane by Karis Walsh. Accompanied by the buzz of honeybees and the scent of lavender, Paige and Kassidy must find a way to compromise on their approach to business if they want to save Lavender Lane Farm—and find a way to make room for love along the way. (978-1-63555-286-7)

Spinning Tales by Brey Willows. When the fairy tale begins to unravel and villains are on the loose, will Maggie and Kody be able to spin a new tale? (978-1-63555-314-7)

The Do-Over by Georgia Beers. Bella Hunt has made a good life for herself and put the past behind her. But when the bane of her high school existence shows up for Bella's class on conflict resolution, the last thing they expect is to fall in love. (978-1-63555-393-2)

What Happens When by Samantha Boyette. For Molly Kennan, senior year is already an epic disaster, and falling for mysterious waitress Zia is about to make life a whole lot worse. (978-1-63555-408-3)

Wooing the Farmer by Jenny Frame. When fiercely independent modern socialite Penelope Huntingdon-Stewart and traditional country farmer Sam McQuade meet, trusting their hearts is harder than it looks. (978-1-63555-381-9)

A Chapter on Love by Laney Webber. When Jannika and Lee reunite, their instant connection feels like a gift, but neither is ready for a second chance at love. Will they finally get on the same page when it comes to love? (978-1-63555-366-6)

Drawing Down the Mist by Sheri Lewis Wohl. Everyone thinks Grand Duchess Maria Romanova died in 1918. They were almost right. (978-1-63555-341-3)

Listen by Kris Bryant. Lily Croft is inexplicably drawn to Hope D'Marco but will she have the courage to confront the consequences of her past and present colliding? (978-1-63555-318-5)

Perfect Partners by Maggie Cummings. Elite police dog trainer Sara Wright has no intention of falling in love with a coworker, until Isabel Marquez arrives at Homeland Security's Northeast Regional Training facility and Sara's good intentions start to falter. (978-1-63555-363-5)

Shut Up and Kiss Me by Julie Cannon. What better way to spend two weeks of hell in paradise than in the company of a hot, sexy woman? (978-1-63555-343-7)

Spencer's Cove by Missouri Vaun. When Foster Owen and Abigail Spencer meet they uncover a story of lives adrift, loves lost, and true love found. (978-1-63555-171-6)

Without Pretense by TJ Thomas. After living for decades hiding from the truth, can Ava learn to trust Bianca with her secrets and her heart? (978-1-63555-173-0)

Unexpected Lightning by Cass Sellars. Lightning strikes once more when Sydney and Parker fight a dangerous stranger who threatens the peace they both desperately want. (978-1-163555-276-8)

Emily's Art and Soul by Joy Argento. When Emily meets Andi Marino she thinks she's found a new best friend but Emily doesn't know that Andi is fast falling in love with her. Caught up in exploring her sexuality, will Emily see the only woman she needs is right in front of her? (978-1-63555-355-0)

Escape to Pleasure: Lesbian Travel Erotica edited by Sandy Lowe and Victoria Villasenor. Join these award-winning authors as they explore the sensual side of erotic lesbian travel. (978-1-63555-339-0)

Music City Dreamers by Robyn Nyx. Music can bring lovers together. In Music City, it can tear them apart. (978-1-63555-207-2)

Ordinary is Perfect by D. Jackson Leigh. Atlanta marketing superstar Autumn Swan's life derails when she inherits a country home, a child, and a very interesting neighbor. (978-1-63555-280-5)

Royal Court by Jenny Frame. When royal dresser Holly Weaver's passionate personality begins to melt Royal Marine Captain Quincy's icy heart, will Holly be ready for what she exposes beneath? (978-1-63555-290-4)

Strings Attached by Holly Stratimore. Success. Riches. Music. Passion. It's a life most can only dream of, but stardom comes at a cost. (978-1-63555-347-5)

The Ashford Place by Jean Copeland. When Isabelle Ashford inherits an old house in small-town Connecticut, family secrets, a shocking discovery, and an unexpected romance complicate her plan for a fast profit and a temporary stay. (978-1-63555-316-1)

Treason by Gun Brooke. Zoem Malderyn's existence is a deadly threat to everyone on Gemocon and Commander Neenja KahSandra must find a way to save the woman she loves from having to commit the ultimate sacrifice. (978-1-63555-244-7)

A Wish Upon a Star by Jeannie Levig. Erica Cooper has learned to depend on only herself, but when her new neighbor, Leslie Raymond, befriends Erica's special needs daughter, the walls protecting her heart threaten to crumble. (978-1-63555-274-4)

Answering the Call by Ali Vali. Detective Sept Savoie returns to the streets of New Orleans, as do the dead bodies from ritualistic killings, and she does everything in her power to bring them to justice while trying to keep her partner, Keegan Blanchard, safe. (978-1-63555-050-4)

Breaking Down Her Walls by Erin Zak. Could a love worth staying for be the key to breaking down Julia Finch's walls? (978-1-63555-369-7)

Exit Plans for Teenage Freaks by 'Nathan Burgoine. Cole always has a plan—especially for escaping his small-town reputation as "that kid who was kidnapped when he was four"—but when he teleports to a museum, it's time to face facts: it's possible he's a total freak after all. (978-1-63555-098-6)

Friends Without Benefits by Dena Blake. When Dex Putman gets the woman she thought she always wanted, she soon wonders if it's really love after all. (978-1-63555-349-9)

Invalid Evidence by Stevie Mikayne. Private Investigator Jil Kidd is called away to investigate a possible killer whale, just when her partner Jess needs her most. (978-1-63555-307-9)

Pursuit of Happiness by Carsen Taite. When attorney Stevie Palmer's client reveals a scandal that could derail Senator Meredith Mitchell's presidential bid, their chance at love may be collateral damage. (978-1-63555-044-3)

Seascape by Karis Walsh. Marine biologist Tess Hansen returns to Washington's isolated northern coast where she struggles to adjust to small-town living while courting an endowment for her orca research center from Brittany James. (978-1-63555-079-5)

Second in Command by VK Powell. Jazz Perry's life is disrupted and her career jeopardized when she becomes personally involved with the case of an abandoned child and the child's competent but strict social worker, Emory Blake. (978-1-63555-185-3)

Taking Chances by Erin McKenzie. When Valerie Cruz and Paige Wellington clash over what's in the best interest of the children in Valerie's care, the children may be the ones who teach them it's worth taking chances for love. (978-1-63555-209-6)

All of Me by Emily Smith. When chief surgical resident Galen Burgess meets her new intern, Rowan Duncan, she may finally discover that doing what you've always done will only give you what you've always had. (978-1-63555-321-5)

As the Crow Flies by Karen F. Williams. Romance seems to be blooming all around, but problems arise when a restless ghost emerges from the ether to roam the dark corners of this haunting tale. (978-1-63555-285-0)

Both Ways by Ileandra Young. SPEAR agent Danika Karson races to protect the city from a supernatural threat and must rely on the woman she's trained to despise: Rayne, an achingly beautiful vampire. (978-1-63555-298-0)

Calendar Girl by Georgia Beers. Forced to work together, Addison Fairchild and Kate Cooper discover that opposites really do attract. (978-1-63555-333-8)

Lovebirds by Lisa Moreau. Two women from different worlds collide in a small California mountain town, each with a mission that doesn't include falling in love. (978-1-63555-213-3)

Media Darling by Fiona Riley. Can Hollywood bad girl Emerson and reluctant celebrity gossip reporter Hayley work together to make each other's dreams come true? Or will Emerson's secrets ruin not one career, but two? (978-1-63555-278-2)

Stroke of Fate by Renee Roman. Can Sean Moore live up to her reputation and save Jade Rivers from the stalker determined to end Jade's career and, ultimately, her life? (978-1-63555-62-4)

The Rise of the Resistance by Jackie D. The soul of America has been lost for almost a century. A few people may be the difference between a phoenix rising to save the masses or permanent destruction. (978-1-63555-259-1)

The Sex Therapist Next Door by Meghan O'Brien. At the intersection of sex and intimacy, anything is possible. Even love. (978-1-63555-296-6)

Unforgettable by Elle Spencer. When one night changes a lifetime... Two romance novellas from best-selling author Elle Spencer. (978-1-63555-429-8)